About the Author

Lauren Lowther has been reading and writing for as long as she can remember, with a strong love for anything fantasy and romance. When not with her nose buried in a book, she can usually be found at the barn, where she rides competitively. Lauren lives in Western Canada with her husband and two rescue pups. You can find her online at laurenlowther.com.

A Kingdom of Dark Truths

Kelly,

love & gratitude,

xo

Lauren Lowther

A Kingdom of Dark Truths

Olympia Publishers
London

www.olympiapublishers.com
OLYMPIA PAPERBACK EDITION

Copyright © Lauren Lowther 2023

A CIP catalogue record for this title is
available from the British Library.

ISBN: 978-1-80074-791-3

First Published in 2023

Olympia Publishers
Tallis House
2 Tallis Street
London
EC4Y 0AB
Printed in Great Britain

Dedication

For anyone struggling to achieve their dream. It is possible, keep going.

Acknowledgements

It feels surreal to me to actually be writing acknowledgments — this is a dream I've chased for a long time. Thank you, God, for giving me this story to tell and the words with which to tell it.

I have to start by thanking my amazing family. Mom: for reading every single chapter one by one as I sent them to you, and always asking for more. Dad: for your unwavering support and for reading the book even though you are a strictly non-fiction man. Hayley: for never failing to make me laugh and lighten my heart. Also for keeping me humble (even when I don't ask). Evan, my love, you are the reason I can do what I do. Thank you for your heart, your words of encouragement, and for being the first person to read this book. I love you. And finally, to Milo and Lucie, who both kept me company, on my lap or by my feet, while I wrote this book.

To the amazing team at Olympia Publishing: a HUGE thank you for taking a chance on my book and on me. Thank you for your support, and for working with me every step of the publishing process. Because of you, my book could be shared with the world!

To my beta readers, you know who you are. Thank you so much for being the first critiques I received and for being completely honest and straightforward. It was a scary step for me to give my baby to strangers to read, but I'm glad it was you.

For all the authors I have loved so much over the years who filled my childhood with wondrous adventures and characters to fall in love with, thank you. From the bottom of my heart, I know I would not be able to create stories without you.

And you, reader, thank you for giving this book a chance. I'm so excited to share this world and cast of characters with you. I believe this story to be an important mirror to today's world. Without you this would all be for naught. Thank you for helping me chase my dreams!

If you enjoyed reading 'A Kingdom of Dark Truths', please consider leaving a review. Good reviews go a long way towards helping authors. It is much appreciated!

PROLOGUE

Darkness, then light, then agonizing pain.

Where was it coming from? I tried to assess my body amid the burning fire that had settled in my mind, robbing me of my sight.

My abdomen. I put a hand there, feeling the warm slickness of blood soak it instantly. Not good.

I tried to take a deep breath — painful, so painful — and force my eyes to see past the fire ripping through my brain. Where was I?

Blinking groggily, I could make out only my very near surroundings. Trees, lots of them. Evergreen and pine and dogwood. It smelled of cedar as well, but I didn't see any nearby. Mossy undergrowth beneath me, blue sky above me. The sun was there, but I didn't feel any warmth. Would I be able to feel the sun anyway with this injury? I couldn't be sure.

With a snap, I remembered how I got here. The portal. I could vaguely feel the ebb of its magic touching mine, greedy and unflinching. It was still holding the edges of my essence. I gritted my teeth as I twisted my body and my open stomach wound to look behind me.

It didn't look like it had before I walked through. It didn't look like anything, really. It was an absence of air and space, clear and shimmering and only about the size of my fist.

Wait—what had it looked like before? Where had I come from?

Shit. *Shit.*

The damn thing was meddling with my memories. I could feel its magic still wrapped around mine.

I delved deep into my own magic and wrenched it from the portal's grasp in one mighty heave. I roared in pain at the effort and toll it took on my bleeding body. Which was still bleeding—way too much.

At this point, I could barely remember my name. *Stand, Spense,* I willed myself. *Stand, and go find supplies. You need to stop the bleeding.*

I kept a hand pressed tightly on my abdomen to hold in as much of the blood as I could. I pulled a knee up and braced it under my body, preparing to push off it and get up. I pulled the other leg forward and pushed off. I was down on the grass again before I realized my legs weren't supporting me. My head swam with dizziness. *Too fast.*

I waited for my head to clear a bit before trying again, but it was only getting fuzzier. Some primal instinct told me this was not a good sign.

No, I couldn't die here alone, with no memory of how I got here or why. Blackness creeped over the edges of my vision. *Fight it!*

Somewhere in the near distance, I heard shouting. Voices, getting closer.

"It's here, Embris!"

Stomping, the clattering of armor shaking the ground. *Soldiers,* a piece of my addled brain offered up.

Wouldn't it be so lovely to let go of the pain right now? Another piece of my mind suggested. *It would be so quick, like falling asleep.* It would be easy, much easier than holding onto my body and my magic inside of a fire-torn mind of pain.

I was vaguely aware of a gruff hand grabbing my face and turning it sideways. I grunted, willing my eyes to open and take in the new threat, but they betrayed me, staying firmly shut.

"Dark fae. Look at his horns. Must have come through this rip he tore in the realm." The hand dropped my face. The same voice continued.

"We need to get Queen Vera out here now so she can decide what to do with him. You two—retrieve the queen immediately. You three—guard the rip. We're not going to allow anything else through."

Footsteps around me shuddered the grassy earth as the soldiers changed positions.

"We should kill him, Captain. Too much risk."

Yes, kill me. Take me from this misery and agonizing pain. Let me slip into peaceful nothingness.

The voice from before—the Captain's—countered. "Look at him, he's on Death's door as it is. He's not a threat like this. It's the queen's right to decide what to do." A pause. "He may not even make it till she arrives, anyway."

It would be so easy—to slip into the darkness that surrounded me now, wrapping around my magic and dulling my senses. Maybe I would. It seemed a better alternative to facing the fire blazing through my body.

"There—she's coming."

How much time had passed? Why hadn't I slipped into oblivion yet? Was death too merciful for me? Why did I have no memory of myself but still feel as though I deserved to be punished?

A female's voice, strong and clear, rang through the trees. "Grab him, we're taking him to the palace healer straight away."

"All due respect, your Highness, he's almost dead. He won't make it, especially not if we move him."

A warm, comfortable touch was on my abdomen. My consciousness registered the heat around my wound—cauterizing it. The smell of lilac filled my brain.

"This will hold him for now. Let's go."

Hands gripped under my arms and legs. They hoisted me up, and everything went black.

ONE
Rituals & Things
DIANA

Ten years ago.

Large, soft hands encapsulated my own, squeezing gently. I sat on the edge of the four-poster bed, looking into my grandmother's half-lidded eyes. "Don't be afraid, Diana," she whispered. Her voice was creaky from disuse.

From the corner of the room, I could hear poorly disguised sniffling. My great-aunt Lily, crying for her sister. The bedchamber, vast and intricately decorated, was lacking its usual luster. The tangy smell of herbs and illness hung in the air like a cloud, threatening to choke me.

Teardrops fell silently from my eyes onto our joined hands. "I don't want to lose you," I said, trying with all the might of a twelve-year-old to keep my voice steady.

"My dear, you won't be losing me. I will be joining our ancestors, and I will guide you from Gaia's realm. I will always be with you." Maeve took one of her hands from mine and softly stroked my chestnut hair. Hers was white now, but it was once the same exact colour as mine.

The head healer, Yvonne, stepped forward to offer

Maeve another mouthful of tonic, to which she shook her head.

My mother, acting Queen of Eira, cleared her throat once from her spot on the other side of the bed. "Mother, take the medicine. It will ease your pain."

"No, Vera. It is almost my time. I want to be clear-headed when Gaia comes for me."

That caused another wave of tears from me. Why did Gaia have to take her, the one fae in my life who understood me? It wasn't fair. In all my lessons I had always accepted the eternal circle of life; our ancestors guiding from a realm invisible to us. It had been easy to accept the eventual fate of death when I had never faced it myself. Now, I felt abandoned by our mother.

"Diana," Maeve said again, pushing my chin up to look her in the eyes again. "You were named for Eira's first Queen. I know you will do great things in your life. Fret not, dear one. It will all seem clear one day." Her words might have seemed vague to my mother or any other fae in the room, but I knew she referenced my fear of being Queen. It was something I had sought her counsel for often, to which she had always succeeded in helping me with.

"Will I see you at my ascension ritual?" My voice trembled with hope.

"That is up to you, my child." When my brow furrowed, she added, "I daresay we will see each other again very soon."

I didn't know how long we sat with Maeve as her breathing became more and more laboured, but it would be impossible for me to forget the sound of her last breath, a sigh that was heartbreakingly peaceful. We sat with her while Yvonne applied the herbs to her skin that would allow her an easy journey to our ancestors.

Finally, after sending her body into the Sacred Pool, and enduring hundreds of condolences from region Princes and court officials, I was released to my bedchambers. That night was the first time I was unable to sleep, even with my over-exhaustion and need to escape reality.

It wouldn't be until many years had passed that I would be able to sleep soundly again.

Today

Morning birds sang loudly, sending a jolt through my body as I realized it was time to get up. I had watched the night sky change from twilight to midnight to dawn, unseeing as sleep evaded me. I hadn't even been able to close my eyes longer than a few minutes; I had just laid on the bed of ivory sheets with my eyes wide open, listening to the owls and crickets all night.

Not being able to sleep was a common ailment of mine, and it was more than likely that I wouldn't have been able to sleep even if today wasn't the biggest day of my life. It was my ascension, and I was to be crowned the High Princess of Eira, a high honour, and not one to be taken lightly. My mother, Queen Vera, presided over all the regions in Eira. She had worn her title for almost three decades, and I was her sole offspring.

Now that I was twenty-two years old, our court's tradition dictated that I was to be coronated as the Heir to the throne of this realm. That is — if I was accepted by the ritual. I had a long line of powerful fae females before me that had all passed exceptionally well. And I could count on the fact that my magic was strong, maybe even stronger than my mother's. Certainly, it was stronger than any of my peers growing up, and my tutors.

It was this legacy that caused my breath to hitch. Centuries of being in the spotlight of Eira was one thing. Being the sole fae responsible for keeping the peace and balance between the regions — not to mention the Darks that haunted the realm next to us — was another. I had been training for this my whole life, and yet I still felt wildly lost thinking about inheriting the throne and all its splendor.

I thought of my grandmother, Maeve, as I sat up in bed and rubbed my hands over my face.

"But what if I'm not ready when I ascend?" I had asked her one spring after a particularly long winter of watching her take countless meetings with the region officials, deciding how to settle the squabble that had come up between two lords regarding illicit activities at the Winter Solstice.

"Diana, my child, this was always meant to be, and everything is as it should be. When fate calls you forward to lead, you will be ready." Maeve had never wavered in her convictions, and I had always felt peace after speaking with her. Now, ten summers after Maeve's passing, I felt her absence like a missing limb. Maeve had understood me more than my mother and great-aunt. She never disparaged me for my endless questions, and always knew what to say to ease me when I had a heavy mind. Time promised to heal all wounds, but time was a liar.

There was a rap at my door, ripping me from my thoughts.

"Diana?" I recognized the voice of Maisie, my maidservant. She had arrived to help me get ready for the ritual. My stomach fluttering wildly, I got up from my bed and settled down at the vanity, where I caught my own eye in the mirror. The girl looking back at me had my face, my long chestnut hair, my pointed ears and dark brows, but I didn't recognize the wariness in my eyes; the purse in my lips.

Might as well get it over with.

"Come in, please, Maisie."

The heavy oak door swung open, and Maisie entered, arms full of fabric and an exquisite iron box. I was struck by her put-togetherness this early in the morning. Maisie made a point to always represent the palace well.

"Your hair is stunning, as usual," I said by way of greeting.

She was constantly trying new braided and woven styles on her curly honey-yellow hair, and they only added to her beauty. I paid her very well, much more than expected for a maidservant — even one who worked at the royal palace in Nevelyn. But Maisie was invaluable to me. We had grown up together, her mother being a cook in the palace and her father a royal guard. We had spent countless hours as children running through the halls, through the woods, through the city, or wherever we could explore without restraint. As adolescents, we did not train together, but I moved her as close to my wing of the palace as I could so we could spend our free hours chatting about new things we had seen or learned, or whatever male was grabbing our attention that day. With her, I only had to be myself.

Maisie smiled and dropped the fabrics down on a mahogany chair by the door gently setting the box on the matching table beside it. A thrumming started in my head. Wordlessly, she walked over and started running her fingers through my hair. The peaceful silence between us was comforting.

Maisie met my eye in the looking glass. She arched an eyebrow and pointed a glance at the dark shadows that had found a home under my eyes.

Finally: "I couldn't sleep last night."

"I thought as much," Maisie said, sweeping my unwaveringly straight hair into an intricate twirl. "I don't think there is as much pressure on you as you think, Diana."

"Isn't there? Every fae in Nevelyn will be there to witness, not to mention the court officials traveling from every region in Eira. And everyone knows who I am descended from. I have greatness in my veins, but I've never done anything great."

Maisie clucked her tongue disapprovingly. "Not true, you have been homing youngling orphans since you were a youngling yourself."

There was a dull tug at my heart. Maeve had started a program to protect orphaned youth not long after her coronation, a beautiful addition to the palace's already large list of charitable programs. She had always said that the younglings were the future of the fae, and to provide a home and education for the youth without one was not only kind, but *necessary*. Considering how rare of a blessing children were, the program was not very busy. It practically ran itself.

I shook her head. "I love doing that work, but it wasn't my idea. The youngling programs have been instituted in the palace for centuries."

"Maybe so, but Nevelyn has never seen a royal work with the younglings personally—let alone a High Princess—before you," Maisie countered. She was speaking of the time I had taught a rather enigmatic young girl how to ride a horse. Her name was Ebi, and she was reeling over the tragic loss of her parents to a shipwreck. Understandably so. Once she had an outlet in riding, she was easier to approach, and a couple from the city of Kallfrom adopted her soon after.

I knew Maisie was trying her best to lift my spirits. So I didn't counter her there. Instead:

"I'm not the High Princess yet."

That got a wry smile from Maisie as she shook her head at my stubbornness.

"Diana, you have been an exemplary royal for the Northern Peninsula. You've never given anybody a reason to dislike the idea of you as Queen one day. Except maybe the ambassador from the Southern Isles," she added teasingly, reminding me of the summer we were seventeen.

The court from the Southern Isles had made the trip north to Nevelyn, the glittering capital of the Northern Peninsula. They had come along with the other two regions for the celebration of the Summer Solstice. The week-long party was one of the North's favourites, with gourmet spreads of delicious food, dancing to music beating from beautiful, hand-crafted instruments, and of course, the opportunity to catch up on all the court gossip.

At this particular celebration the newest Southern ambassador, Hestor, was freshly twenty-two and feeling quite happy to be at the ruling court for the celebration. He was very much enjoying the chestnut ale when he decided to try his luck by asking me to share his bed that night. I had declined, maybe too quick for his pride. Even if I had found him to be attractive, I was nursing a freshly broken heart. That night, I recalled the story to Maisie, laughing for hours about it while fabricating hilarious ideas of Hestor and I together, and what our children might look like with Hestor's unfortunate nose and my uncommonly long ears.

The memory faded around me like a mist; as much as I wanted to try and hold onto that lightness and tinkling laughter, I could only grasp at the air.

For the first time in a few days, I felt a small smile creep onto my face. It felt foreign, lifting a pitifully small amount of pressure off my chest. "Well, you may be right about that, Maisie."

We met eyes in the mirror. Both striking in our own right, both strong and capable, both kind. Maisie would have made a great queen too; I had this thought often while growing up. *But would she be different if she had transitioned from child to adult with a crushing weight on her shoulders, a constant worry about the inevitable crown in her future?* I mused. That was why Maisie was at peace. She could live this marvelous life experiencing it all from the palace, without having the future of the realm in her hands.

Maisie cleared her throat. I realized that I had been staring and dropped my gaze to my hands, where I rolled my emerald family ring over and over around my left middle finger. Emeralds were the representative jewel of the North, and I incorporated it into everything I wore. Maisie wore a small emerald in a hairpin that was keeping strands of hair from falling into her face.

It was a blessing that I didn't have to make awkward small talk with my friend, so I let her continue my hair while I gazed unseeingly at myself, trying to picture what I would face in the ritual today. The sun moved slowly higher, reminding me with each passing minute that I was getting closer and closer to what I had been dreading. As if in response, my head's thrumming grew.

With a flourish of her hands, Maisie wrapped the last piece of hair around her masterpiece and stepped away from me. "What do you think?"

I moved around in the mirror, trying to get a good angle. The top layer of my hair had been delicately braided in small pieces and wrapped around a knot in the back of my head. The rest cascaded down my back in one big fishtail braid. A few loose strands of hair had been left out, framing my face. It was a work of art, and yet something was missing.

"The finishing touch."

Maisie had retrieved the small box and brought it over to me. She was practically vibrating with excitement to show me what was inside. The thrumming in my head was impossible to ignore now, each beat stronger as Maisie got closer.

Inside the box lay a magnificent emerald with jagged edges, as big as my fist. It caught every ray of sunshine coming in the room and turned it out tenfold. It radiated beauty — and magic, I realized with a start. It looked... so familiar. The magic emanating from it felt ancient, older than I had ever sensed before. Suddenly, I pictured it, sitting in the palms of the realm's very first Queen, a glow coming from both. I had seen this portrait almost every day of my life in my mother's office.

My breath was weak. "Is that — "

"Yes."

My knees threatened to give out. This was the emerald depicted in every story, song, and painting of the first female to rule the realm. The queen I was named after. I had heard every version of the legend, but they all revolved around one plot: The Queen had pulled this emerald from the very bottom of the Sacred Pool herself, and with it was able to channel her power to banish the Dark to its own realm. The Lights revered the first Queen for bringing peace to the North and the entire realm of Eira. I had been hesitant to believe all I had been told, as stories tended to get bigger and grander with time. But how could I refute them now with the emerald winking at me, verifying every whisper I had heard about it?

"How?" My throat felt dry and swollen. I tried to keep my voice steady, but it wavered anyway.

The legends were unclear on what happened to the emerald after the Queen died. Many said it died with her, fading to grey and losing its power completely. Others said her daughter threw it back into the Sacred

Pool to keep it safe. No one had seen it with their own eyes in millennia

Maisie's voice was gentle. "It appeared this morning on the Well at the Sacred Pool."

Now before me, this emerald had magic woven into it by the first Queen herself. It had seen the war between the Darks and aided in banishing them to their own realm. The magic in its green light was similar to the kind I could sense from the eldest fae in the realm; powerful, old, and wise. I felt with shocking absoluteness that this emerald had its own mind. Where had it been for over eight thousand years? And why appear now?

More anxiety knotted in my belly.

Maisie gently took the emerald from the box, shuddering where the emerald's essence mingled with her magic, and carefully wove it into the empty knot in my hair. From its spot there, I could feel the power tickling me, touching my own lightly as if in permission. My magic, which I kept woven in a tight ball, tugged at me, wanting to merge with this new light source. At my acceptance, my magic pulled the emerald's power into the depths of me.

At once, I glimpsed a young female, with chestnut hair similar to my own. She stood behind the mirror with her hands clasped in front of her. Her eyes were deeply green. The fae was magnificently beautiful, and there was power coming off her in waves. I instantly knew it was the first Queen. She had been depicted in so many ways, and yet seeing her now, I realized that every painting and drawing was wrong. Her eyes were not hazel brown with a touch of green like every artist seemed to think. In fact I had never seen such a clear, unmistakable colour in anyone's eyes before.

They were emerald.

She was gone as quick as she came.

"Did you see that?" I whispered.

"I didn't catch that, what did you say, Di?" Maisie stepped back, admiring her work. Without waiting for an answer, she said warmly, "I think this is very befitting a High Princess. Wait until your mother sees this, she's going to be speechless."

I shook my head slightly enough that Maisie wouldn't see, but enough to snap me back into the present. The queen's image evaporated from my thoughts. *The emerald remembered*, I realized.

With the gemstone's thrum of magic pressing into my skull, I felt the heavy weight of the ritual settle back on my shoulders with a vice grip. Would I speak with the first Queen later in the Sacred Pool, among my ancestors? The pit in my stomach gripped tighter.

I was barely aware of Maisie guiding me into a beautiful floor-length white gown. White was the colour worn for spiritual holidays and ceremonies, whereas green was for celebrating life and death, and blue was for weddings.

The sleeves became more delicate as they traveled down my arm until they turned to lace and stopped at my wrists. The bodice was tight, the neckline a modest V shape, and once the dress hit my hips it flared out, revealing a few layers of beautiful silk fabric. It was simple, but quite possibly the queenliest dress I had ever worn. I didn't deserve this dress. I hadn't done anything remotely fitting of a queen.

Maisie interrupted my thoughts by insisting that I eat something before the ceremony. I declined.

"Unless you want to clean that breakfast off this dress later today, I suggest we skip the dining room altogether," I said, my hazel eyes boring into hers, a deep pool of blue.

"Fine," she rolled her eyes at my theatrics, but looped her arm through mine. It was a friendly, sisterly act, not one of authority or protocol. She guided me down the hall to the foyer of the palace, where we would meet Queen Vera and my great-aunt, Lily, before heading down to the Sacred Pool.

Maisie stopped us at the top of the stairs. Waiting there, dressed in a crisp suit of cream, was Aedan Thesand. I smiled, feeling a bit of calm as his familiar handsome face and pine scent washed over me. His golden hair was swept cleanly to the side, and his pointed ears just poked through the length of it. He wore an emerald on his breast pocket and smiled back at me as he offered his arm.

I had met Aedan when I was twelve, running amuck in the stables. His father was the head of the Queen's Army and was well respected for breeding exquisite, athletic warrior-mounts. Aedan had known how to ride before he could walk, growing up with the mounted soldiers in the back of the palace. Thankfully, his father had invested in a tutor for him, which reversed all the foul language he had picked up from the rough soldiers in the army.

He and I had been so excited to meet someone our own age, such a rarity growing up inside a court. Maisie had started her own lessons, learning to cook and sew and the other necessities of a maidservant, so I was missing company of my own age. We started riding together whenever I could get away from the palace. I invited Aedan and his father to as many dinners as I could, until they became like family to us. Vera gave them a ward in the palace, and we started training together. His wish was to take his father's place one day, so my mother had agreed that he should be involved in the same lessons as I.

Aedan at the head of Nevelyn's army was one thing about someday ruling that I could be certain of.

"Don't you look nice," I said by way of hello, accepting his arm to lead me down the stairs. Maisie trailed a few steps behind, watching the train on my dress for any hitches or snares. I sometimes felt guilty about her having to be behind me instead of an equal by my side, but she insisted she was happy this way. And I knew my friend well enough to believe her.

Aedan smiled as he took in my dress, his golden skin stretching to reveal a glittering smile with matching dimples on each side. "I am unnoticeable compared to you."

He was handsome by every right. When we rode through the city, it was not hard to notice the females that smiled and stared when he passed. The longing on their faces to receive some of the attention he reserved for his beautiful gray mare, Kali, or for me. But I never felt a prick of longing for him the way those females did.

I supposed it would be easy and beneficial for me to pick him to rule by my side, but I was a hopelessly waiting for a real partner, who loved me with the same ferocity that I loved him. A soulmate, through and through.

Many of the fae were lucky enough to meet their true soulmate to spend the rest of their long lives with. To feel a piece of their souls living in someone else. I knew my mother had been mated, not just married, to my father. They had been given a gift from Gaia herself in each other. It became obvious to them, and their peers as matching tattoos sprang into life on their left arms, swirling and spiraling from elbow to shoulder in unique patterns. That was the sure sign that a couple were each other's true soulmates.

My father died when I was very young, but Vera had told such vivid stories of their adventures together that I felt like I knew him. If I ever felt envy for mated couples, I recalled the sadness in my mother's face, times when she thought no one was watching, and reminded myself that I didn't need to rush it. My mate would come eventually if I were so lucky.

Sometimes I wondered if Aedan also felt that patience in awaiting a mate. There were some — mostly in the Western Shores region — that married for practicality, for position in a court. Aedan would be a very powerful male in the near future, and I could think of a few high-born families who would love to be married to the Head of the Queen's Army. I had never asked him about it. He had taken a few lovers over the time I had known him, but nothing serious. Not like me, who'd fallen in love with the first male brave enough to flirt with the Queen's daughter and then promptly gotten my heart broken into a thousand pieces.

I almost pictured his face then, and abruptly stopped myself, snapping back into my conscious mind with a thud.

We had reached the bottom of the stairs, my body mercifully staying upright on the slippery marble while my mind was elsewhere.

Our party was already assembled. My mother stood at the front, ready to lead us out. Maeve's sister, my great-aunt Lily, was beside her, hand in hand with her newlywed husband, Polis. Half a dozen of our most trusted court members were present, including Aedan's father, Embris. They all watched as we approached.

My mother's face glowed as she saw me. Her gown was white and gold, with glittering jewels all down the front and an entirely open back. Her mating tattoo, now faded to gray, was barely visible through opaque sleeves. The train of her dress splayed out around her feet in a most queenly way. Her long, auburn hair flowed freely around her shoulders in loose waves. A large emerald stone perched at her neck; smaller round diamonds positioned on either side. Her gray wolf, Delios, looked up at me from his ever-constant place at her side with baleful brown eyes.

This, I thought. *This is what a queen truly looks like.*

Vera clasped her hands in front of her with glee. "Diana, you look absolutely stunning! Maisie, what a wonderful job you've done."

I felt heat rise in my cheeks as the party all voiced their agreement.

"Truly beautiful!"

"A vision, just like her mother."

"You look amazing, Diana."

Aedan squeezed my hand on his arm gently, in comfort. He was much more comfortable in the spotlight than I was.

Lily beckoned her head towards the entrance of the palace. "Shall we go? It's almost time." I always appreciated my aunt's to-the-point nature.

And so we went, walking in a V shape with Vera at the head. The court members were placed along the wings, and I walked a pace or two behind my mother, flanked by Aedan and followed by Maisie. Every so often, Delios came into view, always scouting ahead, keeping to the shadows, and returning to see his queen.

It was a mild day, thankfully not raining. Freshly spring, flowers and shrubs had begun to bloom again, and the wind had turned warmer. The sun was shining, but here in the North that didn't fool us. We knew we wouldn't get much warmth from it until we grew closer to Summer Solstice.

As the bird flies the palace entrance was only a short walking distance to the Sacred Pool and the Gaian Abbey that stood proudly nearby. Maybe twenty or thirty minutes at most if you strolled through the gardens to get there. But as this walk was part of the ceremony, we followed the cobble path all the way into the heart of Nevelyn, where anyone wishing to witness the ritual would join our group, adding more and more bodies as we paraded through the streets.

To me, Nevelyn was always beautiful. The stone

buildings were never more than a few stories high, and they were built from mismatched materials in the most endearing way. It was lively and warm, with vendor stands in the streets and colourful artwork everywhere it could possibly be displayed. The fae who dwelled here were equally lively and colourful, most of them artists, mason workers, singers, and dancers. The theatre just a few blocks off the main street was the longest-running song and dance company in all of Eira. I loved going to every new production they showed.

Today, Nevelyn was humming with life. Banners of green with a silver wolf, the insignia of the Northern Peninsula region, were hung from windows and looped from rooftop to rooftop. Fae of all ages waited in the streets for us to pass, wearing outfits of varying elegance in hues of white. The children waved at us and eagerly joined in our ensemble, chattering to their parents about the queen, and about me.

It was odd for me to hear my name so much. I was used to hearing *Queen Vera* skittered throughout conversations I would pick up from strangers. Now I heard *High Princess Diana* in a constant wave of voices. I couldn't focus on one conversation if I tried. *"I'm not High Princess!"* I wanted to shout at them. *"They haven't accepted me yet!"*

Aedan's low voice was soft in my ear. "It will quiet down soon. They're just excited for you." Grateful for his attempt to focus me, I nodded to him, unable to draw my eyes from the celebration around us.

Onward we marched, through Nevelyn's busy streets, walking through the cheers and well wishes. I found myself shocked at how my fellow patrons of the North rooted for me. Were they really supporting me as their next queen, or were they just excited to be a part of the North's history? Did it make a difference to them what my ritual outcome was if they got to be included in a royal ceremony? Some I knew personally from my time spent in the city, but with over fifty thousand fae living in Nevelyn there was no way I had touched every life gathered around us.

My thoughts an ever-constant swirl, I barely registered my steps. I could see the white hooded figures of Gaians standing in wait for us around the Sacred Pool. My heart rate quickened. It was almost time.

As we reached the grassy clearing before the Pool, I noticed a large group to our left. Members of the other courts; come to be witnesses of the ritual and report back to their regions. Most of the males and females were wearing white, some were not, but all were noticeably different as they each incorporated their court's insignia in unique ways. I trailed over their familiar faces, noting the Princes of the West Shore and the Southern Isles regions, respectively. The Princess of the Eastern Plateau was unsurprisingly vacant, her court members to witness in her stead. As long-standing officials and leaders, this group was skilled at keeping their faces neutral.

My mother stepped forward first into the glen to meet High Mother Cretis. "Hello, old friend."

Cretis had been the High Mother of the Gaians since Maeve had been in rule. As lovely a fae she was, the passing of time was starting to show on her face, in wrinkles along her mouth and crow's feet accompanying her piercing blue eyes. Her long red hair had silver woven through it, and the pale hands she clasped in front of her bore spots and scars, denoting her long life.

I had spent much time with Cretis while completing my training as an adolescent. After coming home from my extensive war training in Mt Nord, I was sent straight to the Gaian Abbey, where the priests and priestesses taught me of our religion and how to focus my meditations into visions. I had definitely needed the calm quiet of the Abbey and their comforting words after suffering heartbreak in Mt Nord.

As High Mother, Cretis did not train the adolescent pupils. But as the queen's daughter an exception was made. I was her shadow for three months. She claimed the best way to learn was to be fully immersed. I was at her side as she performed her routine jobs; mostly blessings and weddings. She led prayers to our Mother Earth, Gaia, in the Abbey, in healer's clinics, at the palace, wherever she was called to bring her divine words. By the end of my time there, I could lead newborn baptisms and daily blessings all by myself. It was good work, healing for my soul, but I didn't complain when I finally returned to the easy comforts of training at the palace.

Cretis and my mother joined hands for a moment and bowed their heads together. I knew they were sending a prayer of thanks and a request for guidance for me. When they rose, Vera turned towards the congregated crowd.

"What a special occasion," she said, her voice projecting across the Pool's surface. "Thank you for being here to witness my daughter, Princess Diana's ascension ritual." A low drumming started, accompanied by quiet percussion instruments. I tried to swallow, but my mouth was dry. Aedan squeezed my arm, a reminder that everything would be okay.

High Mother Cretis was speaking to the crowd, leading them in prayer and instructing them on where to sit and what their role would be in the moments to come. Words did not register to me. Before I knew it, the citizens of Nevelyn and the visitors from the other regions were sitting on the grass around the water, a few feet back from its shoreline. I was the only one left standing, along with the High Mother. I hadn't even noticed Aedan leaving my side.

Just focus, I told myself. *Breathe. It's fine. I'm fine.*

I joined Cretis at the Well a few paces back from the shore. It pulled water directly from the Pool—if it so desired to, that is.

She said a blessing over the bucket, then lowered it into the Well. Behind me, the witnesses had started singing along to the music. Gentle, soothing hums.

High Mother Cretis pulled the bucket up, up, up, until it rested on the side of the Well. There was water at the bottom, enough for one drink. She poured the contents into a wide-brimmed bowl and handed it to me.

The Well was a source of life for us. The water pulled from it was said to have threads of ancestral magic running through it. If it allowed the user to pull water from it, one could use the water to heal, protect, or create. But the Well was fussy; legends said it could judge the purity of the user's heart. It was not often that water was present when the bucket was pulled up.

"Drink, my child, and allow your ancestors to speak with you today."

I steadied myself before taking the bowl so my hands wouldn't shake. I raised the bowl to my lips and drank the water down in one smooth motion. It tasted… like normal water. *That was underwhelming.* Cretis took the bowl back and motioned widely for me to enter the Pool.

I tried not to furrow my brow as I walked to the shore. I hoped the Pool had a plan for getting me to dream, because my body sure as hell wasn't going to sleep with all the adrenaline coursing through me.

Kicking off my silver flats, I dared a glance around behind me before stepping in. My mother watched intently, her eyes aglow with pride and support. She sent a tendril of her magic to touch mine as if to say, *"You can do this."* Her sweet, lilac magic met mine of snow and cedar. Everyone else around me had their eyes closed, singing the sweet and strange music of our ancient language.

I turned back towards the Sacred Pool. It wasn't very big in size, more of a pond. Willow trees lined the back, where it touched the wooded land. The red brick Abbey lay beyond there, down a worn walking path. The water was the blue of robin's eggs, with aquatic plants of all kinds—even some that were not native to this landscape—decorating the surface. It was clear enough that I could see some minnows and frogs just below the surface. But the longer I looked, the less I could decipher what was at the bottom. It had at first looked like stones and some seaweed. Now it looked like sand. Magic flowed through the water, making silvery streams.

Alright then. Time to go in.

Hypothetically, I knew the protocols of what would happen should I be rejected from becoming Heir. The High Mother had informed me in case of it, even though she said we had no cause to worry. I would exit the Pool and finish the ceremony by taking one of Cretis's hands. If I took her left hand, I was the new High Princess and Heir of Eira. If I took her right hand, it meant that I was not being chosen to lead, and that a new successor would be brought forward. That had not happened in the Northern Peninsula — ever. The other regions had been known to change ruling lineage every few centuries or so, but my family had always been chosen to be Queens.

If I was rejected, what would happen to me? All my years of queenly, court training? I was sure my mother would still offer me a position in her court, but one day we would be forced to leave the palace, and what then?

I pushed the thoughts from my mind. Useless to worry about the possible outcomes before they were in front of me. *What will be, will be.*

I had been to the Sacred Pool before but had never been in it. Children were warned from an early age not to dare swimming in it. The water had been known to drown fae who waded in for selfish or hateful reasons.

I stepped into the water. It was warm, inviting. I waded farther and farther in, and it was only until the water was at my waist that I realized my dress was not getting wet. I continued farther, surprised at the depth of the water. I went to take another step to find there was no surface left for me to walk on, just open water. A small noise of surprise escaped me as I became completely submerged.

I was not underwater, or on land either. I opened my eyes, to find darkness all around me. My body — wait, was I in a body? I couldn't tell. I was just my consciousness, unable to move as I stared into the black. It should have been terrifying, I supposed, but I felt an inexplicable calm. A small prick of thought in the back of my mind wondered if this was similar to what death may feel like.

A soft chuckle. *"You aren't wrong, child. But not quite correct, either."* The voice was both male and female, high and low, husky and chirpy at the same time.

All at once, the darkness was filled with orbs of light. They were beautiful and glowing bright enough that I knew my waking eyes would not be able to look upon them. I knew, then, that the lights were my ancestors. Was Maeve among them?

"Welcome Diana." An orb dissolved into a female fae. She was tall and lean, with dark skin like molasses. Her black hair was shorn into a bob of curls that framed her oval face. Her eyes were just light, pouring out.

"I am Iave, one of the first Queens of the Light Realm. I must say, it's very interesting that you summoned me first."

"Hello Iave," I said, surprised to find my voice steady and firm. "I didn't try to summon anyone. I don't even know how this works."

Iave cocked her head to the side. *"It is not your*

conscious mind, but rather your soul that calls the first ancestor forward. Only one of us appears at first, to welcome you. I have never been tasked with the welcome before."

This was starting off weird already. Of course I was causing a commotion, changing things before even starting.

"I hope that's not an inconvenience for you."

"Of course not, I am honored. It has been so long since the North have even remembered my name, I'm glad I could be a part of this history. It is rather awe-inspiring to see what my daughters and granddaughters created in you. The same blood that runs in your veins, used to run in mine."

It was true, I had never heard Iave's name in all my history lessons. That seemed strange to me. I had tried to memorize all the past queens when I was a child. Over two hundred queens was a lot for one to remember, and I did not recall even seeing Iave's name or portrait anywhere. But this beautiful female was one of the queens in a long line of Northern history. One who upheld our traditions and kept the peace. As would be expected of me one day, too.

"Quite a legacy to live up to."

A quiet pause.

"Mm, it is only what you make of it."

"What does that mean?"

"Do you not wish to be queen?"

Honestly, I didn't think I'd ever asked myself that before. If I had the choice, if I had a sister that would take my mother's place, would I walk away from the responsibilities and pressures? Would I want it then — if I couldn't have it?

"I... I think I do want to be queen. I want to do good.

I want to *be* good. But... I'm scared that I'll let them down."

"Let who down?"

"Every fae that lives in this realm! My mother, my aunt Lily, Maisie, my friends," My voice raised in emphasis. Was I coming off frustrated? It laced my voice without me meaning it to. I tried to will it out of my voice as I continued. "The other regions — I know they can be hard to please. I don't know how to keep everyone happy. The fae that live in Nevelyn are so different from the rest of the North, let alone the other regions."

Iave shook her head softly. More figures came forward, some I recognized from paintings in our halls. I found myself looking for Maeve. Had she not hinted we would see each other again at this ceremony? Then — the fae I had seen this morning with the chestnut hair and emerald eyes came to me. I recognized her even with her eyes being pools of light. Queen Diana. The first true queen this realm had seen.

Her gaze was gentle but unyielding as she took me in. I could feel her magic swirling around us. It was frosty white, like mine, but with a raspberry scent that contrasted my cedar.

"You cannot please everyone, Diana."

I blinked. Wasn't that what being a queen was — the impossible task of keeping all her subjects happy?

Queen Diana laughed, *"It does come with the job. But you must trust yourself, and the decisions you will make for the good of the realm. It won't be easy, your rule."*

I stuttered. "Does that mean — am I...?"

There was laughter all around, then.

"Yes, my sweet Diana. An honor for me, you know, to

have my name rule again. A little surprise Vera gave us. It's almost as if she knew."

Relief sagged through me like a knife. But… "Knew what?"

Queen Diana grew grave then. The lights around her started blinking out, one by one. Iave disappeared without a word.

"Listen, my child. We are running out of time with you. I cannot tell you everything, but there are big changes coming. You must be ready for them, to do what must be done. You will be one of the greatest queens this realm has ever seen. But it will be hard-earned. There is a darkness coming. Sooner than you think. I cannot see much of what lies ahead – too many ways the future could go right now. Fate is truly in your hands. We know you will do what is best; we know because we are you, and you are us. We will be guiding you, have no doubt."

Thoughts were racing through my head at breakneck speed. All the lights were gone now except for Queen Diana.

"No, don't go! What do you mean, what's the darkness coming? I'm not even queen yet! Please, tell me what to do, give me anything!" I scrambled to find the thread of magic around her, to try and pull it back. It was too slippery; it resisted me as I flailed my magic around myself wildly. I needed answers, I couldn't go back with so many unknowns.

"We are with you, Diana. The emerald's name is Jweira. Treat her well."

Her light winked out. *No, no, no, no,* I thought. Why me? I tried to fight the darkness all around me, lulling me back to my body, to the realm where I belonged.

"Come back!"

The blackness was too strong. I succumbed.

I awoke, facing the willow trees as I tried to get my bearings back. Sight. My sight was a bit blurred on the edges but fine. My feet were standing on sand, and I was still in the Pool. I wiggled my toes. Yes, sand.

There was no drum beat echoing off the water. No music at all, in fact. I turned around to face the shore again, my head spinning as I moved. Even with my ominous message, I still felt a thrill go inside me that I would be able to take Cretis's left hand.

But I didn't see the High Mother with her hands outstretched to me.

All I saw was chaos.

TWO
Chaos Ensues
DIANA

Not a single fae was in the same spot I'd left them in. Citizens of Nevelyn were running back into the city, grabbing their children close as they ran. The court officials had weapons drawn and were speaking with the Gaians in low tones. My mother, Embris, and Aedan were nowhere in sight.

Maisie, seeing my return out of the Pool, ran to me and helped me out of the water.

"Diana! Thank Gaia you're alright."

"What's happening?" I asked, noting the fear in her face.

"Hurry, come with me," Maisie said quietly, not meeting my eyes as she slipped my shoes back onto my feet. She grabbed my arm and started leading me back to the palace, forgoing the cobble path and heading straight through the grass into the gardens.

I whipped my head around wildly, trying to find my mother in the crowd.

We had reached the middle of the palace gardens, where a statue of Queen Diana made of rosebush stood proudly, surrounded by roses of every colour. They were just about to come into bloom.

Seeing her reminded me of everything that I had just witnessed in the Sacred Pool. Heir. Darkness. Queen. Emerald.

"Stop!" I dug my heels into the grass and wrenched my hand from Maisie's grip. She reached for me, and I sent a flare of snowy white magic around me, shielding myself. Maisie's mouth set, not in fear—but in hurt, I realized. I had never used my magic against her before.

"I'm not supposed to tell you anything. I'm just supposed to bring you back to your rooms." Her voice was pleading.

I shook my head. "Tell me now, Maisie. Where is my mother? What happened? Did—did my ritual... go badly?"

Maisie reached for my hand, and I let my shield drop. I took her hand as she led us back to the palace at a hurried pace, taking a deep breath.

"After you disappeared under the water, a guard came running in yelling about Dark intruders in the forest. Of course, that got everybody screaming and running. It disrupted the ceremony completely. Embris was *pissed*. He went to go investigate and not long after, your mother was called to join them. The High Mother tried to keep everybody calm but it was mass hysteria. And you were still under the water! Queen Vera came back to the Pool to find me. She said when you came up, I was to bring you straight back to your chambers and she would meet you there. And then she left."

Thoughts swirled in my head. Dark fae? My conversation with Queen Diana rang in my head. *Darkness is coming. Sooner than you think.*

I tried to get my bearings. If the Dark fae were intruding, we would be flat out running towards the palace with armed guards flanking us. But it was just Maisie and I, walking with gumption.

"So we're not being intruded?" I asked. "It was a false alarm?"

Maisie cleared her throat. "I haven't been given any official details... but you were under for about fifteen minutes, and I did hear some things while I was waiting for you." She looked around as if we might be overheard. "The officials from the other regions were told that it was only one Dark fae, and that he was badly injured. Not a threat. They were bringing him to the palace healer."

I stopped in my tracks again. "They're *healing* him? Why not just kill him?" But as I mulled that over, I realized why they made this choice. If he was alive, they could get answers from him. He was useless to them dead. And knowing my mother, she would be relentless to wring every bit of knowledge she could. Vera was a good queen, merciful and just, but I knew that a big reason she was those things was because of her need for control in every situation.

Maisie tugged on my arm, pulling me towards the palace again, resuming our quick pace. We entered the foyer, and I was surprised to see the regular guards at the front door, looking as calm as ever. We flew up the staircase and down the halls to my chambers. I didn't feel any need to rush once we were in the palace; we were more than safe here. I couldn't tell whether Maisie's hurry was caused by fear or drive to do as she'd been told.

Once we were inside my drawing room with the oak doors firmly shut, Maisie slumped against the wall and sighed. I would not be able to stay here waiting around to be summoned. If I was to be a true High Princess, a true heir to the throne, then I had to start thinking like one. Where would my mother be right now? The healer's ward. Getting briefed on the graveness of the intruder's wounds, and how long until he could be questioned. I nodded once to myself. Then that's where I would be, too. I deserved to be a part of this process. My training was to resume, if and when I was deemed Heir, in a much more hands-on way, shadowing my mother and sitting in on her meetings with the officials. It would start right now. I could prove myself a worthy successor.

Maisie would never let me just saunter out of here, against the orders she was given. I could easily subdue her, but that was out of the question.

I turned to her, now sitting on a wide futon by the lovely fireplace I had created a sitting area in front of. She had her hands in her lap and was staring into the fire, her brows set in a furrowed line. Still, she sat with grace and poise, the picture of a noble. She fit in at this court better than I did.

"Hey Maze?" I said in a singsong voice. She drew her eyes to me, and I plastered a sweet smile on my face. "I'm feeling quite faint with everything that just happened. Would you mind please fetching me some water?"

Maisie glanced pointedly at the glass pitcher and matching cups sitting on a silver tray on a side table

46

beside the futon.

Damn.

I wanted to kick myself. How hadn't I noticed that?

I poured myself a glass to keep up my ruse. I would have to go a different route. Start by distracting her. "I was chosen as Heir."

That got Maisie up, clapping her hands with glee. "Oh, Di! I knew you would be! I'm sorry I forgot to ask, everything got so hectic there."

She wrapped me in a hug, her blonde ringlets brushing my cheeks. "We should celebrate! Oh! That mulled wine that we had last Winter Solstice — it would be perfect right now. Summon a bottle up to us!" Maisie's eyes had lit up, her woes temporarily forgotten.

Instantly, I felt my plan click into place.

"It would be delicious," I agreed. "But my mother put wards around the wine after we went through so much of it at Solstice — I can't summon any out of the cellar."

A lie. But Maisie didn't question it.

"Okay. I'll go get some. But you have to stay here — I mean it, Diana."

I nodded gravely. My gut twisted a bit in guilt.

Maisie, ever trusting, left through the heavy double doors. I waited a minute and then followed. Easier than I had anticipated. I told myself I would bring her some candied apple later and apologize.

I was swift and quiet as I made my way through the halls, down the staircase that opened to the wondrously spacious ballroom and passed through the kitchens. There were fae at worktables in black uniforms, busy as worker bees, preparing for the feast tonight in honour of my ritual and our visitors from the other regions. Clearly no one had brought them up to speed. They didn't so much as glance my way as I slipped through the back entrance and out into the hall behind. I was passing the library and rounding the corner into the healer's wing when I rammed straight into my mother.

Her face was shock and confusion. "Diana—I was just coming to get you. Why aren't you in your room?"

"I—I'm Heir. I came to see what was happening, and how I could help." The words came out more rushed than I'd meant, with less conviction.

Delios appeared shortly, stopping at my mother's side as always. He watched me curiously. I had known the wolf since I was very young, and used to chase him around the palace, trying to get a hold of his fluffy tail. His tawny fur always managed to slip out of reach. To this day, I could count on one hand how many times he'd let me pet him.

It wasn't uncommon for wolves and the North to be intertwined. They were on our crest, after all. But to see a wolf as a domesticated companion was extremely rare. As fae, we didn't like to keep animals against their wills, and wolves were extremely independent. I had wondered on more than one occasion why Delios chose to spend his abnormally long life by my mother's side.

Vera's face softened as she smiled, reaching out to tuck a strand of hair back that had come out of its braid. "Oh, my darling, I'm so pleased to hear that. I'm sorry I wasn't there when you came out of the Pool."

She really was sorry. She would probably harbor

some guilt about it for a while.

"It's okay, I'm just glad everyone is alright. I can't believe a Dark got through the realm. How did that happen?"

Vera's eyes narrowed. "Maisie filled you in, did she?" She sighed. "We don't know. As far as we're aware, only one got through. He was nearly dead, so I assume the rip he tore wasn't stable. It's unlikely he was followed. As soon as the healers are done with him, we'll know more. I've sent scouts around the forest to patrol for anything unusual in the meantime."

I nodded. "Don't blame Maisie. She thinks I'm still in my room, actually. I want to be involved in this, mother. Let me shadow you." Besides my own curiosity for the Dark fae currently being healed less than a hundred feet from me, I felt duty for this land which would become my responsibility one day.

My mother considered this. "It is your right, of course. As you are now Heir, it is on my shoulders to prepare you for the throne. You may come with me to question the fae when he is awake."

My heart leapt. I was anxious at the thought. Should I be excited? *No,* I thought. *It's good that I'm taking this seriously.*

I opened my mouth to ask when they thought he might be awake when a healer, clad in a simple tan dress and white gloves reaching to her elbows, rounded the corner.

"Oh," she said, her eyes widening as she realized she may be interrupting a conversation between the Queen and the Queen's heir. She cleared her throat and looked to her feet. "Head Healer Yvonne sent me to find you, my Queen. The Dark male — he's awake."

At once, my mother snapped to attention. "Thank you, Doris. Please lead the way." She followed the small female down the hall, glancing once in my direction to indicate that I follow. She whispered to Delios, "Wait for me in my office," to which he paused but obeyed, his tail swishing as he trotted down the hall.

I trailed a step behind my mother. As we neared the waiting area, I saw Embris and Aedan standing near the door that led to half a dozen patient rooms, a scared-looking healer blocking their way. "I'm so sorry, Captain," he said, his voice calm despite his contradictory facial features. "No one in or out — queen's orders."

"Embris." My mother's clear voice rang out. The healer slumped in relief. "Leave my healers alone. What good would you be as a healer's assistant anyway?" The tease softened the blow of the order before it. Vera and Embris had been close friends for many years, but my mother never let the lines of their relationship be blurred. I noted that, tucking it away as good queenly practice.

Aedan smiled in relief as he saw me. I smiled back, glad for his familiar presence here.

Embris was not smiling. "I need answers, my queen. I am absolutely appalled that this happened on my watch — and during such an important ceremony." His eyes betrayed some of the embarrassment and anger that lurked beneath. He looked to me. "My apologies, princess. I will take the blame for your ritual's failure."

Vera waved her hand at him, brushing him off. "You could not have prepared for this, my friend. Even my own wards around Nevelyn didn't catch it. And as for Diana's ritual, well that was no failure at all. She is now High Princess, my Heir." She smiled proudly at me.

Embris bowed his head, while Aedan wrapped me in a big hug, lifting me off the ground. "Congratulations, *High* Princess." Aedan said, grinning. I was glad to have these males in my life. They were family to me as much as my own blood.

I laughed as he set me down, his pine scent washing over me, but the laughter died away as Head Healer Yvonne appeared through the door. She was wearing the same tan dress that all the healers wore, with a black trim to signify that she was the one in charge. The wolf insignia of the Northern Peninsula was stitched over her left breast pocket.

Yvonne, a small and portly female, had never smiled in the years I had known her. She was impeccably good at her job and didn't take her title lightly. She was rough around the edges but cared deeply about her patients. Today, her raven-black hair was pulled into a tight bun at the nape of her neck, making her face taut. She surveyed us all.

"My queen. The intruder is awake and stable. He had severe internal injuries—caused by magic. Nothing I've seen before. He lost a lot of blood, and he needed several different healings on his abdomen, so he will need some time to recover. I wouldn't push him too much. In fact, I would prefer you not see him at all today. But I know that's not going to happen, so I'm giving you ten minutes." Yvonne crossed her arms. She was standing in front of the queen of the realm, the Queen's Heir, and the Captain of the Queen's Army. But in this ward, she was the queen, and she made the orders. Not a flicker of uncertainty crossed her face.

Vera nodded slowly. "I understand. Thank you, Yvonne."

I watched, the respect for the Head Healer obvious on my mother's face. Yvonne had helped her deliver me over twenty-two years ago, and had been promoted to Head a year later. She oversaw her staff of twenty healers here in the palace and was often called to hospitals all over the region to consult on difficult cases.

Yvonne stepped back into the hallway, and we followed her down to the last room. She paused as her ebony hand wrapped around the door handle.

"There's something else you should know. He doesn't have any memory."

My jaw almost dropped, but I clenched it shut.

Embris snorted. "A ruse, I'm sure, to save his own ass."

Yvonne's eyes flared. Internally, I flinched. Wrong thing to say, Embris. "Do you think me incapable of my job, Captain? I verified his claim myself. His mind has been—altered. I think the rip he tore had its own magic that was damaging to his body and mind. It's almost as if it sliced through him as he came through. That's what his mind feels like, sliced and jumbled. He can recall basic things, like how to walk and talk and how to use his hands. He knows he is fae; but has no recollection of his life before waking up here. His memory may come back, and it may not. There is no way to know for sure. I need time, and to monitor his progress."

I stepped back as I felt the air around Yvonne grow thicker with her power. Embris mumbled something about not doubting her.

"Of course, Yvonne. I trust you have done everything in your power. May we see him now?" Vera's tone was the perfect queenly pitch, not too soft and not too commanding.

Yvonne pursed her lips. "This many fae at once may overwhelm him. I would suggest only two go in."

My mother dipped her head, acknowledging Yvonne's grasp at power over the situation and choosing to adhere rather than push against it.

"Diana, you and I will go in. Come," she said, allowing Yvonne to lead us both through the door. I stole a glance at the two males behind us. Aedan was quietly surveying, whilst Embris looked ready to punch through a wall. While I was a bit surprised my mother chose me to go in with her, I felt a little surge of pride as I closed the door behind us.

The room was not very large, but big enough to hold a small metal bed and a chair in the corner by a window. The blinds were pulled down, but the window was open, blowing a spring breeze into the room with the smell of rosewater from the gardens. It barely masked the smell of blood and medical supplies. There was a long table along the opposite side of the room to the bed, housing roots and vials and powders. Extra gauze strips were folded neatly, ready for use, beside a wastebin that was almost filled completely with bloodied gauze.

There on the bed lay a fae male, not much older than

me. To my surprise, he looked — normal. Much like the fae I saw and conversed with every day. He was tall, his frame almost spilling over the bed. He wasn't wearing a shirt, and even with all the bandages around his abdomen it was very clear he was muscular. He was pale — so, so pale. I wondered absurdly if I would be able to see through his hand if he were to hold it up to the light. His arm was covered in swirling black tattoos, matching ones on his chest.

My gaze went up his body and landed on his face. He was incredibly handsome, with strong features and grey eyes. His hair was jet black, slightly curly and twining around his forehead. And poking through his hair — horns. Black and about a finger's length, curling just a bit at the top into a soft point. I had never seen a fae with horns, not even in the pictures of the Dark fae from my history lessons. Instinctually, I wanted to touch them, just to know what they might feel like. Unyielding or pliable? Ridged or smooth?

He watched my mother as we came in, his eyes alert.

"Do you know your name?" Vera asked, a bit sharply. I looked at my mother, noticing a different expression on her face, one that I had grown used to over the years. It was her queen mask, hiding any of her vulnerable features. Her eyes were fixed, and her mouth stern. A mask that said, '*do not cross me.*'

He was quiet for a moment. "Spense." He said it with reluctance in his smooth voice, as if he didn't want to give up a piece of himself — the only piece he remembered.

My mother took a breath. "Well, Spense, my name is Vera, and I am the queen of this realm. I have been informed you have no memories before today. That is certainly inconvenient, as we would very much like to know how you were able to rip through the realm and enter ours. It has been sealed for millennia."

Spense was silent, his face neutral. He took in her words with calm reverie.

"Should you recover any memories, you will come forward immediately. If you cooperate with us, we are willing to be merciful to you."

Spense smiled drily, sarcasm filling his face. "Meaning you won't kill me right away."

Yvonne cleared her throat. "My queen, I believe we may jog his memory by repeating things he may have done in his life before. Daily tasks, maybe a job once he's fully healed. Muscle memory is very real, and it may trigger something for him." She deftly steered the conversation around something too heavy for the first meeting.

I watched as my mother took in her words, nodding. "A good idea. When will he be healed enough to start?"

Spense looked between Vera and Yvonne, his face still a mask of his thoughts.

"Give me two more days to watch the healing of his abdomen, and he should be able to take care of himself as long as he still gets lots of rest."

Vera looked at me, then turned back to Spense. "When you are healed enough to leave here, you will move into the palace where we will be able to monitor your progress. You will experiment with skills and hobbies as we move forward. My daughter and High Princess, Diana, will be your guide and guardian for the foreseeable future." She gestured to me as she turned back to the door, her dress sweeping around her.

Spense looked to me as if he hadn't realized I was there, and we locked eyes. A chill went up my spine. He was so sturdy, so confident even without knowing who he was. I tried to make myself look as queenly and commanding as I could, even with thoughts screaming through my mind in surprise at the bomb my mother had just dropped.

I felt heat rising in my cheeks as his gaze raked over me, taking me in. Unlike a lot of the males in this court, it wasn't a predatory look. It was more... calculating. Taking in his new situation, new guardian, and trying to make sense of it all. I was sure he must be in quite a bit of pain as well, with such a serious injury, but it didn't show on his face.

I didn't want to give him the power of me looking away first, but I felt my reserve faltering as his gaze bore into mine. I tore my eyes away from him, stealing one last glance at his horns, and I followed my mother to the door. Yvonne opened it for us and led us out.

"Rest, Spense. We will be waiting anxiously for your memories," my mother said softly without turning back to look at him.

Embris' and Aedan's faces were full of questions when we met them in the hall. "Come," my mother said, her queenly mask still in place. "Let us discuss this in my office."

Without a word, the queen marched through the palace, her ownership evident. In that moment, we were nothing more than her subjects as we followed her through the halls.

THREE
Permanent Damage
DIANA

"This is absurd," Embris growled, pacing back and forth on my mother's beautiful hand-woven green rug. The four of us were in her office, a grand oval room with a stunning mahogany desk at its center and seating around it for fifty bodies comfortably. My mother sat at the head, regal as ever, and I sat to her left. We had been joined by the court officials from the other regions, who sat down the sides of the table beside us. Aedan had chosen to leave a few spots empty between them and him, knowing he was only present as a courtesy.

For the first time in my life, I felt wary of the grand portrait of the first Queen Diana hung over the fireplace, her green eyes watching us all.

The Prince of the Southern Isles, Leo, sat to my left. Around the same age as my mother, he had tanned skin from endless days of sun in his region, and blond hair that was tied back in a long braid. He wore a suit of sky blue and white and a gold chain at his neck bearing the symbol of the Southern Isles; a rattlesnake. His brown eyes watched Embris pace, his expression matching the captain's. The southern court officials were similarly tanned with light hair and blue ensembles.

On my mother's right were the members of the Western Shore region. Their Prince, Kashdan, was much older than anyone else seated here. His grey hair and beard were a stark difference to the violet robes he wore. An emblem of a grizzly bear was stretched against his chest, a large statement. He only had one official with him, his lovely wife Amatha, who wore a long-sleeved dress in a matching violet.

The members of the Eastern Plateau region were quiet and cold. They adorned white out of respect for my ceremony, with red trims around their fine clothing. They all wore the same necklace of pearls around their neck, a small eagle silhouette pendant hanging from it. Their Princess, Hollaina, was absent as usual. I had only met her once, when I had accompanied my mother on a festive trip to all the regions when I was thirteen. Hollaina was a withdrawn, strange female, with white hair despite her young age and fire in her eyes. I didn't know much about her, only that she had witnessed the brutal slaughtering of her parents and entire court as a youngling. She rarely left her court, and sent her Second, Lord Nimshar, to be her dapifer. Her representation with full authority to make decisions on her behalf.

The North officials, whom I had known my entire life, sat at the other head of the table, effectively closing the other regions in. My mother's seneschal, Solis, claimed the head opposite the queen, his dark eyes flicking over everyone present.

Nimshar cleared his throat. He was tall and lanky, with strawberry blond hair and pointed features. "Captain, while we appreciate the commentary, perhaps we should get back to making a decision on the matter at hand."

Vera looked sharply at him, while Embris bristled where he stood.

"Lord Nimshar, there is already a decision on this matter. You are all here as a courtesy."

Nimshar narrowed his eyes. His associates shifted in their seats.

"My queen, surely you cannot expect us to all *let it slide* that a Dark fae ripped into the realm — causing permanent damage, I might add — and be on board with your decision to do nothing while he lives here, gaining valuable knowledge on this court and our people."

I raised my eyebrows. Permanent damage? I had not heard of this. I glanced to my mother, but she did not look away from Nimshar, her steady look commanding.

"You may have left your manners in the East, Nimshar, but surely you have not forgotten that I am your *queen*. I have made my decision based on reputable healers and many years of experience leading the fae. Leading your citizens." Her voice was steel.

All the officials had dropped their eyes. Even I focused on a knot in the mahogany, counting the rings around it. Nimshar licked his bottom lip, undoubtedly biting his tongue from getting him into further trouble.

Vera continued. "What would you have me do, pray tell? The boy is no threat to us; he is insurmountably outnumbered. With him dead, we may never know how he was able to open a rift into our realm."

Nimshar muttered under his breath. "We may never know with him alive, either."

Kashdan, however, was focused on a different aspect. "Boy? You mean to say he is a youngling?"

My mother dipped her head. "He looks to be not much older than Diana or Aedan. Not a youngling; he has maybe reached his mid-twenties."

Kashdan was contemplative. "Interesting. And his magic? You are sure he is not using it to appear as something he is not?" The way he used his words did not come off as abrasive as Nimshar's sentiments. This was an old fae, a Prince for many years, much older than my mother. He respected Vera as his queen, but also asked for respect in return.

I watched as the officials around the table quietly exchanged words among themselves.

"I assure you; he is not. In fact, my healers were able to put a band on his arm to block his magic until such time we decide to remove it. He will not be able to get it off himself or have any access to his magic." My mother's words were a sharp hit to the gut. I had a brief moment of empathy for him, being cut off from his life source, the magic of his soul, until I reminded myself where he came from.

This information was significant to me in a different way. I realized that while I was allowed to be here in this meeting of the most important fae in the realm, I didn't truly belong. Not when I did not know even half of what was under discussion. I remained quiet, keeping my face neutral as I had been trained to do. I would be able to get more answers when my mother felt she could speak freely.

Kashdan nodded solemnly. "I expected as much

preparedness from you, my queen. You understand, of course, that I must ask for the sake of my own subjects." Amatha gently placed her hand on top of his on the table. He squeezed it comfortingly.

I watched the quickest pang of sadness in my mother's eyes before she settled back into her queenly mask. "You've been quiet, Leo. Anything to add?" This was a slight challenge on Vera's part, but also a true question. Prince Leo was new to his throne, having only been coronated two years ago when his father retired. While he was a practiced general and a clever strategist, this was new to him. My mother had been quietly monitoring his rule for any unrest or changes to his court.

The male looked to Vera, a small smile forming at his lips. "My queen, who am I to question your authority over something that happened in your own region? I would have more to say, perhaps, if this had happened in my own courts and had to yield to your flag, but I have no qualms against this." His head tilted to the side as his amber-brown eyes poured into Vera's. I could not imagine her strength, staring down these powerful princes who would leap at any weakness she showed. Something in the way Leo sat, poised, while he watched everyone reminded me very much of the rattlesnake he wore around his neck. Calculating, dangerous.

Vera's voice was just as dangerous as she responded. "If this had happened in the South, would it be my decision about the boy that you are against, or the idea of yielding to your queen?" I sucked air through my teeth. My mother would not be joining his wordplay.

She wanted clear answers from him.

Leo smiled farther, stretching his lips over white teeth. "You are right that it would be hard to see my fae in the hands of another, but I do agree with you about the Dark boy. If we can get answers from him, we will gain a significant advantage against any other attacks." A snake indeed.

A warning growl sounded from Delios, who was sitting at my mother's side. She hushed him with a gentle rub on his ear.

Kashdan cleared his throat. "May I remind you, Prince Leo, that while you may sit on a sandy throne in the Southern Isles, you are nothing more than an emissary to those fae? You are not a monarch. You serve our queen, and everything you have is hers to take from you if she wishes." His voice was thundering as he stared down the younger prince.

Leo's smirk turned into a sneer, baring his teeth.

My mother waved her hand into the air, disrupting the males' glares.

"Thank you for your loyalty, Kashdan, but I am sure Leo is well aware of the oaths he swore to me. This is a strange new obstacle for us, one we have only heard stories about our ancestors facing. If this is indeed the start of a war against the Darks, then we must be united as one realm. Eira must remain strong."

Everyone murmured their agreement at that.

Nimshar spoke again, his words less venomous. "So what shall you have us do while we wait for the boy to regain his memories—if that is even possible?"

My mother stood now, addressing all of the fae in

the room. "You will all return to your regions and not breathe a word of what happened to anyone. As we speak, a glamour is being dusted over my city. My subjects will not remember the intrusion; and will instead believe Diana's ritual went smoothly and uneventfully. We will be monitoring the intruder carefully. Our healers already have a plan in place to trigger his memories. I will keep you informed of any progress. If nothing changes, we will meet again at the summer solstice celebrations as per usual. You are to act as if nothing has changed except for Diana now being Heir. Understood?"

A glamour over Nevelyn. I hadn't even known that was possible. I understood why, but it felt incredibly *wrong* to alter with the citizens' minds without their knowledge. Was it really so important to keep the intruder's existence here a secret? He would stick out like a sore thumb with his horns anyway. Judging from the officials' lack of reaction, it wasn't as huge of a shock to them as it was to me. Clearly this wasn't an uncommon occurrence, which made my stomach roll uncomfortably.

The princes all agreed and stood to leave, the meeting now over. They each addressed my mother separately on the way out. Kashdan shook my hand and offered his congratulations to me as he passed.

I stood next to Aedan, his face blank as his thoughts were obviously elsewhere.

"A copper for your thoughts," I said lightly. He blinked. His eyes focused on me, his normally happy smile a bit grim.

"I don't like that there's a Dark here. But I do think it's wise to get as much information from him as we can." I nodded in agreement. We watched in silence as the officials took their leave. They were always welcome to stay in the palace, but all would be leaving before the celebratory feast. I realized now that I had no idea what time it was—if the feast had gone on without us or been cancelled. With the exhausting summer solstice celebrations less than three months away, I was perfectly fine skipping tonight's planned festivities.

Then it was just my mother, Embris, Aedan and I left.

"I think that went well," my mother said to her captain.

He grunted in agreement. "As well as it can with those stubborn males."

Vera chuckled gently. "They are nothing I can't handle." She then grew somber. "In two days, we start work on getting the intruder's memories back. I need your soldiers vigilant until we can get anything out of him."

Embris nodded seriously. "You have my word." Then: "What will we do with him?"

"We will guide him through routine jobs and daily activities. The healers think regularity will help," Vera said.

"I'll assign my best males to guard him, my queen." Embris straightened his jacket lapels with pride. I looked to my mother.

"No," she said, and Embris blinked in surprise. "Diana will be his guide and only guard."

The males looked to me; Aedan's eyes wildly concerned. I put on my best show of looking confident, even though I wondered what I could do that the best soldiers in the Queen's Army could not.

"Alright," Embris said slowly. "Let me know what I can do to be of service to you."

Vera nodded. "Diana and Aedan, you are dismissed. I would like to go over details with my captain."

Aedan immediately bowed his head and made to leave. I went with him, turning at the door to say to my mother, "I would like to speak with you — soon." Vera studied my face and nodded once.

Aedan escorted me back to my rooms. We walked through dimly lit halls, the world dark around us. Night had fallen without notice. If today had gone according to plan, I would've still been at the celebratory feast, dancing into the dawn. I didn't hear any music or lights coming from anything except the dim hall light orbs, so I assumed it had been cancelled. Even though I hadn't eaten all day, the thought of forcing something down my throat now was enough to almost make me gag. I needed a good sleep to think. To be ready to talk to my mother about what exactly I was supposed to do with Spense.

When we got to my room, Aedan took my hands. "Are you okay — with this, with all of what's happened? You haven't really had time to adjust to your ritual, and now you've been given this dangerous job—"

"I'm fine. Really," I lied, forcing a bland smile on my face. I squeezed his hands. "Thank you for your concern. I'll see you at breakfast." He was a wonderful friend, but he was overprotective. He was under enough stress as it was without adding my worries to the pile.

Aedan watched as I entered my room and closed the door behind me, his face full of thoughtful concern.

All I wanted right now was to sleep, to calm the racing thoughts that I couldn't decipher through right now.

Maisie stood near my bed, hands on her hips. "I have a bone to pick with you."

Sleep would have to wait a little bit longer.

FOUR
Mercy Over Justice
DIANA

I sat upon an ivory chair bedecked with hand-painted emerald swirls next to the queen in the throne room. Her chair was impressively bigger, and yet even though her legs didn't touch the ground, she still commanded the space. Delios lay curled at her feet, his fluffy tail over his eyes.

I had left the emerald, *Jweira,* in its box in my chambers. After speaking with my ancestors, a healthy respect of its power had developed. I didn't want to interact with it too much until I had some time to research and devote my efforts into learning about it.

Vera looked at me, smoothing one last hand over her silk dress. "Are you ready for your first Open Palace?"

I had attended many of these in my life, considering they happened once every month, but never from the dais looking out onto the citizens. For the full length of daylight, the palace was open to anyone who wished an audience with the queen herself.

Smiling, I nodded. Trepidation had gathered in my stomach, but thankfully my excitement overshadowed it. I was eager to begin.

The throne room felt different from the dais. I had

always admired the strong columns and large windows, allowing views of Nevelyn. From here I could see something I'd never paid much notice to before, a motto inscribed over the door. *Mercy Over Pride*, it read. A phrase I had heard before in my history lessons, but never once from my mother's mouth. The inscription was significantly old if it had fallen out of use.

My mother nodded to Anten, one of the queen's personal guards-- and by far my favourite to play cards with. He swung the heavy door to the throne room open in one motion. Looking out into the hallway, fae were lined up, wrapping all the way around the curve. Through the glass windows, dawn was breaking, initiating the start of the Open Palace. These fae must have been here all night to wait in line.

Anten welcomed the first citizen in, guiding him to step up onto the pedestal in the middle of the room. A middle-aged male with a neatly trimmed beard smiled at us as he bowed his head. Anten introduced him as Vikter.

"Welcome, friend," Vera said. "What brings you to the palace today?"

"My queen, I have come to humbly ask your blessing to use the Well."

My mother nodded. "A frequent request. What are you planning to use the water for, should you be successful in pulling any?"

Vikter's easy expression darkened. "My wife, she's expecting our first born any day now."

"How wonderful!"

"It is my queen; except I fear the babe is ill. My wife

stopped feeling any kicks or movement a few weeks ago. We have seen healers, but they say we will not know anything until the birth. If I could use the Well—perhaps the water could heal the babe, or at the very least ease our minds." Vikter wrung his hands as he spoke, his fear etched clearly on his face.

My heart was filled with sorrow for him. Children were a rare blessing, and many couples could try for decades to no avail. I looked to my mother, whose face was sympathetic.

"Alright," she said. "I give my blessing for you to use the Well." Vikter's face lit up. "But I must give these words of warning also. The Well is its own entity, created by Gaia herself. It may not present you with any water, though I wish you luck."

Anten escorted the male, saying an endless stream of thanks, off the pedestal, and motioned for the next citizen to join us.

The day continued in similar fashion, many asking for the queen's blessings, some coming to air grievances about their neighbours, or give insight on who they believed might be selling contraband. It was both exhilarating and exhausting. I was in utter awe of my mother, how she remained so patient and kind and firm.

When we broke for lunch, she asked me over a bowl of hibiscus soup what I thought so far.

"I don't know how you do it, mother," I said, shaking my head. "I hope one day I can rule like you."

Vera smiled gently. "Your rule will be greater even than mine, I'm sure, my sweetness." She paused. "Are you worried about the role I have assigned you?"

I gently dropped my spoon into my half-eaten bowl of soup. "In all honesty, it does seem like a big first task as Heir."

She nodded. "I understand you are probably overwhelmed. But I urge you to look to your training, your wisdom. I know you are ready to do this."

"Can you not assist me with this?" I asked, anxiety settling in my chest.

"You know my door is always open."

I nodded. Where would I even start? Would this Dark even be willing to work with me? I was hardly an intimidating figure.

As if reading my mind, my mother spoke. "Start at the beginning. Learn what he knows and doesn't know how to do. Like Yvonne said, regularity will help."

I breathed in a long suck of air through my nose. Start at the beginning. I finished the rest of my bowl in silence, mulling over my daunting task.

Right before the doors opened to the North again, Vera said, "It is vital that no one discovers who he is. I do not want to cause unnecessary panic, and I don't believe the public will openly welcome the Dark into the heart of the city." That was true. Although no one alive in Eira had ever seen a Dark, scary bedtime stories usually involved one.

"Of course, Mother. We will be discreet."

"Good. He will also attend dinners with the royal family each night."

What? My mouth opened in shock. "But—but he is a prisoner."

Vera gestured at Anten to bring in the next citizen.

"He cannot be treated like one, or our palace workers will be suspicious. It is hardly our custom to have a guest stay in the palace and not attend dinner." When she saw my incredulous face, she added. "Relax, Diana. It's just one meal a day."

Anten led a frail, elderly female to the pedestal and helped her—excruciatingly slowly—climb up. It took enough time that I was able to picture the Dark sitting around the dining table, sipping wine and eating grilled vegetables like an esteemed guest. I almost laughed. Seriously, what was I getting into?

I missed the introductions as I pulled away from my daydream.

"Welcome, Eteya. How can I help you today?"

The bony female looked up at us with milky eyes. She looked like she was on Death's doorstep. Her white hair was wispy as it fell around her like a curtain. In a shaky voice, she spoke. "Queen Vera, I have come to ask for your assistance. I am dying."

"I can guide you to the best healers in the realm—"

"You misunderstand me." I bit back a gasp at her outright interruption of the queen. "I do not wish to get better. I have seen many healers, I have tried to use the Well, but I will not hide from it any longer: my body is failing. It is almost time for me to return to Mother Earth. I have spent almost a century in Nevelyn, creating clothing, feeding the economy. I ask very little in return for all I have given this city."

Vera had kindness in her eyes as she surveyed the elder. "You are wise, Eteya. And we thank you for your years of servitude. But if you do not wish to be healed, then I'm afraid I don't know what I can do to help you."

"What I am asking is to be administered the Draught of Eternal Sleep."

My eyes widened. It was forbidden to use the concoction of deadly herbs, including oleander, belladonna, and hemlock. The drinker immediately fell unconscious, to greet Death within minutes. It had been outlawed years ago after becoming a widely used poison. Even the plants required to make it were forbidden to be grown, and were frequently removed from the forest surrounding Nevelyn. Only the palace's private garden had a store, safely monitored.

My mother cocked her head to one side, her eyes narrowing. "A female of your wisdom should know that draught is illegal."

"Of course, I know that, otherwise I wouldn't be here, would I?" Eteya was exasperated, her shaky breaths rattling in her chest. "I do not wish to be a prisoner in my body as it decays. I do not wish to see the anguish of my sons, my granddaughters, as I fade away. I wish to die with dignity."

"Eteya, ending your own life is not dignified."

The old female shook her head. "I am willing to take my chances that Gaia will understand these circumstances." My mother did not reply. "Please," Eteya added. "I am not strong enough to fall upon my own sword, nor will my family agree to do as I wish. I — I admit, I do not wish to see that pressure on them. I wish to pass in my sleep, peacefully and happy in the knowledge my family will not have to see my decay." My heart sank at her words, at the sadness that flowed through them.

Vera clasped her hands in her lap. "I am truly sorry for what you are going through, but I cannot grant you this."

"Please, queen, have mercy. I have nothing left to offer this life. You would be sparing a lot of pain. Your subjects' pains." My eyes flicked to the words above the door. *Mercy Over Pride*. Surely an exception could be made. This fae had been a dedicated member of the North, spending her days sewing and creating clothing for her peers, her fellow North.

The air turned cold as my mother's queenly mask slid into place. "The answer is no, Eteya. That is my final word. I wish you a peaceful passing." She nodded to Anten to dismiss the elder.

It didn't take much for Anten to gently pull her down the steps, but she was firm in her steady gaze at Vera. She pointed a crooked, bony finger at her as she was escorted from the throne room. "It saddens me greatly to be disrespected so. Maeve would never have been so blindly arrogant. When I pass, I will make sure the ancestors know about this. In fact, they already do. May your punishment be deserving of this disgrace, queen."

With strength I did not believe of someone so frail, Eteya shrugged off the arm Anten was guiding her with. She wrapped her shawl tightly around her as she left, her chin held high.

Vera sighed. I turned to her. "Surely, it would be no harm to give her the Eternal Sleep."

"This is an example of when being queen becomes

the hardest job in Eira. It is against the law to even *make* the draught, let alone administer it. If I do not uphold my own laws, how can I expect my citizens to do so?"

My brow furrowed. "But there are extenuating circumstances. This is hardly — "

"Diana. I do not wish to have this argument twice. What if she was lying? What happens if I give the poison to Eteya, and she turns around and uses it to kill someone? That death is on my hands. I cannot risk it."

My stomach churned. My mother's words were wise, but it still felt wrong. I felt with utmost certainty that Eteya spoke the truth about wanting to use it to die on her own terms. And after hearing her side, I had to admit that it seemed a peaceful way to go. Were we really so shackled to our own laws that we no longer had room for humanity?

Feeling dizzied with the guilt and confusion, the rest of the day passed uneventfully. I barely spoke in the hours that passed, soaking up all of the interactions and lessons my mother offered. She was so clear in her convictions, her decisions. Until now, I had thought our morals were aligned. And maybe they still were, but I could not get Eteya's pleading face from my mind.

My brain whirled as I saw the throne room from newly opened eyes.

FIVE
Warrior Bred
DIANA

I had given Maisie the day off and dressed myself, choosing a long green tunic and tan riding pants, paired with leather walking shoes. Two days had passed since the Open Palace, and today I would have my first meeting with the Dark. My plan for the day was to give Spense a tour of the city and gauge his reactions. It pained me to skip another day of riding, but all things considered, adding a riding test to the first day probably wasn't all that wise. The best way to see Nevelyn was by foot, anyway.

I made my way to the healer's ward, smiling and saying brief hellos to some of the palace workers as they flitted around doing their daily duties.

I stopped by the kitchens to give Maisie's mother, Ada, a quick peck on the cheek and apologize for her feast not being enjoyed. She waved me off of course, saying the palace workers always welcomed leftovers and sent me on my way with a freshly picked gala apple.

I munched the fruit as I rounded the corner into the healer's ward. This time, the smell of blood greeted me right away, strong and metallic down my throat. I scrunched my nose and tried not to breathe too deeply as I met the healer in the waiting area—Doris.

"Good morning, princess," she said, her heading dipping towards me. "Sorry for the smell—we just received a soldier who fell off his horse in the training arena and landed on his knife. Not serious, but it is a long enough gash on his arm to bleed a fair amount."

I shook my head at her as though I didn't smell anything, even with my nostrils burning. I stuck the remaining half of the apple into my pocket, my appetite gone. "I'm sure he'll be healed up in no time with your expertise here. I don't want to get in your way—I just came to retrieve the Dark male. Is he ready to go?"

Doris nodded eagerly. "Of course, princess, he should be through the door any minute." She paused, and then added gently, "His name is Spense, by the way. I don't want to impose, but calling him by his name will most likely help him find himself easier."

I pushed down the shame that flushed my cheeks. I could push the trepidation aside if it helped get the memories we were looking for.

I nodded at Doris, unsure of what to say, and thankfully I was saved by the entrance of Yvonne, her ever-present scowl and tightly wound bun, leading Spense behind her. He towered over her short frame, his shape barely fitting through the door. He looked as pale as he had two days ago, but some colour had returned to his eyes. They were still gray, but now they were platinum instead of faded steel. And his horns—wait, where were his horns? I was momentarily confused until my magic flicked at my forethought, suggesting a glamour in front of me. They had hidden his horns away to make him blend in. *He'll still stand out,* I thought to myself. Even just standing there eyes flickering over everything in the waiting room, he looked... different. He looked like us, but didn't.

Yvonne addressed me. "Don't do anything beyond walking and easy work for a week. If he has to come see me again to fix that complicated abdomen wound I spent hours healing to perfection, I won't be happy." I didn't doubt that.

Without another word, Yvonne turned around and left, clapping Spense on the arm as she went down the hall towards the blood smell. Doris bowed and backed into the hall, following her head healer. This left Spense and I alone in the waiting room. Regaining his memory seemed like a small feat in comparison to the thought of having to fill the awkward silence between us. Small talk would be ridiculously mundane. I looked at him wordlessly as my brain spun for something to say.

"Hello again," Spense said, breaking the silence. He wore common Nevelyn attire, loose tan trousers and a white long-sleeved shirt. The pants were a bit too big and the shirt a bit too small, which didn't help with his disguise. I noticed a wide black band on his wrist, plain and unassuming. If I didn't know any better, I would think it a piece of male jewelry. But I did know better, and that bland piece of fabric had been spelled to keep him from accessing his magic.

I straightened my spine and mustered a smile. "Spense. I don't know if you remember me from a few days ago — I'm Diana," I said, gesturing for him to follow me out the hall. I was desperate to get away from the reek of blood.

"I remember." Spense walked beside me, and though my training yelled at me to walk a pace in front of him, I did nothing to change our side-by-side stride.

I looked sideways at him, straining my neck to meet his eyes. "Well it's good that your memory works now," I said, instantly regretting the weak attempt at a joke. He said nothing.

I was about to lose my nerve.

"I thought we could start slow for today. If you're up to a full day of walking, I was going to show you around the city. I think you'll enjoy seeing it, and maybe you might find something you remember doing," I looked down at my hands, which had begun wringing themselves together.

Get it together, Diana. You are the Heir of Eira. If you can't keep your head for this simple task, how will you ever be queen?

Spense only nodded, sighing through his nose.

We walked in silence through the palace, save for times when I would point out a wing or room that might be important for him while staying here. The kitchens, the library, the dining hall. He took it all in, not saying much, sometimes reaching up to put a hand through his wavy black hair. I wondered if he could still feel his horns with the glamour on.

We made our way out into the sunshine, which touched our skin but didn't warm us too much. Thankfully, there was no breeze today, making it bearable to be outside without any coats. I was pointing out the royal gardens when he abruptly asked, "What season is it?"

I blinked in surprise. "It's spring. The Equinox was two weeks ago. We are pretty far north, so the sun won't be hot until we get closer to summer."

Spense nodded, reaching out to brush a hand over a rhododendron bush as we passed. I ventured a question. "Is it familiar — this kind of weather?"

He was thoughtful for a moment and then answered, "It's odd... I feel familiarity towards things, but I cannot place why. I know that spring is supposed to be warm and blooming, but I cannot remember experiencing it before. I know that we are walking on cobblestone and that these are flowers, but I don't know why I know that. Does that make sense?"

Sympathy rose its head, but I pushed it down.

He is your enemy, Diana. "I can imagine it feels quite overwhelming."

Again, he said nothing. We walked together down to the city, through the streets. Even though he and I were plainly dressed, fae recognized me and bowed their heads or offered their congratulations as we passed. Some I knew on a more personal level, but I kept a clipping pace in order to keep attention off of Spense. I didn't know whether it was working for or against me, as many stared at Spense quite non-discreetly, taking in his informal wear and the fact that he was not a regular walking partner of mine.

When we got to the heart of Nevelyn, I decided to turn us around for the day and head back. The sun was up high, meaning that it was past noon, and I was starting to get hungry. On the other side of the city square was the Marketplace, where vendors from all over the North came to sell and trade goods. It was a busy, hectic place with bodies moving relentlessly. Easy to get swept up in—easier to get pickpocketed in. It seemed too frantic and wild of a place to visit on his first day.

I watched Spense on our way back, tired of making idle chitchat with almost never a reply back. He was taking everything in extensively, his gray eyes darting from building to building, his gaze sometimes landing on a walking passerby, or in the window of a shop. He was alert, I realized. Perhaps he was doing a better job of looking for something familiar than I was. *Or,* a voice in my head countered, *he's planning an escape route.*

I shoved that thought from my mind. He would be stupid to run with his magic bound and no memory before two days ago. Judging on his awareness, he knew that too.

A soldier rode by nearby on a prancing bay stallion. I recognized it as one of Embris' palace-bred athlete horses. It really was magnificent to watch, and I knew from experience that they had more gumption and stamina than any horse from the other regions.

Spense watched the pair, and asked, "Do you keep horses at the palace? I noticed the stallion is wearing your insignia." Indeed, the horse's breastplate was adorned with green stitching and a wolf on the front, over his heart.

"Yes, we have a stable in the back. Actually, our Captain of the Queen's Army has been breeding these horses for his entire tenure. You won't find a more suited battle mount in any of the regions. Their caliber is unmatched." I tried to keep my voice factual, but I heard the pride creep in. "Would you like to see it?"

Spense nodded, showing more life in his face than he had all day. "I would like to see it very much."

We made our way back to the palace, forgoing the cobblestone to the grand foyer entry, and instead weaving around on a lesser-known dirt path that led directly to the soldiers' entrance to the stables.

The birds were loud here, usually undisturbed on this path. The freshly budding trees were filling in nicely, the small animals scuttering around as they woke from their winter naps. This was always my favourite time of year, watching everything come back again. It reminded me that life was a circle, never-ending.

We followed the dirt path until it just became grass and led us up a small hill. On the other side stood the considerably large white barn, with windows all along the side. Some had horse's heads hanging out, surveying. Other horses roamed in paddocks nearby, and others tied up at the tacking post, where soldiers and stable hands were getting them ready to exercise for the day.

The smell of fresh shavings and timothy hay met us as we entered the barn. It was immaculately kept, with bright light coming through the skylights and a nice breeze floating through the open doors. This was familiarity at one of its highest points for me, and in that moment, I felt a pang of empathy that Spense could not experience any feelings like this.

The head stable hand, Rolfo, grinned as he walked

towards us.

"Princess! Can I get Finnvarra saddled up for you?"

I shook my head. As much as I would love to take my fiery chestnut mare out for a rip on this fine day, I did not see that being something I had time for in the next few weeks.

"Just a tour for my friend today, Rolfo. Hope you've been taking good care of my girl for me!"

Rolfo smiled, his gap-toothed grin alluring with his tiny frame and big personality. "The boys are scared of her, you know. She drags them around and terrorizes them. But it's good for me, gives me something to threaten them with when they get behind on their chores," he laughed.

He waved as he walked away, leaving us to wander the aisles. I stopped at Finnvarra's stall, and she came to greet me, her soft breath tickling my face. She was such a lovebug around me, but I knew that part of her personality was the exception and not the rule. She was a warrior bred for battle, through and through.

"Is she yours?" asked Spense, coming up behind me with soft footsteps.

"I like to think that we're each other's," I replied.

He reached out a hand to gently rub Finnvarra's cheek. She eyed him up but allowed it. With him this close to me and the updraft going through the barn, I caught Spense's scent for the first time. It was fruity with a hint of chocolate. I wouldn't have guessed that for him, but as I took him in it seemed to fit perfectly.

"So, are the horses doing anything for your memory?" I asked, stepping away from Spense's scent.

82

"I—I think they might. It's like grasping at air, or trying to hold on to mist. But I do recognize horses, and I think that I might know how to ride. I recognized the equipment the boys were using to tack up the horses outside. I think my body would remember how to assemble it, even if my brain doesn't."

I nodded, an idea forming. "Why don't I see if Rolfo has any positions available for work? Nothing too strenuous, of course, so I don't get beheaded by Yvonne, but maybe it will help regain your memory."

Spense pursed his lips, looking around. "I could work here," he said.

I left him at my horse's stall and tracked down Rolfo, who readily agreed to take on a new set of hands. That didn't surprise me—there was always work to be done around the stables. I left out Spense's background, just saying he was a family friend who moved here recently, and he had basic knowledge of horses but may need refreshing.

Not too shabby for my first day.

We spent some more time wandering around the barn. I found peace from being here, and I could tell it was nice for Spense after the liveliness of Nevelyn. When our bellies grumbled audibly, we headed back to the palace, where Ada was more than happy to fix us up a plate of fruit, cheeses, and cured meat. We ate in the grove outside the dining hall, the sun touching us gently and the birds chirping as the only noise. I peered at Spense over my plate, studying him. He knew how to hold a fork properly, and what cheese to pair with what fruit. *Could be coincidence*, I thought, *but could be muscle memory as well.* Either way, I decided, everything he tried was a step in the right direction.

After our plate was empty, I decided we could both use a rest before dinner.

I showed Spense his chamber, a grandly decorated room big enough to house a family of four with its own private bathing room, in the west hall, opposite to the royal family's quarters. Most of the west hall was made up of guest rooms for visiting court officials and their families. All were empty except Spense's now. He would have the wing to himself, although I knew there would likely be guards stationed at intervals close to his door.

"It's nice," was all he said as he took in his new arrangements. Nice was an understatement, I thought as I took in the views of the garden and the copse of trees in the far distance.

"Dinner's at sundown in the formal dining hall. Someone will be by soon with clothes for you to wear, and to escort you there. I'll see you then," I said, leaving him to his own thoughts.

Back in my own room, I noticed an envelope addressed to me on my side table. Turning it over, I broke the seal of the West Shores, a grizzly bear head encircled by roses. I almost squealed in delight, knowing who it was from right away.

Opening the letter confirmed my suspicions. My dear friend Jamey Pinois from the West region had written to me. As the daughter of Prince Kashdan's first son, she traveled with the court to all our solstice and equinox celebrations. I had befriended her at a young age, and we kept in touch via letters back and forth, staying relevant in each other's lives.

Dearest D, she had written. *I absolutely cannot wait until I get to visit the north court for the summer solstice celebration. It has been way too long since our last visit. On another note, I wanted to send this letter with a warning. My court will not like me divulging this in you, but I want you to be safe. We have had shadows appearing around the cities. They are black as night and move with their own magic. They suck things up and don't give them back. I dread the day a youngling gets too near. Some fae have reported hearing the shadows whisper to them. I've never heard of such a thing, and of course no one will tell me anything. Hopefully, I will have more to tell you when I see you in three months. Until then, please be safe and wary. –J.*

That was troublesome news to hear. Knowing the loyalty of Prince Kashdan, he would have filled in my mother about this. It was unsurprising that she hadn't shared it with me considering how hard I had to push for the small amount of knowledge I had been given so far.

I sat on the edge of my bed for a long while, thinking about today and contemplating what to pen back to Jamey. When I finally stood again, the sun had set low, almost ready to disappear for the night. I was already late for dinner, and I'd effectively left Spense to the wolves. The sun had almost disappeared from the horizon, meaning I was probably already late.

I jumped into motion, dressing for dinner in a simple dark blue gown, one I particularly liked because of its lack of complicated lacing at the back. I could easily get in and out of this dress without Maisie's help. I ran my fingers through my hair to comb it out and left it down around my shoulders. I placed emerald earrings in my ears and called it done. Maisie would have done something a little more interesting for dinner, but I was running late and definitely didn't have the skillset to whip up a new hairstyle.

When I got to the dining hall, everything looked as it normally did. The long table was set with a floral tablecloth to celebrate spring, and the light orbs on the walls were lit with a pinkish glow. It was warm and inviting here, with the smell of herb-crusted fish and a variety of mushrooms. The same familiar faces of my mother, Lily, Polis, Embris, and Aedan sat around the table. What stood out though, was seeing Spense, rigid-backed, next to Embris. I was amazed at how being given a properly fitting outfit made him seem as though he belonged. He had bathed and tidied his mess of curls; I could see his pointed ears for the first time.

There was one open seat at the table; my usual spot on my mother's left. Aedan sat at my other side, but instead of facing Embris as I normally did, I sat down and met eyes across the table with Spense.

"Good evening, Diana," said my aunt. "Nice of you to join us."

I looked down at my plate and noticed it was full where the others were already half eaten. Hastily I picked up a fork and started eating.

"Nice of you to wait for me, Auntie," I said drily, earning a chuckle from Lily as she raised an eyebrow and took a long sip from a goblet of white wine.

I locked eyes with Spense over the table and caught

him smirking a bit. I had never seen anything but a blank, calculating look on his face, so it caught me off guard. It was an extremely cocky look on him.

My mother addressed me, tearing my gaze away. "You didn't miss too much. Spense was just telling us how he is to start working in the stables." It seemed unlikely to me that Spense offered up this information without prompting, which made me wonder if I *had* missed much. Vera looked at me like she would've liked to have known this information from me directly. *I know the feeling,* I thought.

"Yes," I said, chewing on the fish. "I figured that would be okay. Yvonne suggested he get a job and he seemed drawn to the horses. Made perfect sense to me." My tone was dangerously close to being snippy as I felt annoyance rise in me at my mother. Wasn't I being tested on my problem-solving skills?

I didn't dare look at any of my family's faces around the table as I scooped more food into my mouth, trying to look indifferent.

"It was a smart idea, Diana," was all my mother said.

Embris growled, "I wasn't aware of anyone asking if that dirty rat could touch my horses."

"They are the palace's horses, not yours," I snapped, instantly defensive.

The table got tense at that moment, and Aedan being the wonderful friend he was, filled in the silence.

"Speaking of horses, would you have time to go for a ride with me tomorrow?" he asked me, drinking some wine as he leaned back in his chair to better face me. "I've just started training some of our yearlings from the foaling three years ago, and there is this one stallion who I would love to get on an open field and test out." Aedan's face was alit with passion as he spoke about the horses he loved helping his father breed and train.

Which made it so hard for me to have to shut him down.

"I would love to; I certainly could use a good open field gallop. But I think I'll be too busy in the next few weeks with current situations—" I glanced swiftly in Spense's direction, "—and now Heir training," I said, grimacing at the thought of how much was on my plate. I hadn't realized until I'd said it out loud. My mother met with her advisors and councilors biweekly, and had at least one meditation with the Gaians a week. On top of that, the Open Palace was held monthly. I would be expected to sit beside my mother and observe everything until I was well-versed enough that she could start delegating duties to me, which could take years.

Aedan hid his disappointment well, but the look of disgust he threw Spense's way was much more obvious. I looked around the table, and noticed how everyone seemed to bend away from Spense. If they did look in his direction, it was with distaste. He seemed oblivious as he ate his meal, not touching the wine, but when he met my eyes again, I could tell that their behavior towards him didn't go unnoticed.

Dinner finished uneventfully, with small talk spattered here and there. At the end of the meal, everyone got up to leave except Spense, who seemed unsure if there was some protocol to the order we left the table. With no one else noticing him, I walked to his chair and offered to escort him back to his room. "The palace can be kind of a maze," I added.

He nodded and we left the dining hall together, heading towards the west wing. I called goodnight over my shoulder and noticed Aedan watching us leave, his brow furrowed.

Spense snorted as he saw the other male's look as well. "He's worried I'm going to attack you — or worse, invite you to bed."

I tried not to gape at the absurdity of his words, or at the surprising amount he had just spoken at once.

"Aedan is hardly the jealous type," I said, shaking my head. "And he knows I can hold my own." That was an understatement. I could have Aedan on the ground in a few moves. He was impeccably trained, but so was I.

Spense dipped his head, a small shrug appearing at his shoulders. It made him seem smaller — more alive, I realized. Less gloweringly tall and mysterious. *Although still tall*, I amended, as the top of my head only reached his upper chest.

He toyed with the band around his arm, the fabric that was stifling his magic down to some unknown place inside him. No matter how hard he tried, he would not be able to remove it. I had heard stories of fae who chopped off their hand and found the band sitting around their bicep, as present as ever, and a hand on the ground with a naked wrist.

I don't know what compelled me to ask it, but I did:

"What does it feel like? Not being able to use your magic?"

Spense sighed. "It's darkness. I don't remember how my magic feels, but I *know* what it feels like, if that makes sense. I know that it's there, and it wants to be used. But it feels like trying to hold water in your hands. If I reach for it, I sometimes feel like I have a grasp on it, but I always come away empty handed." He gestured with his hands. "It feels like I have a limb missing."

Sympathy pooled in my stomach. My magic was always readily available, strong and willing and comforting. It was as much a part of me as my arms and legs. I wouldn't be able to function without it, flickering and tasting the air, the animals and other fae, the whispers of life from the trees. I wondered if Spense would be able to ever find his true self without his magic. It was such a raw, integral part of the fae. It wouldn't be much for me to snap it off his wrist, but that would *not* go over well with my mother.

Could he even be that much of a risk with his magic intact? I knew he was wearing it not to stop him from attacking others, which would be useless on his part, but to stop him from using glamours or manipulating others. Still, the band was almost inhumane. For his sake, I hoped he proved himself trustworthy enough that it could be removed.

"I don't know who you were before, or what you were planning when you ripped through into our realm, but I am sorry for the situation you're in. I can imagine you feel very alienated," I said finally.

Spense looked at me, his gray eyes questioning. "Don't you think I deserve this?"

I paused. "I don't think that's for me to decide."

Truthfully, I didn't know what to make of this — or him.

He continued, "It seems like everyone is ready to kill me over what I did. I could take the glares and comments if I knew why."

I nodded. "It's fair for you to know the history between your fae and ours. It may help to bring your memories forward as well. But that will have to be saved for tomorrow, as it's much too late to get into that now," I said. "I was thinking I could show you the other side of Nevelyn tomorrow, and maybe stop by the library in the afternoon."

We had reached Spense's door, and he paused before opening it. "Would it be possible to tour the city on horseback?" he asked.

I considered. "I don't see why not, provided you know how to ride."

He nodded. "I guess we'll find out. Goodnight, Diana."

He stepped into the room and inclined his head towards me before closing the door.

"Goodnight, Spense," I said to the empty hallway.

SIX
Prophecies, Mostly
SPENSE

I didn't know what time to expect Diana in the morning, but considering her late arrival to dinner last night, I was confident she wouldn't be rapping at my door at the break of dawn. That fact made me smile a bit—the perfectly poised princess, never on time.

Yesterday had been an utter fiasco. My life had turned into chaos, but maybe that was normal for me. I wouldn't know. Admittedly, having a bottomless, empty pit for a brain was frustrating to say the least. But there was a certain amount of peace that came with it, unburdened by anything except the present.

Although the citizens in the colourful city of Nevelyn didn't look at me with anything other than curiosity, the inner circle of the queen certainly did not think highly of me. With that knowledge, I could surmise that for whatever reason, my presence here was secret. I hadn't been able to get much from the healers, only small bits here and there, but with it I was able to piece together that I was from another realm—and I was not welcome in this one.

That healer—Yvonne—had been gruff and full of attitude, but I could tell she was not prejudiced against me, she only saw a patient. The queen practically radiated hate towards me, not to mention her brick-looking captain and his too-pretty son. And Diana... she feared either me or the idea of me, I couldn't tell. But there was no hate exuding from her. I often caught her staring at me like she was trying to put together a puzzle. I wanted to tell her that if she solved it, I would love to know.

A palace worker had come by my room and dropped off a variety of clothing in different colours and elegance. They fit me better than the old, well-worn scraps that the healers managed to dig up for me. Despite the queen's unapologetic promise that I was only allowed to live until they got answers from me, I was being treated like an esteemed guest. Clothing, food, work, all in the name of keeping my existence under wraps. It was almost pitiful.

What they didn't realize was they had inadvertently given me all the power. I could control the narrative if anything did return to me. I wasn't sure yet if I was the kind of person who would yield that power against them.

I studied myself in the mirror as I dressed in plain pants and a shirt that would be easy to ride in. I could see my horns even if no one else could, twirling out of my mess of dark hair. My right arm and chest were covered in swirling black lines of tattoos, depicting symbols and languages that didn't match anything I'd seen on the fae here.

I paused to look at the scraggly scar running down my abdomen before pulling a shirt over my head. It was pink and slightly raised, a vast difference to the other scars on my body, faded white lines scattered around. I'd also noticed a rather large, deep scar running across my left shoulder blade, which must have been a serious injury considering the twinging pain it wrought when flexed at a certain angle.

There was a faint deep breath at the door before a light knock. No doubt Diana, steeling herself before meeting me for the day.

I opened the door, and she greeted me with that same close-mouthed smile that didn't reach her hazel eyes. She took me in, tucking a piece of chestnut hair behind her pointed ear.

"Good morning," she said, her voice much lighter than I had last heard it.

"Good morning," I echoed back.

She turned toward the hallway, gesturing with her head. "Shall we?"

I nodded and walked with her through the palace and across the back gardens to the stables. Unlike her rambling yesterday, she was quiet. I liked it better when she was talking, so I prompted:

"How long have you been Heir? The conversation at dinner last night made it seem like it was new to you."

One side of her mouth lifted as she answered, "The day you arrived. Actually, you kind of… arrived right in the middle of the ceremony."

A slimy feeling started in my gut. Was it shame? Guilt? I had a hard time placing it.

"I apologize for that," I said, and Diana nodded. "Tell me about it. The ceremony."

She gave me a sideways look, flipping her hair around her shoulders. At the same time a breeze blew towards us. It sent her scent right to me, overwhelming cedar and... fresh snow, I realized. Smiling inwardly at my revelation, I focused on Diana's story.

"In our realm, Eira, we have always been ruled by a queen chosen by our ancestors. We have four regions; the Northern Peninsula, where we are now, the Western Shores, the Eastern Plateau, and the Southern Isles. They all have a prince or princess at their heads but ultimately, they all bow to the Light Queen. My mother. Once I turned twenty-two, the tradition is that I meet with my ancestors so they can decide whether I will be the next queen or not. The Heir. That's what the ceremony is all about. The whole city comes and there's usually a big feast and party afterwards." Diana spun an emerald ring around her finger while she spoke, keeping her eyes trained on the white barn in the distance as she spoke like a well-rehearsed tutor.

There was a lot to digest there. I understood the ruling system they used. The ancestor one was new to me, although my addled brain offered a thought that it could be linked to meditation.

"I suppose I ruined the party pretty well. Did you get chosen at least?" Of the array of questions I had, this one slipped out first, almost inadvertently.

Diana smiled, still close-mouthed, but I noticed it reached her eyes this time.

"Despite your efforts, yes, I was chosen," she said, her voice teasing. "I don't really mind missing out on a grand event with me at the center. It would've been one hell of a feast though."

I nodded once, and tried to return the gesture, the slimy guilt softening in my stomach slightly.

"So are you saying that there was a chance you wouldn't be chosen as the Heir?" I asked.

"Theoretically, yes. It's happened before in some of the other regions; a prince or princess' child will go to their ritual to be told that the ancestors would be choosing a different fae instead. Sometimes they are noble born, sometimes not. It never goes over particularly well, from what I've heard." She paused. "Power is an addiction."

"It's never happened in the North?"

She smiled again; a little bit proud. "No. I am directly related to our first Queen. I guess my family is worthy of ruling in our ancestors' eyes."

I was feeling confident, so I ventured: "You truly communicated with your ancestors during your ceremony?"

Diana nodded gravely. "Yes."

"And what did they have to say?"

She looked at me, clearly contemplating whether or not to tell me the truth.

"Prophecies, mostly."

"Anything come true yet?"

That small smile again. "I guess we'll find out."

*

After we had both successfully mounted our horses, we rode down the same path we came in yesterday to get to the city. It was a bit of a shock to us both when I was able to effortlessly swing myself into the saddle and grab the reins correctly. I hadn't thought about it too much when I walked up to the quiet black mare, Plum, and my muscle memory took over. It felt a bit jagged and clumsy, but the smooth movement was there. I had looked to Diana, who just shrugged, mounted her copper-coloured horse, and said "let's go". It was probably best not to put on a show in front of the stable hands who had led our horses out. I was pretending to be one of them, after all.

As we walked, I noticed the interactions between the palace workers we saw passing by on the grounds. They seemed cheerful enough, and all stopped to say a hello to Diana, and some to me as well, even though I had never met them. They all bowed their heads to her but were comfortable talking with her casually. She knew them all by name.

She's well-liked, I mused. *The captain's son is sure smitten as well.* That hadn't gone unnoticed by me, the long glances Aedan stole in Diana's direction, how he lit up when she spoke to him. I wondered if she even realized.

We hit the cobblestone road and the farther we got from the palace, the less fae we saw. Soon it was just us, escorted by the sounds of the horses' shoes clip-clopping and some birds in the distance.

"So it was your birthday recently?" I asked.

"A week before the spring equinox."

"And you're twenty-two?"

She nodded. Then: "Do you know how old you

are?"

"I... don't know," I admitted, feeling my stomach leap at the reminder of the vast emptiness taking ownership inside my brain. It was a black pit, swallowing everything that made me, *me*, and refusing to let any light in.

Deciding to make light of the horrifying realness of not knowing who I was, I asked, "How old do I look?"

Diana narrowed her eyes, studying me. "Hmm," she said. "Not a day over seventy-three."

A sound came out of me that I realized was a laugh. The first time feeling any sense of lightness in my chest since waking up in the healer's ward. She laughed once too, a look of surprise crossing her face, then said, "In actuality, probably around my age. Maybe a bit older."

I liked talking with her. She felt real. Even if nothing else in my life did.

"You promised me a history lesson," I reminded her.

"I suppose I did." When she turned her head to me the wind caught her hair and blew it into her face. She dropped the reins on her horse's neck and used both hands to tie her hair into a ponytail, a blatant show of comfortability and trust in her mount.

"Where should I start?"

"At the beginning of course," I said. And because I liked to see her smile, I added: "But leave out the boring parts."

Something fluttered at the wry grin I got from her.

"Well, the oldest records we have say that Eira was created by Mother Gaia, the spirit and life force of the land. It used to be full of fae of all types: Light, Dark, and even some other Folk like sprites, nymphs, and elves. The realm was split into two territories: The Lights ruled in what used to be called the Seelie Court, and the Darks ruled in the Unseelie Court. The Dark fae were powerful and delighted in the misery and misfortune of others. They played tricks and pranks, like knocking over vendor stands, pickpocketing, and occasionally lighting houses on fire. It was annoying but never went too far.

"But a new King came to power, Urdan, and he was bloodthirsty. Under his rule, the Darks began pushing the limits of what they could get away with. They started hoodwinking, robbing homes, vandalizing Gaian temples. When they realized their new king did not punish them for these acts, they started fighting and murdering freely when it came to it. The king's army pushed the border back, taking more land for the Unseelie. The Lights finally decided to put an end to their malintent, and the Seelie Queen met with King Urdan to talk about a peace treaty. He killed her on the spot and set to take her throne for his own as well. Her only living relative, her daughter, was consumed by grief and rage and in her anguish was able to open up a rift between all the realms in the world. She had considerable magic herself and was able to send a large chunk of the Unseelie army through the rip. But when her magic was spent, she could not fight against the king. The Seelie court, in a selfless act of love towards their queen's daughter, sent her all the magic they had, and with it she banished every last one of the Darks through the rift.

"As the days passed, the Seelie rejoiced and set out

to explore the edges of the world where the Unseelie had prevented them from travelling. But the rip grew unstable and would suck fae in without warning. Sometimes it would spit things out, horrible, gruesome things from realms much older and darker than ours. So the queen's daughter decided she would have to close it. She waded into the Sacred Pool to ask for her ancestors' advice, and came out wielding a giant and powerful emerald. With it, she was able to close the rip forever. Eventually, the fae receded into their own corners of the land and formed their own courts. The queen's daughter became their official High Queen and changed their name from Seelie to Light, as they were all the same now. The rip had been closed for eight thousand years. Until you."

The tale, however mesmerizing, was heavily biased towards the Light fae, but I knew she believed every word. That I was part of the fae that this realm had driven out for being murderous and bloodthirsty and *bad*. No wonder they hated me so much.

Was I a killer?

Why did I risk my life to get into this realm?

What was I capable of?

Diana played with a piece of Finnvarra's fire coloured mane as I silently digested.

"I know why you hate me now. Why you're keeping me magic-bound and glamoured from the rest. I understand," I managed to get out, my throat tight. A small flare of hatred for the royals receded—although, not by much. Which made me feel even worse.

Diana met my eyes, her hazel stare unflinching. "I

don't hate you."

"Why?" She'd been raised her whole life to believe that my kind was the villain. Her blood was the same as the queen's daughter, the heroine of their entire history. How could she not hate me?

She didn't drop my gaze. "You haven't given me any reason to hate you. My family cannot see past the rip and the fact that you are Dark. All you've done so far is interrupt a sacred ritual, which was a tad annoying I'll admit, but not something I'd warrant hating you for." Diana paused. "Maybe that makes me a fool, but I don't want to judge you based on something that happened eight millennia ago. That neither of us were alive for. I'm not sure all the Dark fae were bad, just as I've seen for myself not all the Light fae are good. Since neither of us know your true nature, I'm going to give you the benefit of the doubt while we figure it out."

Her words struck me. She was kind and just; the perfect candidate for a queen. She was right, too. I didn't know who I was—no one did. I could become good. I could become whomever I wanted. I was a blank canvas ready to be painted on. And I was eager to start painting.

SEVEN
Dark Purple
DIANA

Spense and I made our way through Nevelyn on horseback, all the while with me telling him stories of the court's history. When we got to the city square, the beating heart of Nevelyn, we had to dismount due to the high volume of foot traffic. We left our horses tied to the hitching posts that had been erected in the city square at its creation, at the post dedicated to the royal guards' mounts, where the wood was painted green with a wolf emblazoned on each corner. It was good that there were no horses tied there today, as Finnvarra was not the sharing kind.

We continued on foot through the busy city, weaving through street performers and adolescent messengers on wobbly bikes, stopping and starting without warning to look for addresses.

I led us down the streets and took a right turn at the corner where my favourite pub stood, The Leaf and Stone. I had spent many nights there with Aedan as an adolescent, with us terribly disguised and trying to order honey mead like what the soldiers in the Queen's Army drank. We always thought we were successful because the barkeep humored us (probably to keep in favour with Embris—who had no idea of our nightly adventures) by giving us cold tea infused with honey in a glass bottle. We would drink it and become silly, believing the alcohol was taking effect on us, and stumble home very pleased with ourselves. Eventually we realized that alcohol tasted much worse than cold tea with honey, and while the effects were fun at first, the next morning was not. We still sometimes met at The Leaf and Stone when we wanted a casual night, away from the grandeur of the palace.

It pained me to think that I could not recall the last time we'd gone to the pub together.

After turning down the street, we were met with so much colour and vivacity that I was surprised it didn't knock over Spense with its ferocity. An arch above us read out 'THE MARKETPLACE' in mismatched letters. The sides had been decorated with streamers and littered with signs advertising goods and services. Past the arch, the street went as far as we could see, and was absolutely filled to the brim with vendor carts. They took up both sides of the road, making for a very small walking aisle. Where there was no room, some took up homes in the middle of the street, forcing the road into a makeshift two lanes. There were fae milling about, shopping or bartering, having to walk so close together that it was impossible not to brush up on another. Fae wearing backpacks of goods tried to sell by foot, walking up to groups and advertising blatantly to them. Anything one would ever want to buy could be found in the Marketplace. Clothing, jewelry, weapons, spices, cured meat, transportation horses, woodwork, paint, books, it was all here.

I looked at Spense, who, to his credit, did not look overwhelmed as he took it all in. His eyes had widened slightly, but he was stoic as he watched the hustle and bustle of Nevelyn's market. *He takes everything in stride,* I thought. *Nothing seems to surprise him.*

We spent almost an hour walking the street, occasionally sampling sweet treats or stopping to admire handiwork on a tapestry or painting. We passed my favourite weapons-maker, Bodin, at his stand, where he was displaying a set of hand-carved throwing knives. They were made from hand-polished steel with an oak handle, the blade curving slightly at the end.

"Exquisitely made," I told him, to which he just grinned at me and named his price.

"Noted," I said, returning his smile as we kept walking. Spense said nothing, not even to acknowledge the astronomical amount that Bodin was asking.

The crowd thinned slightly as we crossed a stone bridge, entering the older section of the market. The River Nord, which came straight from the mountains, was not particularly high yet but flowed quickly underneath us, denoting that spring was here in full force. The merchants got older and testier the farther back they were situated in the Market, and although I had never been there, it was rumored at the end of the Marketplace one could find countless contraband things like opioids, poisons, hired assassins, and other workers of the night.

A lot of jewelers had picked the older section of the Marketplace to sell in, due to there being less pickpockets and more customers who could afford their products. The afternoon sun became a conduit for the gems, making the entire street dazzle and shine. Unlike other sections, vendors here didn't call out to us to take a look at their shop, they hung back in their tented carts, watching fae mill about with eyes that didn't miss a thing. The Northern Peninsula had the largest number of jewelers due to the region's affinity with earth magic.

Now that it was quieter, I asked Spense, "What do you think of the Marketplace?"

He let out a huff of laughter. "This is overwhelming—but in a good way. It feels like it has its own soul here." He wasn't wrong. The atmosphere here crackled with energy, fueled by the amount of transactions by all types of customers and vendors.

"It's definitely overwhelming," I agreed. "But it's nice to be able to go somewhere where I can be lost in the crowd." Now that we had entered the jeweler's section, I knew I stood out, a stark difference to the busier part of the Marketplace, where I hadn't seen many gawkers at all.

He nodded, stopping to look at a table filled with earrings and necklaces made from obsidian. The bird-like female who undoubtedly made the work peered at him indiscreetly. I never liked obsidian, I found it jarred uncomfortably with my magic, but I couldn't deny that it was striking, wholly black and smooth like glass. *Spense is like obsidian,* I thought, smiling a bit at my comparison.

Shimmering red caught my eye at the next table, and I walked over to look more closely. Beautiful rubies in the shape of teardrops, fashioned into earrings that delicately encased the stones without taking away from them. They were so simple, so unlike anything I wore at the palace, but I was instantly drawn to them. I almost bought them without any questions asked, but finally drew away and walked back to where Spense was standing. He watched me return with confusion in his face.

"Why don't you get them? They would suit you," he asked, having seen the awe in my face.

"Oh, I didn't bring any coin with me today," I said, a half-lie. I did not mention how that would not matter here. Vendors were happy to bring items I picked out to the palace, where they would be compensated more than fairly. I rarely bought expensive things from the Marketplace, even if I loved the work. It felt wrong to me, to be frivolous with the palace's money. I knew that it belonged to me, and we gave much of it to charity, but it didn't feel right. I didn't feel as if I had earned the money I was spending.

Spense didn't seem to be listening to me. He had his eyes fixed on a few younglings that had gathered on the apex of the bridge. Two boys, around the same age, and a younger girl. She had her hair beautifully braided on one side, held together by a pink satin ribbon to match her dress. The other half of her hair was knotted and messy, and soon I saw why: the boys were holding the matching ribbon above her head, making her reach for it. My stomach wrenched as I saw the dismay in the girl's eyes, tears starting to fall down her face as the boys laughed.

Spense took a few steps forward, as though he might intervene but wasn't sure if he should. I watched carefully, knowing that he would not have to if this continued much longer, for I would have no trouble marching over there and reprimanding the hucksters.

One of the boys dangled her ribbon over the side of the bridge. I started towards them; this had gone too far. Without warning, the little girl heaved herself towards the boy's arm with her own little arms outstretched. He stepped to the side, deftly avoiding her, but she hit the side of the bridge, and her momentum pushed her over the side. She screamed in panic before hitting the water with a splash.

I broke into a sprint, but Spense was faster. He was racing towards the side of the bridge, pushing through anyone in his way. He didn't hesitate before leaping over the rail and plunging into the water after her.

Adrenaline poured through my body, my blood racing in my ears as I ran. It was impossible to get to the water from here without jumping in, but I knew a spot in the city where the river flowed past a lower bank. I could get to them there and help them out, but I had to be faster than the water.

I tore through the familiar streets, my hair flying behind me. It was impossible to keep this pace through the Market, so I cut down a side alley and ran closer to the water. I could hear the river now in this quieter part of Nevelyn, mostly homes decorating the streets. I followed the road I knew would lead me to the embankment, my feet flying on the cobblestone.

I tried not to let thoughts consume me of the sharp,

jagged rocks that lined the bottom of the River Nord, or of how easily the current could drag a victim under.

I reached the river and slowed down, looking for the telltale bobble of heads in the water. Had I been too slow? I forced myself to drink air into my lungs as I frantically looked through the waves.

Holy hell, what would happen if they were both lost? I wouldn't be able to live with it. I should've been faster, should've gone over before it went this far —

There — dark hair. Spense was bobbing in the water, cutting diagonally against the current towards me. The young girl was in his arms, her chin held as high as she could to fight against the water trying to cover her head.

Relief spilled through me. I made my way down to the riverbank, aware of how slippery the grass was. As I waited for their imminent arrival, I spied a dead tree a few feet away. It was bare and crackling, its branches pointed towards the ground. I ran over and put a hand on the tree, sending magic up the rotting trunk. Picking out a long branch that looked sturdier than the others, I willed it to snap off at the base. My magic had no trouble, considering the condition of the tree.

Wielding the branch in front of me, I got as close as I could to the water's edge. I found a spot where I could dig my feet into a sizable rock, and held the branch as far as I could into the water. Spense and the girl were flowing with the river dangerously fast. My stomach clenched. Would I be able to fight the water's momentum when he grabbed the branch? What if *he* wasn't able to hold on?

They got closer and closer, and I yelled, "SPENSE!"

as loud as I could. He looked up from his diagonal quest and locked in on the branch.

The two bodies flowed right up to it, close enough I could see the panic-stricken girl's face and the exertion in Spense's.

He reached out his free arm and grabbed the branch, instantly pushing his arm around it and tucking it into his armpit for better grip. The weight of them both on the branch was substantial, pushing my heels farther into the muddy grass as I struggled to hold them. The water splashed over the sides of them as it fought to keep its flow.

Magic licked over my hands, begging to be used as it tasted my body's pumping adrenaline. I obliged, letting it wash over me, instantly relieving some of the pressure. It snaked down the branch and enveloped Spense and the girl, tugging them towards me gently.

Spense hit the side of the bank and heaved the girl over the edge. She sprawled on the grass, coughing and breathing heavily. Now that his arm was free, Spense was able to hoist himself on to the bank and drag his body up. As soon as I saw he was safely out of the water, I released the branch and my magic, feeling it gather back inside me like a tide.

I kneeled by the girl, rubbing her back as she coughed up water from her lungs.

"Are you alright?" I asked when she was breathing normally again, checking her for injuries. There was a scrape along her arm, likely caused by hitting the rocks, and even though it bled slightly, it wasn't deep enough to be worried. The girl nodded and launched herself into my arms, trembling.

I held her to me, the wet dress soaking my clothes, and stroked her hair. I looked to Spense, who was on his knees, panting, looking like a bedraggled rat with his hair pressed flat to his head, any curl gone. He nodded to me.

Shouting sounded from behind me. The girl's mother, assumedly, raced towards us. There was a crowd forming behind her, in shock and awe over what had just occurred.

I helped the girl stand and guided her out of the slippery grass towards the cobblestone. She saw her mother and ran towards her. They held each other, weeping. The two boys who had been taunting her stood to the side, sheepish. They were her brothers, I noticed, seeing the similarity between them all now.

I went back to help Spense up, his clothes clinging to him and dripping water as he walked. "Come on," I said, "Let's get you warm." The spring air still had a chill to it, and I knew he would be cold as we rode back to the palace.

I waved off the mother's endless thank yous and offers of repayment, smiling as I grasped her shaking hand and telling her that I was just glad her daughter was safe. Spense trailed behind me, returning the mother's smile and not accepting any praise.

On our way back through the Marketplace, I bought Spense a large black cloak to try to fend off some of the cold seeping through his wet clothes.

As we found our horses again and mounted, I realized the grandness of what had just happened.

Spense had dived after the girl without a second thought, not caring for his own safety. He had been entirely selfless in that moment.

"You saved that girl's life you know," I told him as we began the ride home.

He shrugged, pulling the cloak tighter around his shoulders. "Anyone would have done the same. She was helpless," he said.

I shook my head. "Anyone didn't. You did."

He met my eyes, smiling a bit. "You helped."

We stared at each other for a moment until he looked away when a shiver racked through his body.

From what I had been told about the Dark fae over the years, I'd pictured evil, shadowed figures with twisted faces and no morals. Definitely not handsome with distracting curly hair. Spense had taken me entirely by surprise, first with his easygoing and gentle nature, and now with this act of bravery towards an innocent. Was he truly my enemy?

He interrupted my thoughts. "I felt your magic. When you pulled me out. I remembered for a second what mine felt like. It tried to fight the band – to touch yours."

I let that settle in me. If his magic had been unbound, he would have been able to get out of the water easier, safer.

I sidled Finnvarra close to Spense, leaning towards him. "Give me your arm."

He held it out, questions in his eyes.

I let my magic touch the band, which recoiled against the *wrongness* of the band's ability. It cracked in half as I twisted it in my hand. Spense took a shuddering breath. I knew his magic was now flooding around him, filling every part of him and touching every nerve. I leaned away again, back into my saddle, but still felt his magic touch mine slightly before he reined it in. It was black, like I'd thought, but also swirled dark purple and warm, tingling where it touched mine.

After a long time, Spense blinked and swallowed once, regaining his composure.

"Thank you," he said. "It—it feels like I have a part of myself back."

I smiled, justified with my decision. How cruel it was to have let him wear the band for so long. To rob someone of their entire essence was harsh enough, let alone when he had nothing else to anchor him to who he was. And for him to still be willing to put his life on the line for another made me believe that his magic would not bring forward an evil side of him, only pull out more of his true nature. Which, so far, seemed... decent. Moral.

We walked in silence, Spense reveling in his newfound selfness.

It was only when we had dismounted and entered the palace again, about to go our separate ways when he said, "I didn't tell you about your magic for you to take the band off, you know."

I met his eyes, having to tilt my head upwards to do so now that we weren't on horseback. "I know."

He nodded. "I just wanted you to know that you made me feel like me again, even for a split second." Heat rose in my cheeks as I felt the weight of the compliment settle in me. I was glad to do this for him. He saved an innocent.

He held my gaze for a beat and then turned down the wing where his room was, leaving me to stare after him.

I had done the right thing, I knew that. I was interested to see what would come next; hopefully, memories that could prove he wasn't the terrible, horrible Dark that my family thought he was, that I knew he wasn't.

I cringed as I thought of my family. I would definitely have to tell my mother what I'd done, or risk her wrath if she found out on her own.

Before I lost my nerve, I changed course and set out for Queen Vera's office.

EIGHT
Afternoon Dalliance
SPENSE

"Again."

Diana's voice rang through the clearing.

Focusing my thoughts, I sent my magic into the undergrowth of the forest floor. I could feel it whirring as it went deeper, sensing beetles, worms and moles. A clang in my head as my magic hit a patch of bedrock. It sucked back a bit, but I urged it forward. We hadn't found what we were looking for yet.

There. I could feel the pull of the gemstone reaching to me. Tourmaline, I confirmed. My magic wrapped around it, and I willed it to come up through the dirt to me.

It obliged, and with a satisfying *pop* the gem broke through the grass, glinting at me. Diana knelt to pick it up. She inspected it and nodded, adding it to the pile of half a dozen tourmaline I had already collected.

"Good work," she said. Almost every day for the past two weeks, Diana had been teaching me how to yield earth magic, the element that those in the North excelled at. On the rides to and from the forest, she'd give me history lessons and teach me about the politics of her court.

So far, I had been able to bring up rocks, clay, and now take out small gemstones as well. I could also sense how far along in its life a tree or animal was, and where in a river might be the best spot to look for gold.

Having my magic back felt like I had been healed in places that I didn't know I were broken. Colours seemed more vivid, and I felt a greater understanding of the land and its citizens with my magic being able to taste the air and the energies around me.

I was panting slightly from the strain. "Not that good," I said back. "I haven't been able to find anything other than tourmaline."

Diana shrugged. "You're not being specific towards a particular gemstone when you search. Tourmaline is made up of many different minerals, so it would make sense that you would be able to find it first." She spoke so matter-of-factly. What she was saying *did* make sense, but…

"Or maybe there's nothing to be found here."

Diana smiled sweetly. "Oh, there's lots here. Garnet, amethyst, topaz," she rattled off names.

I smiled back. "Let's see it then."

We held eye contact for a beat before she tilted her head as if to say *fine*. She closed her eyes and took a deep breath. Instantly, I could feel her magic reach down into the earth in a beautifully straight line. The power radiating from her was palpable. I remembered the feeling of her pinkish-white magic as it grabbed hold of me when she pulled me out of the river. It was cool and smooth and full of light that filled every corner of my soul. Even though it failed against the magic-binding bracelet, I had felt my own magic leap to try and connect with hers, to be close to something so pure.

Diana had told me that the Queen had been upset to hear about the removal of the band but had eventually agreed to it remaining off. While I believed this to be grave downplaying on Diana's part, I was relieved that I wouldn't have to wear it again. And if I was being honest with myself, I would fight with every force of my being if it came down to resisting the band that would snuff out my very essence again.

In almost no time at all, a glittering ruby the size of an acorn had broken the surface. It sat there in a bold show of Diana's power. She was doing a bad job of holding back a smirk as I picked it up. I held it to the sun, watching the light rebound off it in countless rays.

"Alright, you win this round," I conceded.

She smiled, a real smile this time, one that made the corners of her eyes crinkle. Smiling at me like that, with the sun turning her chestnut hair auburn and her hazel eyes green, I couldn't help but think *beautiful*.

"What?" she asked. Had I said that out loud?

"The ruby. It's a stunning gem," I amended, shaking my head internally. "What do you do with these after you find them? Turn them into jewelry? Sell them?"

She gathered the tourmaline into her hands and turned them over. The gems fell softly to the ground and sunk back into it, disappearing. "I put them back. I have no use for them, really, and this way a miner will be able to find them and make a living."

I nodded. Of course, I thought. What else would a perfect, beloved princess do?

"Would you mind if I kept this ruby?" I said, an idea coming to mind.

Diana shrugged, and I pocketed the gem, joining her where she sat on a mossy log. "Sure. Although in a true miner's market, you'd have to trade me a lot more than your pile of tourmaline for it," she added with a wry smile. She bumped me with her shoulder playfully. The effect of her small frame hitting me in the chest was not near enough to push me off-balance, but it sent a thrill up my spine.

I laughed softly. "Well then, princess, I sink farther into your debt."

She smiled and then grew serious. "We're not keeping score, you and I."

That changed the mood, the severity of her words sinking in. How could she think that when I was an intruder to her peaceful lands? Even if someday my memories came back, even if somehow this whole situation went away, I would never be her equal.

I cleared my throat. The air had grown thick between us.

"The mountains are clear today," I said lamely, gesturing to the expanse of towering mountain range hugging the forest. The tops of the peaks were almost visible, a change to the ever-present fog that got thicker as the mountain grew taller.

She nodded, looking away from me and breaking the tension.

"It's strange, sometimes I think I can see flying beasts at the peaks if I look closely," I added. "But then the fog shifts and I realize it was just the clouds."

Diana looked at me sharply. "You can see the pegasi?" Her voice was incredulous.

I was taken aback. "Wait, there *are* beasts at the top of the mountain?"

She looked at me in confusion, then laughed softly and shook her head. "I should really stop being surprised by you.

"The mountain is called Mt Nord. There's a warrior tribe that lives up there; the Nordians. They ride winged horses, called pegasi, into battle. Terrifyingly impressive creatures."

"Am I not supposed to see them?" I asked.

"No one is. There's a glamour over the entirety of Mt Nord. Although the magic is different up there. It's ancient and flies on the wind like its own entity."

"Can you see them?"

Diana's stare bored into mine. "Yes."

"Why?"

"You're full of questions as usual today, Spense." Diana sighed but continued on. "I've spent time up there. The pegasi know me. They miss me." She smiled. "And I miss them."

She was being honest with me, but I could tell there were things she was leaving out. A very real part of me wanted to respect that and leave the subject alone, but my curiosity won out.

"How long were you up there for?"

"A full summer when I was sixteen. It was part of my training." Diana's eyes glazed over as she was lost in memory. I envied that, being able to recall her life and relive it.

"What's it like in Mt Nord?"

Her expression changed; it grew solemn. "It's a different way of life up there. It's harsh and unforgiving. While they've sworn fealty to the Queen and to the North, they live by their own laws and customs. They rarely ever come down, and we rarely go up. For the most part we leave each other alone. But I still enjoyed my time there. What I learned."

I raised my eyebrows. I couldn't see her in an unforgiving landscape. She was too pure.

She noticed my skeptical face and snorted. "I learned skills that will serve me my entire life. I was always good at yielding my magic, but the Nordians taught me real battle skills and how to fight like a warrior. It gives me confidence to know that I'll always have that."

As she said it, I understood. Even with her small frame and soft eyes, there was a warrior lurking beneath that had been hidden to me before. She was merciful and strong. Every bit of her a queen.

"I'd love to see those skills in action one day," I said, a bit of a challenge.

She smiled wryly. "If you're lucky, you never will."

"Why, because you'd best me before I saw it coming?"

"Something like that."

I smiled, looking back to the foreboding mountain that stood proudly before us. "Will you take me to Mt Nord sometime? Maybe they can train me too. So I stand a chance of besting you," I added, returning her shoulder bump.

Diana didn't laugh or return the jab. She stood abruptly and brushed moss from her pants. "No. I don't go up there anymore." Her voice was firm enough that I didn't push it. I just nodded, following her to where we had left Finnvarra and Plum a few feet away. We mounted our respective horses and rode through the trees for a short while, and when Diana still did not relax her shoulders, I suggested we race back as we often did. That seemed to snap her out of her reverie, settling an unwelcome lump in my chest that I hadn't realized had made itself at home. We whipped through the trees blindingly fast, the horses' keen senses and breeding making them perfectly agile as they charged through the forest.

I thought about her reaction towards Mt Nord. She spoke with respect towards the tribe and the way they trained and yet would not consider returning. Something must have happened to her up there. Even though I saw her as my only friend and ally here, she probably didn't see me in as high regard. I would stay in my place.

It wasn't until we had reached sight of the stables again that I realized I had a slim chance of finally winning one of our races. I urged Plum faster, and the mare quickened her pace even with her chest heaving. The mare was full of heart. But it wasn't enough.

Diana won.

After we cooled down our horses, she left me in the stables, her mood lightened.

"I have a quiet day tomorrow, I'll be able to ride with you around noon," she said. I nodded and watched her go back towards the palace, feeling the absence of her presence heavier than usual.

*

"Tell me about the politics here."

Diana narrowed her eyes at me, looking up from where she sat cross-legged in the grass, trying to teach me simple healing magic. "I take it you're not concerned about the cut on my hand, then?" A fine trickle of red painted her delicate fingers, trailing from a small incision she had made on her palm with a sharp rock.

"I know you can take care of yourself," I said, giving her an easy grin. I had seen her demonstrate half a dozen times now how to close the skin of a small wound, and had the faint scars on my own hands to prove my messy understanding of the skill.

She rolled her eyes, but I saw the faint smile she tried to hide. The sight made me fight my own smile. "Should I be worried that you're asking to know how our governing system works?"

My bravado slipped a bit. Of course it would seem suspicious. "I didn't realize your monarchy was such a big secret."

Diana held my gaze for a beat before turning her attention to her hand, where the cut shrunk smaller and smaller until the skin was soft and fresh. "It's not a monarchy, but you already know that," she said. "In Eira, there are four regions —"

I waved my hand, cutting her off. "Yes, you've told me about that. North, South, East, West, princes, all that.

What I want to know is how the regions differ from each other. Are there fights between them?"

"I didn't take you for a gossip, Spense," Diana said, raising an eyebrow at me. I held her playful stare until she sighed. "For the most part, yes, the regions are peaceful with each other. However, I believe that is because they are all under my mother's direction. If they were the sole leaders of their own regions, I think there would be… friction.

"Prince Leo of the South is new to his position, and from what I've heard, he has some radical ideas about how Eira should be run. Kashdan is loyal, I don't think there would be any problems there, but in the East—that relationship is already tumultuous."

Warily, I asked, "How so?"

Diana chewed on the inside of her cheek. "Princess Hollaina is a deeply damaged soul. She witnessed horrific tragedy when she was very young, and rules from afar. I've only met her once; when I visited the East. She has Lord Nimshar attend all the celebrations and meetings in her stead. *He* is the one I would look out for if I were queen. He's vain, outspoken, and seems only loyal to himself. What the North has been trying to figure out is if he is acting alone or if Hollaina has molded him that way." She cut herself off, and I wondered if she thought she shared too much.

"Is there anything beyond the land?" I asked.

"We have spent a lot of time exploring the ocean, and how far it stretches. Seemingly, if you continue far enough you will eventually find yourself back where you started. I've never tried, but I'll take the adventurers' word for it. I'm not a huge fan of open water."

If I tried, really concentrated, I could picture a vast open ocean, with glittering waves and no land for miles. My heart quickened, thinking this was a possible memory. But it didn't seem... familiar. Was I just picturing what I thought the ocean would look like?

The only sound beyond the birds chirping in the clearing was the ripping of moss from the log Diana perched on.

"How nice to have such a peaceful kingdom," I said finally. "No fights, no wars, just four regions flourishing."

Diana shook her head softly. "I think it's naïve to think that just because there are no wars, the kingdom is at peace."

"You don't think Eira is at peace?"

She shrugged. "The word peace is up to interpretation. The world's not black and white, you know. Most of it's gray. Which is not really a bad colour at all," she added.

I scoffed, taking on a joking tone. "Gray? Gray is a boring colour."

"I don't think gray is boring. It's the perfect mix of dark and light. It's like your eyes." Her lips parted softly in surprise at the admission.

We stayed in that moment, the quiet compliment filling me with warmth. I only looked away when I realized I had been staring too long. My stomach fluttered gently.

"If you live too much in black, or too much in white,

you lose your sense of empathy. If you're not consistently challenging your outlooks, then you can never grow," Diana finished, her voice smooth. I took her in as she gathered her coat and untied our horses, seemingly done for the day. She was wise beyond her years. This reasoning was surely why she did not regard me with hate the way her family did. Eira would be lucky to have her as their queen one day.

If you're not consistently challenging your outlooks, then you can never grow.

*

I had spent most of last night *not* sleeping, so I was unsurprisingly weary when I started work at the royal stables before sunup.

Finding it hard to sleep at night, I found myself in the habit of slipping out of the palace to Nevelyn, unbeknownst to anyone. It was surprisingly easy to avoid detection, my body bending to a skill it undoubtedly knew well. Perhaps I was a spy in my previous life.

I witnessed the night life and practiced my blending in. It was so interesting to observe the colourful characters of the pubs and dance bars. There were a small number of seedy fae (I had surprisingly only been offered narcotics *once* so far, which I politely declined), but for the most part all the patrons just wanted to dance and enjoy themselves. They let their magic loose as they moved and flowed with the music, creating a haze of aura and colour over the dance floor. It was mesmerizing. I wondered if Diana knew about this wild and free nature of Nevelyn after dark, or if she would ever be able to experience it like I had. It certainly was nothing like the palace where she spent most of her time.

Dinners with the royal family and their associates were no less awkward as time went on with me there; certainly, it didn't help with the newly assigned guards in the corners of the room, watching me eat as though I were a caged animal. I felt rather stupid, sitting at the table and dining with them and never contributing to the conversation. I would have preferred it if they treated me like the prisoner I was, taking meals in my room. Mercifully, Diana had taken it upon herself to escort me to and from dinner, so I never had to be alone with any of the royals who hated me. I was endlessly grateful for her company, even if it was inconsistent now as she was getting busier shadowing the Queen.

But she remained strong in her belief that if I kept up work and routine, I stood a good chance of regaining my memory.

Working at the stables wasn't bad work at all. It was repetitive and therefore boring, but easy to master. I was able to keep up some of the muscle tone that I had no recollection gaining, and sometimes a soldier would come through who wasn't too stuck up to converse with me. They would talk about the shifts they enjoyed, like accompanying royal visitors, and shifts they did not, like breaking up border squabbles.

Since I was a "real" worker, Rolfo paid me a weekly wage. It wasn't much, but it allowed me to have some fun for myself, since I didn't have to worry about buying food or necessities at the royal headquarters. Although some guilt had settled in me about not disclosing my nighttime activities to Diana. I wanted to, but this was the only thing that was just mine. Something that I enjoyed doing, and didn't have to share with anyone.

Today was a quiet day for Diana. I was looking forward to it; Plum and I had been training on stamina and speed bursts. I always held out hope that we could finally win against Diana and her Finnvarra, who seemed to move as fast as the flames she resembled.

An unfortunate drawback to getting whisked away for magic training was how it affected my relationships with the other stable hands and grooms. I heard the whispers when Diana would come to ride and request that I join her, only for us to return much later. I started coming an hour earlier than everyone to get a head start on the work I would inevitably miss later, but it was easy to see that it didn't make me very well-liked. If it wasn't a complaint about me missing work, it was that I was making them look bad by coming to work early. Clearly their opinion of me wasn't going to change, so I had no choice but to ignore it. It was harder, however, to ignore the vulgar rumours of what we were doing on our rides in the forest. Those made my blood boil, hearing them talk about Diana like that. Not only was she their High Princess, but she was always kind and polite to everyone in the stables. How could they betray her like that?

It went against every instinct in me to stay quiet from retaliating against their obvious baiting. But I knew I would be betraying her if I made a scene when she asked me to keep my head down.

There are probably hundreds of suitors lined up eager to defend her honour, anyway.

Today the stables were busy, with high-ranking soldiers of the Queen's Army taking advantage of the sunny day to practice swordsmanship on horseback. The stable hands were tasked with getting the horses ready for the soldiers and putting them away after they were done. With over two hundred warrior horses stabled here at the palace, this made for quite a lot of work.

With the amount to get done around here, I could theorize that my fellow workers would not be happy when Diana came and took me away for an hour.

And I was right. From where I was standing outside the entrance to the barn, holding a rather testy roan stallion while a surly soldier mounted, I could smell her cedar-and-snow scent carried on the breeze. Sure enough, her small frame came into view leaving the palace, clad in navy riding leathers, making her way down the dirt path, her chestnut hair flying around her. Fenn, an outspoken groom with three missing fingers was nearby, and also caught her scent.

Instantly, he looked to me, a wicked smile forming.

"Spense's afternoon dalliance," drawled Fenn, catching the attention of some nearby grooms. "Right on time."

There were some low chuckles from the others. I noticed the soldier I had been helping pause. He was facing away from us, fiddling with his sword sheath's buckle. It would seem to any other that he was not paying attention to us at all, but something sparked in the back of my mind, questioning his slow, calculated movements and the slight tilt of his head.

He's listening, I thought suddenly. *And he doesn't want anyone to know.*

One of Fenn's comrades, Branner, sidled up close to me as I collected the discarded gear from the soldier I'd helped.

"Princesses are always on time," he purred. "It's something they're good at. But I've heard they're good at *other things* too."

I ground my teeth. "She is your High Princess," I said in a warning tone.

Fenn shrugged, stepping closer to me as well. I was aware of two more males at my back, quietly closing in.

"Hey now, we're just wondering when we'll get a turn, that's all."

I focused on my breathing, sucking air in and out through flared nostrils. My magic swirled inside me, begging to be released.

"Yeah, bet I could teach her a few things," drawled Branner.

Diana was almost close enough now to be in earshot. The grooms had never been so testy before; not while she was here. I didn't want her to hear any of the poison coming from their mouths.

"But then again," said Fenn. "Do we really want Spense's sloppy seconds?"

The words were barely out of his mouth before I exploded. My magic flared out, pushing the males back a step from me. It hovered around me like an aura, daring them to draw nearer.

Instantly, Fenn grew feral. *"How dare you, boy!"*

He advanced on me, swinging his fist at my face. Without thinking, I sidestepped and caught his arm, twisting it away from me as my other hand coiled into a fist and made contact with his stomach. He let out an *oof* and stepped back. Branner came running at me, the other males following suit.

It was so fast and yet so slow. The adrenaline in my body coursed thick, heightened my senses, my magic coiled inside me like a snake, ready to strike.

The males didn't hold back, obviously trying to impress the visiting soldiers. They came at me with brute strength and force. I easily blocked and retaliated their sloppy technique. Without conscious control, my body moved and struck with speed and precision. I didn't feel the exhaustion that was showing on their faces.

No. I felt invigorated. Alive.

The males all backed off except Fenn, who faked a left punch and came at my right side. With his weight sent forward, it was easy for me to grab the front of his shirt and yank him to the ground. I instantly had my boot on his throat, pinning him below me. His face showed fear as he took me in, but it was replaced with a self-righteous attempt at a laugh as his eyes flicked behind me. Rage shuddered through me, and I pushed my boot down harder, feeling a choke in his windpipe.

I was aware of yelling behind me, but I could only see Fenn's horrible face, see the veins engorging on his beet red skin, see his eyelids slowly drooping.

"That's enough, boy."

Rough hands gripped my shoulders, yanking me back and snapping me from my prey. I ripped around, magic soaring towards my new enemy. I realized it was the soldier I'd been helping just in time to see him flying backwards through the air.

"Spense."

My magic was forced back to me with a slam. My head throbbed instantly. I looked around and caught eyes with Diana, her face terrifying. I had never seen her like this, her eyes glowing and the power coming off of her in waves. She had a hand held up towards me, and her magic created a barrier around mine, strong as granite and unforgiving. The shock of it all faded the endorphin high and any residual anger. It settled around me like a mist, the realization of what I had just done hitting me. My magic dropped and receded as I took in the groaning males and the soldier laying in a heap a few feet away.

Oh, shit. I was in *deep shit.*

What had I done?

Diana did not take her eyes off me as her magic released its control. It swirled around me menacingly like a cat stalking its prey.

"What did you do, Spense," she said, more of a resignation than a question. Her voice was angry, a tone I had never heard from her.

I fumbled to find words that would explain, that would exonerate me.

But I did not deserve it.

She had placed her faith in me, that I would blend into her world and stay hidden. I had betrayed that trust, all because I couldn't control my anger. Stupid. Shame filled my stomach as I failed to meet Diana's eyes.

Soldiers were gathering around us now, helping up their comrade and shaking him off. The grooms had backed away into the shadows, away from the action but close enough to eavesdrop on what my inevitable punishment would be.

Diana was the picture of a queen as she ordered the soldier to the healer's ward and told the small crowd to get back to whatever they were doing. She looked to me, the light faded from her hazel eyes, and beckoned with her head to follow.

She led me back towards the palace wordlessly, two steps in front of me the whole time while her magic encircled us. My gut clenched as I thought about her dumping me at Queen Vera's feet, abandoning me to whatever cruel fate her mother craved for me. From what I knew of Diana, I wasn't sure she would do that, no matter how much I may deserve it. But before today, I hadn't seen this side of her before; the true Heir.

I tried not to dwell on it as I followed Diana into the palace and up to the second floor. If this was my end, I was glad that I was able to show those filthy bastards their Heir was no joke. We reached a magnificent oak double-door, where she paused in front of the brass knocker shaped like a wolf's head.

Even while craning her neck to look up at me, she stared me down. Her small height did nothing to diminish the power in her stance.

"Follow my lead and don't speak until you're told," she said. Without waiting for me to acknowledge her, she knocked once on the wolf head and pushed the doors open.

She led me into a room I instantly realized was the queen's office, as Vera herself stood from behind a giant desk and took us in with a confused look on her face. The giant, oddly docile wolf that never left her side lifted his head as we came in, his ears alert.

I wasn't afraid of Diana, even after feeling her magic easily pin mine down. It probably made me pretty stupid, but I still trusted her.

"Diana? What is this?" the queen asked, walking over to meet us in front of the fireplace. I kept my eyes down as Diana said, her voice clear as day,

"I've come to report a crime."

NINE
Considerations
DIANA

It was all I could do to keep from wringing my hands with nerves as I stood in front of my mother.

"A crime?" she echoed, taking in my set shoulders and the submission in Spense's energy and body language. Her eyes narrowed. "Do continue."

I knew how my mother would react to what had just happened in the stables, so it was imperative I got to her first to control the narrative. While Spense had just displayed extreme violence and a clear anger issue, I didn't feel like he deserved a punishment that my mother would have chosen should she have witnessed him instead of me. She may have killed him on the spot for hurting one of her soldiers. She was already on edge with the other regions breathing down her neck about the rift, and Prince Leo was getting more and more forward about contradicting her. I had to be calm and collected and report what happened. I could deal with Spense on my own.

I straightened my spine farther, feeling my bones crack. "Spense was attacked in the stables today."

The queen looked sharply between us. "Attacked? By whom? No one knows his true identity."

I could feel my mother's patience wearing already. I wanted to send a tendril of my magic to take some anger from her energy, but it would likely not be well received.

"Some grooms ganged up and attacked him. Four against one. Likely to show off in front of the soldiers. Everyone is fine, I was able to diffuse the situation."

"If this was but a mere squabble, then why bother bringing this to me? Tell me what you're leaving out." The queen was, of course, highly perceptive after being on the throne for so long.

"I wanted to tell you because a soldier was involved and got hurt. He recovered but I sent him to the healer's ward to be checked out."

Vera just looked at me as sucked air through her teeth. "One of my soldiers? I find it very hard to believe one of my own would be involved in such a petty show. Did you not say it was easily diffused?"

I could see she was trying to get me to back track on my own words, one of her tactics of exposing a lie. But I knew where I was going. And I'd spent the last few weeks with a front-row seat to my mother's tricks.

"He got involved because the grooms were taking it too far, they were going to hurt themselves."

More narrowed eyes. "And not Spense?"

I inclined my head slightly. "Spense held his own impressively."

"Meaning?"

"Meaning he had them all down easily and they still kept coming back for more. The soldier stepped in to stop the embarrassment." That part was a bit of a lie, I admitted to myself. Shockingly, I didn't feel the guilt I normally did when I tried to pass something over on my mother.

Vera looked at Spense, her lips in a thin line. "So he's been trained."

"That's what I'm thinking. He fought like a true soldier. This is great news; we're making progress on his past! I think if we continue — "

"I do not see this as 'great news', Diana." My mother's voice was hard. "All this proves to me is that he is unstable and dangerous. And without the band, who knows what else could be discovered accidentally? What if he had released his glamour?"

"He was *defending* himself." I steadied myself again before my voice started to sound pleading. Spense's eyes flicked to me, but he said nothing.

"I am not comfortable with this continuing, Diana. I'm going to call the region heads to meet, we can decide what to do — "

"*No.*"

"Excuse me?" At her tone, Delios stood up and nudged at Vera's hands, which were now splayed on the table as she rested her weight on it.

My mother cared for me and the well-being of her kingdom, but she was also looking for a way to regain her footing amongst the other regions. This was a rushed decision.

"You gave me the power on this. I know this is a breakthrough. He's not dangerous, mother. I'm going to see this through."

My mother set her jaw. "You have one month to bring forth a memory — a real one. If you fail, he will sit trial with the regions."

A pit settled in my stomach. One month?

"Please—that's not enough time," I said.

Vera settled her icy stare on me as she sat down behind her desk again.

"Then you may be excused from your Heir duties until the month is up."

That was a jab to the gut. Intended to punish me for speaking against her, that was blatantly obvious. Bubbling anger was rising to my mouth—I was going to say something I would regret if I didn't get out. And I wanted to, *so* badly.

I wet my lips and bowed my head slightly, turning to leave without another word.

It wasn't until we were safely out the door and down the hall that I let go of some anger in the form of blasting my magic into a wall. The stone cracked at the impact, a thin line spreading down to the ground.

Spense stood behind me silently. Softly, he said, "Thank you."

I whirled to face him. "Don't start, Spense. I only defended you to save your damn life. I can't deal with you right now—go back to your room and stay there. You better have a hell of an explanation for me."

He only nodded, keeping his gaze lowered as he made his way down the halls. I noticed Maisie standing nearby. Close enough to have witnessed everything.

Wordlessly, she held out her hand. I walked to her and took it, letting her lead us back to my room.

"I can see the toll that being the Heir has already taken on you," Maisie said as she sat us down in front of my fireplace. She put a cup of peppermint tea in my hands after using her small cache of magic to heat the water instead of waiting for it to boil over the fire. As it usually did after she used magic, the smell of honey filled the air. Maisie was not strong in her magic, an attribute of the fae whose bloodlines had been heavily diluted away from the royal line. It was something I think she could have improved with years of training, but she was happy that way. It was befitting of her unpowerful position.

I filled her in about what had happened, relieved to be able to tell the whole truth to my confidante and friend. She listened intently, then blew out a puff of breath.

"Wow, a Dark fae with an anger problem? I didn't see that coming."

I nudged her with my elbow. "He's not like that, though. He wouldn't attack first."

"How can you be so sure?"

"He's endured dinner with my family every night since arriving—surely he would've punched someone by now. The snide remarks are enough to make *me* want to."

Maisie became lost in thought. "I wonder why they felt the need to attack him anyway. He doesn't really talk that much so I can't see him annoying them; and even if they were trying to make a show for the soldiers, why pick Spense? He doesn't exactly look like someone that would be easy to beat up."

I considered this. It was true, Spense was toweringly tall and filled out, his muscle even more defined since working at the stables. I didn't have an answer for her. I intended to get one from Spense later.

After some silence between us, Maisie said, "Was it impressive watching him fight? I can imagine a male of that… structure would be terrifying and beautiful to watch. Like a battle-stained warrior."

I raised my eyebrows at her. "Do you have a thing for Spense?"

Maisie rolled her eyes at me. "Of course not. That would be like a rabbit going after a wolf. But I can certainly admire something beautiful, can't I? That mysterious, dark brooding thing he's got helps. It's just this aura that he puts out. There's no one in this entire region like him."

"You're right about that," I admitted. "As much as we try, he doesn't really blend in here."

"You know, I can see him in Mt Nord. At least they'd stand a better chance of beating him in a fight. Hey, maybe you can send him there for punishment."

My heart plummeted. She was right, he would fit right in with the Nordians. And maybe it would be good for him to go there, get some training on how to fight without exploding his magic outwards. *Thank Gaia my mother didn't ask about his magic,* I thought.

I had less than zero desire to make the trek up Mt Nord and live amongst them again, even for a short time. That would have to be my last resort.

Sensing the change in me, Maisie steered towards the topic of the summer solstice celebrations coming in less than two months, how preparations were coming and what days of the week-long party she was most excited about.

We talked for a little while more before she got me ready for dinner early, so I could have time to speak with Spense. We decided on a pale pink dress with an empire waist and flowing sleeves that started off my shoulders. Maisie tried to get me to wear the emerald *Jweira*, but I talked her out of it, opting for a pearl-and-emerald strung necklace instead. I hadn't been able to find any research on magic-bearing stones in two weeks, and I wasn't ready to delve into its essence yet, not without a full day devoted to focusing on it.

I set off down the hall after a kiss on the cheek from Maisie. "I want to know what he says," she told me as I left.

I came across Anten on his way to my mother's office. By his chagrined look as he saw me, I knew he had come to report on the soldier who had met Spense's rage.

"Is he okay?" I asked, stepping into his path. Anten hesitated. "Princess, I think it's best I give the report to the Queen first."

I had known Anten for as long as I could remember, and I knew he had a soft spot for me. Before I could even give him my best *pretty please* he sighed and said, "He's completely fine. He was just winded. A bit of a shock is all."

I let out an audible sigh of relief. "Thank Gaia."

Anten started on his way again, but paused. "He said that boy of yours is a real good warrior. He said he hasn't seen anyone fight like that before. If you can teach him to reign in that angry streak, I'd say he'd have a spot in the Army should he be inclined."

Nodding consideringly, I thanked the guard for letting me know.

So softly I almost thought I had imagined it, I heard Anten say as he walked away: "Don't worry, princess, the soldier didn't remember the magic."

Icy cold nerves trickled down my spine. This soldier was so adamant that Spense could be a one of them that he risked hiding information from his queen. I didn't know whether to be impressed or concerned.

Grateful above all else that this situation hadn't gotten too far out of my control, I allowed myself a deep breath as I continued on my way.

*

I didn't hesitate before knocking when I got to Spense's door. He answered equally quickly, the lazy confidence he had grown over two weeks gone from his face.

"Come in," he said, opening the door wider.

I stepped into his room. It was one of the nicer guest rooms. All were decorated equally lavishly but this one had a wonderful view of the gardens. Sunset loomed on the horizon, bringing an orange haze into the room that made it feel homey. Looking around, though, not much would suggest someone was living here indefinitely. Save for some clothing draped on the armoire and the ruby I had summoned for him glittering on the bedside table, the room hardly looked lived in.

Spense perched on one of the armchairs, but I chose to stay standing.

"What happened today?" I asked.

"I got into a fight. You were there. It was dumb, and I'm sorry."

"Not good enough. Why? Who started it?"

Spense bit his bottom lip and looked out the window. "Fenn threw the first punch. But I should've kept my mouth shut. They were trying to bait me."

I didn't understand why Spense would be targeted. From what Rolfo had told me, Spense was a great worker, he always finished earlier than the others and worked harder than he needed to. Was it jealousy?

"Tell me what Fenn said to get a reaction out of you."

Spense kept his eyes on the sunset, his teeth bared slightly.

"I'd rather not repeat it."

"It wasn't a question."

He turned to look at me, his gray eyes mutinous. I refused to look away, holding his stare with what I hope was a commanding face.

"They were saying vulgar things — about you."

My lips parted slightly, the only thing I couldn't stop myself from doing automatically in surprise. I supposed that was something I should have considered, knowing how the males in the stables or the Army, or really anywhere I went, would sometimes stare. I let myself feel the pain of being spoken about like that for a moment before letting go of it and moving on. It was sadly not the first time and wouldn't be the last — although I made a mental note to speak with Rolfo about punishment.

I chewed on the inside of my cheek while I

considered what to do. Even with my fury at Spense for almost blowing his cover and for causing a scene, I was vindicated in my opinion of him. He wasn't violent without cause, and it was a noble one at that, even though stupid. But he still disobeyed me, and clearly had an anger issue, judging at how hard it had been to snap him out of the haze.

Spense had been looking out the window again but snapped his eyes back to me when I spoke.

"Thank you for defending me. It was a kind thing to do. But it was also stupid and reckless. Fae are going to say what they're going to say about me; honestly, it's not my business what they think of me. Only what they think of my character. And you should have been able to see past a couple empty words without getting heated. We're going to work on that.

"And since we only have a month to get something from that dark puddle of a brain, we have to work harder."

Spense nodded, his face splashed with the light from the sun. "I will do it. Where do we start?"

I squared my shoulders. "I had an idea. In the City of Scholars there's a library called the Academy. It's one of our oldest buildings. It houses all of Eira's most important artefacts and texts. There has to be something there about memory loss. It's worth a trip to find out."

At the very least, the scholars there might know something about Dark fae and tearing rifts. And while there I could browse their volumes for more information about *Jweira* and possibly Iave. And as an added bonus I would be able to see my friend Shela who worked within the Academy.

"It's a day's ride there, so I think we should leave tomorrow at sunup. We don't have much time to waste." I had been planning to take Spense to the Academy before the solstice, but now with a deadline on our heads it was important we got there as soon as possible.

Spense stood, running a hand through his black curls. "I'll start packing after dinner," he said.

Dinner. I looked to the window, where the sun was almost done its descent. If we left now, we would be perfectly on time for dinner. But the more I thought about sitting in the fancy dining room, playing nice with my mother while listening to Embris drone on about army configurations, the more I would rather pull my own teeth out instead. Plus, it would not be a good idea for Spense to show his face in front of my mother right now. Even less of a good idea if Embris had heard about his soldier.

I wanted to blow some steam off before traveling all day.

"Let's skip the stuffy dinner. I have a craving for fried potatoes and mead, and lucky for us, The Leaf and Stone is the best in Nevelyn."

Spense grinned, dropping the fancy stitched tunic he had picked up for dinner on the chair he just vacated.

"Sounds perfect."

TEN
City of Scholars
DIANA

I was in the Sacred Pool again.

"Diana," whispered Jweira, the emerald reflecting all the stars of my ancestors, "You are borne of greatness. You are prophesized to continue that line. You know what you have to do. Look inside. I will help you. You know what to do."

Before I could even blink, my world evaporated.

I was in the forest, not far from the Gaian Abbey. I could hear thrumming, a constant drumbeat. As I walked forward, the brown and orange leaves crunching below my feet, the drumming grew louder. From between two trees, a faint light was visible.

"Diana."

I started running, trying to see where the light was coming from.

"Diana."

The drumming was echoing through my whole body, making my head swim. My heart was keeping time with the steady beat.

The light was so strong now that I was closer. I squinted, putting a hand in front of my face. I could see now that it was coming from an impossibly small hole—no not a hole, I realized. A rip. A rift. This was the portal that Spense had come through.

It was strange to behold, with its blinding light and distracting drumming. It was maybe the size of my hand, floating at eye level. Ancient magic flowed from it, but not an inviting one. Its pull was grey sludge, wanting to trap me in it and suck me in.

Still, I was curious. Through the light, I could make out another landscape not unlike the forest I was standing in.

"Diana."

I cried out, the voice reverberating through my head like a ball. It was too loud, too deep, too much.

I backed away, my feet getting caught in roots that were lying dead from a fallen pine tree. I fell, my hands thrown out backwards to catch myself. I looked down, trying to see where I was caught. The roots were moving, crawling up my legs, holding me down. I began to panic, trying to will my magic forward. Nothing came. It was like a dry riverbed.

"You can't outrun fate, child," the awful voice said.

I began trying to unwind the roots with my hands. My arms became flecked with scrapes and slivers.

"Come to me, Diana," it said my name like a purr. "I am the only way through your fate. Come to me, and restore me to my mighty strength once more."

I yelped as the roots wove up my abdomen, clutching tighter as they wound round my chest.

I could no longer get a breath. Spots danced in my vision.

The voice laughed at me, dark and mirthless, as I fell into darkness.

*

I woke up in a cold sweat, panting as I clutched at my chest.

I tried to steady myself as I took in my surroundings, relieved to be in my own bed. The sun was just about to rise, the dawn sending a small strand of light into my room through the wall of windows. The palace workers would be starting to flit around soon.

The low, melodious voice in my dream sounded again in my head, sending a shiver down my spine. I'd had my share of weird dreams and visions, but I'd never felt something so real. My arms tingled and burned slightly; as I ran my hands over them, I was surprised to find them perfectly fine, no scrapes to be seen. The thought of the roots tightening around my body sent my heart into a wild flurry. It felt unnervingly like a real memory — not a memory of a dream.

I had never been great at deciphering dreams like the Gaians who studied them. They believed our souls sent messages to us through dreams for us to use on our paths in life. I didn't doubt that it could be true, but I had never experienced any worthwhile dreams. If I remembered them when I woke, they were usually trivial, like enjoying a good gallop with Finnvarra, or wandering around the garden collecting ripe fruit from the trees.

Running my hands through my hair, I shook the foreboding rift from my mind. I could talk to the High Mother about my dream, but I had more pressing issues at hand. Besides, it was probably one of those weird dreams brought on by drinking too much.

Oh. Last night.

It came flooding back to me as I shoved some clothing into a leather bag. I had definitely drunk too much to be fully in control of my actions. I recalled trying to pull Spense onto the dance floor and just dancing alone after he declined. Thinking about it now, the patrons in the pub dancing with me definitely recognized me, which was embarrassing. I wasn't sure why it was different than when I danced at the palace parties, but for some reason I didn't like the way I had been on display. The High Princess and Heir to Eira, slumming it up, half-drunk in a pub, dancing into the morning hours.

Spense definitely had as much as I had to drink, if not more. But taking his size into account, he probably had not been near the level I was on. How humiliating.

At least I hadn't gone too crazy and gotten myself sick this morning. That would have been a horrible way to spend a day on horseback.

Maisie lightly knocked at the door and let herself in. "Good morning," she said with a twinkle in her eye. "I'm surprised to see you up and about. I was expecting to have to drag you out of bed considering the time you arrived back last night." She smirked at me while she helped me pack some essentials for a small trip.

I stuck my tongue out at her.

"You must have been having some fun if it made you forget about packing," she said, continuing to tease.

"I needed to blow off some steam. And it certainly worked." Fatigue pulled at the edges of my body, shaming me for only getting two hours of sleep.

Maisie nodded knowingly as she pulled out a small

satchel adorned with several pockets and started carefully stowing jewelry inside.

"I'm sure it was nice for Aedan to get out too. I hear his father's been working him quite hard lately."

Oh. I hadn't even thought to invite Aedan, even with The Leaf and Stone being our favourite spot. I had been so focused on spiting my mother and getting out of the palace. I did recall that he'd been quiet at dinner in the recent weeks, his new higher position in the Queen's Army taking a lot out of him. I had meant to carve some time out for him this week. With all that had happened, he had completely slipped my mind.

Guilt washed over me. He was one of my oldest friends.

"I didn't even think to invite Aedan. I feel terrible," I said quietly. I was almost too ashamed to hear myself say it out loud.

Maisie shook her head. "Forget I said anything. I just assumed." She finished with the satchel and stuffed it into the leather bag. She shooed me away to get dressed while she finished packing for me.

"So you went alone? I can't see you enjoying that, but I guess even the Heir needs time to herself every now and then," Maisie continued.

"Uh, actually, I went with Spense." I kept my head down, not wanting to meet Maisie's eyes, as I slipped into riding pants.

She raised her eyebrows in surprise but kept packing. "I can't see him as the dance-in-a-pub kind of male."

"He's definitely not," I said.

Maisie nodded. "You seem to really know him well. I look at him and all I see is shadow. Although I suppose you spend everyday with him."

I narrowed my eyes. Her tone was light, but the words felt targeted.

"I would think it necessary to get to know him seeing how we are trying to find out *who* he is." I kept my voice at the same level.

"I just want you to be careful, is all."

"I keep telling everyone—he's not dangerous, and even if he were—"

Maisie cut me off, closing the leather bag and fastening its snaps. "I know he's not a danger to you physically. That's not what I meant. Di, you have a tendency to get too close to the situation. You act like he's your friend. But how can he be? I'm pretty sure even after all this, he'll still be executed as soon as he gives up the information your mother wants."

The words hit me like a slap in the face.

Was she right? I had been so worried about the consequences of not getting his memory back that I hadn't even stopped to think *what* those consequences might be. Executing him felt like cold blood now. If he gave us the memories, shouldn't he be spared for helping us? What if he had no malintent when crossing into our realm? Or what if the month ended and we had no progress? My mind spun.

I fumbled for something to say. "I... I—"

"I'm sorry," Maisie said. "I'm just trying to spare your feelings later on. I know you give your heart to everyone, and you trust everyone and always give the benefit of the doubt. And I love that about you. I just don't want you to go through emotional hell again. Maybe if you stepped back a little, treated him more as an assignment than a friend, it won't become a situation like Mav—"

"*Don't say his name,*" I hissed.

Maisie just turned her palms upward in resign. "See what I mean? Mt Nord was almost six years ago, Di. You should be able to hear the name *Maverick* by now."

I felt deeply hurt from what she was implying. Firstly, that I didn't know how to detach myself and secondly that Spense was just an assignment for me to practice at queen, to be thrown away when I was done. I also didn't appreciate her flippancy for what she knew was the hardest time of my life.

I was flaming up for a retort when a messenger arrived and handed a letter to Maisie. She thanked him and read the address before handing it to me.

"It's from Jamey," she said, her voice clipped. "I'm going to take your bags down to the front gate. The horses will be waiting there for you."

I eyed the window as I broke the Western Shore seal. It was nearly sunup; I would have to remember to write Jamey when I was back from the City of Scholars.

D,

Things have taken a turn. The shadows are growing more frequent. Sometimes they leave blights in their wake. What's worse — a village along our outer rim, close to the Unclaimed Land, was attacked. We don't know who is responsible or how it happened. There was no sign of a struggle, just villagers in their beds staring blankly up at their ceilings. Most are still alive, in a comatose state. Our healers have never seen such a phenomenon.

I fear if this keeps up, I may be seeing you sooner than the solstice. For once, I hope that isn't the case.

Stay safe.
All my love,
J

My hands shook as I held the paper. What was happening? I had never heard of these shadows, or any sort of malicious being that would attack villages. Eight thousand years of history, not one dark force at large.

I thought back to the story I had told Spense not long ago, about the realm before the Darks were banished. There used to be plenty of rifts for peacefully traveling the realms, but sometimes evil creatures and essences would sneak through. The rift in the forest that Spense created was still open. It was under constant surveillance, but could it be possible something slipped through undetected? My terrifying dream flashed in my head.

I swallowed, folding the paper and hiding it discreetly under my bed sheets. This was something I needed to take to my mother. Spense could wait at the gate for me for a few minutes.

I raced through the halls, following the path I had spent years taking to my mother's quarters.

I was nearly there when I turned a corner and collided into Aedan.

He caught me easily and thankfully neither of us hit the floor.

I should really stop taking these corners at breakneck speed.

His eyes searched my face, two blue pools of concern.

"Hey—are you okay? How come you weren't at dinner last night?"

"Sorry to leave you high and dry there. I just needed a break from my mother. And now, coincidentally, I need to see her. I'm in a rush, but I'd love to catch up with you later," I said, taking a sidestep in the direction of my mother's door.

Aedan's brow furrowed. "Queen Vera left last night to the Western Shores on urgent business. She probably won't be back for a few days. She didn't even get to finish dinner. I thought someone would've told you."

Yes, that certainly would have been nice to know, I thought bitterly. But if my mother was in the West already, that meant she was handling the shadow situation, which took some urgency out of my need to speak with her. She could fill me in when I was back from the City of Scholars—and hopefully I would be able to fill her in with good news of my own.

City of Scholars. Sunup. Spense. The urgency returned, finding a place to settle in my stomach beside the anxiety that had taken up residence since my mother put a time restriction on Spense's memory.

"I guess I didn't make myself very easy to find last night," I admitted. "I'm leaving now for the City of Scholars. I'm taking Spense to hopefully find a clue about curing memory loss."

Aedan nodded; his face still concerned. "That's a

smart idea. Are you taking guards? I can personally assign some good ones."

Irritation flickered through me, but I pushed it aside, knowing my friend was just trying to help in the only way he knew.

"I hadn't planned on taking any. I wanted a quick ride there and back. I haven't been able to tell you, but I've been given a deadline," I said, turning around and starting the walk to the palace foyer to meet up with Spense. Aedan walked with me, his long stride keeping up with my quick pace.

"I heard about that, actually," he said. "That must feel like a lot of pressure."

I remembered Maisie saying how Aedan himself was under a heavy workload and fighting his own pressures. My heart sank as I realized how little I had talked with him lately. He probably needed to talk to someone who understood. An idea formed in my head.

"Hey, why don't you come with us to the City? You can easily keep up and then I'd have the protection you feel that I need. And — you'd finally get to meet Shela!" I gripped Aedan's arm, suddenly full of vigor with my new plan.

Aedan grimaced. "That would be fun, but I have a lot of responsibilities to tend to, with my father away escorting the Queen's Guard. I'm not sure I could drop everything and go."

I considered this. "Listen, it will only be for a day or two. We'll probably beat them home. Who's your Second? Don't you trust them? Plus, my aunt Lily will be here, and she practically ran the Army herself back in the day." Aedan still wasn't convinced, so I put on my best smile. "Please come. You deserve a break."

Finally, Aedan sighed. "Fine. But I'm only coming because my father would flay me for letting you leave Nevelyn unguarded."

I jumped once on the spot. "Perfect! We're leaving right now so I hope you can pack quickly!" We parted ways and I met Spense waiting in the foyer, as scheduled, in black riding leathers. He was leaning against a marble pillar as if he'd been there a while. Farther down the road, I could see grooms holding our horses at the palace gate. Finnvarra's flame-coloured coat stood out as she pranced around, no doubt feeding off the fear of her handler.

Spense smiled when he saw me. A small thrill went through me, unbidden, as he ran a hand through his dark waves. "You're late, princess," he said, pushing himself off the pillar to meet me. "Feeling the effects of your indulgences this morning?" he added teasingly.

"Ha, I can handle my *indulgences* just fine, thank you." I said, probably very unconvincingly. "I'm late because I had to make some last-minute personnel changes. Princess things, you wouldn't understand." That earned a chuckle from him as we made our way down the palace steps to where the horses waited. Plum stood obediently still, the warhorse incarnate, while Finnvarra paced, her tail held high as she surveyed her surroundings.

Spense had a small, worn cloth bag over his shoulder, no doubt holding the very few travel items he possessed. I made a note to get him a better bag. *At least his clothes fit better,* I mused. He looked the part of a regular Light citizen, that was certain. But Maisie was right about the air around him that was different. Even with the glamour over his horns, he drew the eye. He was open and confident and seemingly happy, but there was a mystery to him that made you think there was more to him than that. I supposed it was still a mystery to his own mind as well.

"Last night was a lot of fun," said Spense, unexpectedly. "I've never seen that side of you. The real you — not the princess."

I met his eyes, his face sincere. I thought of Maisie's words, how I got too closely involved in everything. It had steered me wrong in the past — but it was part of me. Was it wrong to deny that part of myself, or was it smart to think like a queen and observe from afar?

I nodded back at Spense. "It was fun, I haven't been able to do that for a while. But don't get used to it; we have to keep focused now."

Aedan was certainly efficient, as his gray mare Kali was led to join ours in no time, her saddle bags filled. I mounted Finnvarra while Spense attached his bag to Plum. "Who's joining us?" he asked as he mounted as well.

By way of answer, Aedan jogged out of the palace towards us. He had changed into riding wear and light soldier's gear.

Spense's face hardened, his openness disappearing in front of me. It was the first time I had witnessed a change in him like that. I knew I had been the most consistent fae in his life here, but I hadn't realized how much he had become unguarded with me. It satisfied a fraction of me somewhere deep down.

Aedan mounted Kali and the grooms waved us off as we headed down the cobblestone. The males surveyed each other from either side of me but said nothing as we went on our way. The air felt inexplicably thick.

"Well, we need to make up some time now," I said, breaking the silence. "I hope you boys can keep up." Without waiting for what would be an undoubtedly *male* rebuttal, I squeezed my heels into Finnvarra's sides. She burst forward faster than lightening, the wind at our backs urging us on as we raced into the forest.

*

By the time we arrived through the iron gates of the City of Scholars, it was nearing dark. The Academy was open into the night, but I thought it best that we get a good rest and try our luck there with fresh minds.

There was a mid-sized house a few blocks away from the Academy that was owned by the palace. We had a place in all of our major cities for times we were visiting or passing through. This one had not seen a royal visitor in quite a few years, so I was expecting a bit of dust or overall lack of life to it. It was surprising to enter the threshold and find light orbs lit along the halls, candles placed on the tables, shining surfaces, and the smell of fresh sage wafting in the air. I had not sent word for servant help while we were visiting, which led me to the realization that the palace was paying for this house to be cleaned and prepared regularly on the *chance* that a royal may stop by. Something twinged in my gut.

We had dropped the horses off at a boarding barn not far from the house, with the squeaky owner repeating over and over what good care he would take of them, his wide eyes taking in Aedan's gear, Spense's stature, and my — well frankly, my well-known face.

We carried our bags to the house, both males trying at one point to take mine for me, which I vehemently declined. Once inside the small home, I showed them their rooms upstairs, sharing a hallway. Although this house was meant to blend with the others in the area, it thankfully had three bedrooms. I couldn't see any configuration of sharing between the three of us that would work well.

After changing into looser, more comfortable clothes for the evening, I rooted around in the kitchen, looking for items I could use to throw together a quick dinner. With absolutely no warning, the front door burst open, the slam shaking the house. I ran to the hallway to see Aedan, small knife drawn, halfway down the stairs and not wearing a shirt. He was staring at the door, where a tiny female with flaming red hair was looking for damage on the wall while closing the heavy door.

"Shela!" I half-yelled, excitement taking over me. She spun around with a giant grin on her face, squealing as she ran to me. She almost knocked me over with the force of her hug.

"Diana," she tsked after pulling away from me. "I can't believe you think after four years you can waltz into town without saying hello!"

I led her to the sitting room, where we settled on some handsome, feather-filled chairs.

"Of course not! We *just* arrived. I didn't even have time to write you beforehand, we only decided to come last night. I was planning to see you though; I would like to sequester your help at the Academy tomorrow."

Shela nodded; her happy face lit up. "I'd love to help! I'm so happy to see you, Di. It's been way too long."

I agreed, then asked, "How did you know we were here, anyway?"

Shela gave me a sideways look. "Did you think you could waltz in here, the *Heir apparent*, and leave your royal warrior horses at the local barn without that spreading around the city like wildfire? If you meant to come undercover, you gravely failed."

Good thing we weren't undercover, I thought. I supposed it would be exciting for the city to have their princess visiting. I hadn't thought of arranging a quick visit with the city's representative, Lord Daqin, who would undoubtedly know I was here now and would think it quite rude for me to ignore him entirely. I groaned internally. This was part of being queen that did not come easily to me. Diplomacy and politics. We would have to stop by Lord Daqin's residence on our way back to Nevelyn.

"What's with the hasty trip here? I assume the delicious half-dressed soldier upstairs is Aedan? He is definitely way more handsome than you've ever described him as, Di. Let me guess, it finally happened? You fell in love and now you're here to elope." Shela was always like this, dramatic and full of life and wildness. It seemed so opposite to picture her working all day at the Academy behind stacks of books and quiet research.

I laughed. "*Gaia,* no, nothing like that. Aedan's here to make sure I come back in one piece. I brought along a male I've been working with at the palace. He lost his memories, and my mother assigned me the task of getting them back. I was hoping I could find something in the Academy to help."

Shela raised her eyebrows at me. "Seems like an awful lot of work for the princess to personally involved in. Why's he so important?" She answered her own question, her face triumphant to her own revelation. "Oh, he did something *bad,* huh?" She grinned wickedly.

I definitely was not going to answer that. Thankfully, the arrival of Aedan and Spense down the stairs was enough to redirect the conversation.

"Shela," I said, standing to greet the males. "This is Aedan, a commander in the Queen's Army."

Aedan approached her, holding out his hand as he said, "Deputy captain, actually. Good to meet you." I blinked in surprise. That was a huge promotion, not only prestigious but also something Aedan had been working towards for a long time. Damn humble boy.

Shela stood, smiling flirtatiously as she took Aedan's hand. "Pleasure. I've heard a lot about you," she said.

I rolled my eyes at her antics. In all the time I'd known Shela, she had never stopped her shameless flirting. There a time when every morning she arrived at the Academy, she was being escorted by a different male or female from the night before. It didn't matter size, gender, age, colouring. If they were attractive, Shela was interested.

I saved Aedan from her grasp, even though I was positive he could handle himself.

"This is Spense," I said, motioning to where the tall fae stood a step back, quiet and still. His gray eyes took her in as she gave him a once-over. She sauntered over to take his hand. I almost laughed at the height difference; she was maybe half his size.

"Well, aren't you mysterious. No memory, hm? Are you sure you want them back? What a great opportunity to create yourself anew." Shela was bold as she kept eye contact.

Spense smiled drily. "I would like to know who I am leaving behind before creating someone new," he said. "Otherwise, how will I know if I just became the same someone I was trying to forget?"

Shela gave him a foxlike grin before sitting back down on the chair. "I like your choice of traveling partners, Di," she said to me.

"I suppose they'll do," I said, thinking in wonder at how I'd managed to keep the two of them from at bay the whole day. They had a strange hate for each other. "Please tell me you're staying for dinner."

"I was ever-so hoping you would ask!"

"Great," I smiled. "Because I'm going to need your help making it."

Shela rolled off the chair theatrically. "A trick!" But she gracefully hopped to her feet and joined me in the kitchen, leaving the males behind. I took her arm in mine, wondering how wise it was to leave them alone together. *They're not children*, I thought. *They are grown males. Gaia forbid I can't leave them alone for mere minutes.*

Once we were out of earshot, with Shela expertly pulling spices out of cupboards and lighting a fire in the oven, I said in a low voice, "I need your help getting into the Secured section in the Academy. I can't tell you what, but I need some volumes that I know won't be in the public archives."

Shela paused; her face serious as she took in my own graveness. Slowly, she nodded. "Whatever you need. I can get you in."

I sighed in relief. Shela was truly a good friend. I knew I could trust her with everything; Spense's true identity, the rift, Iave, the emerald, all of it. And maybe I would let her in on it, maybe I would need her bottomless knowledge to complete the puzzle that sat unfinished in my brain. But for now, I had to see what I could do on my own. I owed it to my ancestors.

"Thank you, Shela. You have no idea how grateful I am."

She bumped my arm playfully with hers. "Put in a good word for me with blondie, and we'll call it even."

We laughed as we cooked together, catching up on stories and what we had been up to since we had seen each other last. Warmth settled in my stomach, giving me a much-needed distraction from the tornado that was my life. I soaked it all up, took as much as I could. The pit of anxiety would be back soon enough.

ELEVEN
Magnets
SPENSE

The food prepared by Diana and her exuberant friend Shela was simple wild rice and vegetables. It didn't have much extra flavour or the grandeur of the palace food, but it was the best meal I'd had since being here. Conversation was bubbly and mostly only between the two females. Occasionally Shela would baldly ask Aedan or I personal questions.

"So, tell me, Aedan, do you have anyone special in your life?"

To which Aedan politely coughed and commended Shela on her outgoing nature and lack of shame. The female only forked some rice into her mouth and smiled genially at him. When she realized it was fruitless trying to get any personal details from him, she turned to me.

"If you had to pick, without thinking about it, would you rather go the rest of your life without food or sex?"

Diana looked mortified but I laughed. "That depends — sex with whom?"

Shela cackled, pleased to have her question matched instead of ignored. "Always wise to answer a riddle with a follow up question, Spense. *Especially* when sex is on the line. Tell me—do you even remember the mechanics?" Without waiting for an answer, she said, "I would gladly help jog your memory, seeing as we're friends now—"

"Alright, that's enough of propositioning Spense at the dinner table," Diana cut in. Shela shrugged while my shoulders shook with laughter. I could see Shela's empty flirts for what they were.

Thankfully, Diana did not mind slapping her friend's arm or redirecting the conversation when needed. Shela did not seem to take it personally. She came across as the type of fae who said everything that came into her head without thinking first. While I could see that being annoying over long periods of time, it was also endearing. It felt—familiar.

I could also see the draw to living here. Where Nevelyn was bright and colourful and lively, the City of Scholars was neutral and peaceful. The buildings and homes were a little less flashy, but as a whole the city presented itself quite neatly. It made perfect sense with so many scholars keeping permanent residence here.

My attention was drawn to the table as Diana asked Aedan about his new position. Deputy Captain. I was lacking on all my military terms, but I knew it was a big deal. He ranked just below his father now.

"I can't believe you didn't tell me," she was saying, scooping more rice onto her plate. "It's such a huge accomplishment. You're not going to have any time for me anymore," she added teasingly.

I saw the shift in Aedan's energy. He smiled grimly

at his plate. "I guess that makes two of us now," he said, attempting without success to match her teasing tone. Apparently, there were some underlying nerves there.

Shela, despite her love of gossip, had some boundaries at least. She hastily began talking about the ancient Head Scholar at the Academy, and the wager between the employees to find out how old he *actually* was. She guessed three hundred.

The mood had been saved again, but as I glanced over to Diana, I could see that she was hurt from Aedan's words. It was only noticeable in the tiny crease between her eyebrows, giving away her pretense of being interested in Shela's story. Warm anger coiled in my core. It wasn't Aedan's place to speak to her like that. She was training to be queen; of course she was going to have less time for him. There was a piece of me that wondered if he wasn't so upset that she was spending time away from him, and it was really about *who* she was spending her time with.

I had let myself become unhinged at the stables the day of the fight. I could have blown my cover if I hadn't been stopped. What if my magic got away from me and dissolved the glamour hiding my horns? All because of my anger towards Diana being mistreated. I wanted to say something. But I wouldn't, because she had told me that she could take care of herself, and I respected that.

But as I glanced sideways at the brooding male at the end of the table, picking at his carrots, I was mad all over again. Sulking like a child. This was to be the fearsome and tactical next leader of the Queen's Army? Carefully, as not to wake the sleeping beast inside me, I tugged on a few tendrils of my magic. It rose willingly and crawled over the table slowly, softly, unnoticeable. It lingered on Aedan's plate before dissolving into his food.

The sleeping beast grumbled its approval.

Feeling satisfied, the rage building in me faded away, and I was able to listen to the rest of the conversation.

"What a wonderful surprise ending to my day," Shela said. "I believe I should get going, though. I am on dawn-duty at the Academy." She made a face that conveyed how little she enjoyed dawn-duty. "Stop by whenever you want. But if you come in the early morning, the price of my help is breakfast scones. Blueberry, or they're useless to me." She got up, stretching.

Diana stood with her, accompanying her to the door. "We'll be there with payment for your services," she said, smiling brightly. "Thanks, Shela. See you tomorrow."

I waved to her from down the hall as she blew us all kisses, leaving as grandly as she entered.

I began to help clear the plates off the dining table. Aedan was sitting frozen in his seat, his eyes glazed over. Diana noticed, and tried to get his attention. "Hey, are you alright? You look kind of pale." Indeed, his complexion had turned ashen. I kept gathering utensils.

"I, uh, I'm fine. I think I just need to lay down," Aedan said. Without waiting for another word, he scraped his chair back from the table abruptly and left.

Diana shrugged at me as we took the plates into the

kitchen. She filled the sink with soapy water and washed them thoroughly, handing them to me to rinse and dry. The kitchen was small, forcing us to stand shoulder-to-shoulder as we worked.

"I assume princesses don't spend a lot of time cleaning dishes," I said. "But the fact that you can doesn't really surprise me."

She laughed softly. "I just think it's wise to know how to do everything. I don't always want to be dependent on palace staff."

"No? Isn't that part of being queen?"

"Seems that way. And I can see where help is sometimes necessary. But when I rule, I'd like to be able to do a lot more things myself, like cooking a meal and cleaning up afterwards or washing my clothes." She smiled darkly. "Although I suppose it's wishful thinking. I don't even have time for that right now, let alone when I take over all my mother's duties as well."

I took her in, the way she had drawn in her bottom lip and was chewing on it, the way she was scrubbing an already-clean dish.

"I think you can make it happen. You have all the resolve you need and more," I said softly.

Diana looked into my eyes, her hazel colour warm. "Thanks, Spence."

I made us each a cup of tea to finish the day. They only had chamomile, which I found out was not a flavor I enjoyed, but I drank it anyway. A good night's sleep would do me some good for tomorrow.

We sat on the floor in front of the fireplace, Diana's magic keeping it glowing lightly. It was too much work to make a real fire for a few minutes, she'd reasoned. I hadn't seen her perform anything but earth magic, so I was more than happy to observe.

"The magic of each region is easier to access when you're in that place," she said. "So, earth magic is easiest to do in the North, fire in the South, air in the East, and water in the West. Some can access all of them from anywhere, but that's a rare gift. It's most common for fae to be affluent in the magic of the land they were born into."

"Are you one of those specially gifted?" I asked.

Diana smiled into her mug. "I can do all the types of magic, I'll admit. But I wouldn't say I'm particularly strong with water. It just seems so—slippery." She laughed at her own joke, her chestnut hair cascading down her back as she tipped her head towards the ceiling. I couldn't help but laugh with her.

After a moment, Diana mused, "I wonder if you can access them all."

I turned towards her. "I guess we'll have to do some more training," I said.

"Good thing you're a quick learner. I wonder how that plays into who you were before. Maybe you were academic, like the scholars here," Diana said, studying my face.

"I would be so relieved if I turned out to be a quiet scholar, happily reading my life away," I said, knowing deep down that could not be true. "I can't shake the feeling that whoever I was—wasn't good."

Diana swallowed. "I don't believe that, Spense. Truly. I've seen your heart in those rare occasions you let it show. You always choose the right thing."

I was suddenly aware of how close we were sitting, where our knees touched, how her scent had wrapped around me so gently.

"You're good, Spense."

This wonderful leader, this fearless, relentless, talented force of a female believed me to be good. I wanted to contradict her, tell her that she was wrong, she had only seen my actions, she had not seen what I wanted to do to those males that spoke about her, to Aedan, to anyone who wasn't worthy. Instead, I found myself looking into those hazel eyes, our breaths mingling, as we pulled closer like two magnets finally finding each other.

The horrific, unmistakable sound of retching filled the air, coming from upstairs. We both jumped; the tension in the air winked out as fast as the flame Diana had been holding in the fireplace.

"I wonder if I should check on him," Diana murmured, almost to herself.

"I'm sure he does not want you to do that," I said, absolutely confident in this.

She nodded, still looking at the stairs. "You're probably right. Goodnight Spense." She didn't look to me again as she glided upstairs and disappeared down the hall. I heard a door close softly.

My brain was a bit fuzzy. *Stupid, Spense*, I thought. *Don't ruin this, don't do something you'll regret.* Shame prickled all over my body. Diana was nice to me because she was nice to everybody. It was her innate nature. Of course she didn't feel the things I was feeling.

Ironically, I thought, it was my own doing that caused the moment to be broken. How suiting. My own fault.

These thoughts continued like a wheel in my head. I laid in bed staring at the ceiling for a long while before sleep came.

*

When I woke, I could hear movement in the hall, and hushed voices. Thinking I'd overslept, I hastily grabbed the clothes from yesterday and got dressed. I ran my hands through my hair and padded downstairs, where Diana was packing a small satchel at the front door.

"Morning," she said, her regular smile on her face, no sign of tension towards me. "Are you ready to go?"

I looked around for the blond sulking child, but he was nowhere to be seen. "Where's Aedan?" I asked.

Diana threw the satchel over her shoulder and opened the front door. "He's too ill to join us," she said. Her face was trying to be sympathetic, but I thought I saw annoyance there. "So it'll just be you and I." She gestured for me to follow her out the door.

Gladly, I joined her in the fresh spring morning.

I couldn't help but smile just a little bit.

TWELVE
Blueberry Scones & Revelations
DIANA

When we arrived at the front gates of the Academy, the familiar smell of dust and old books was already filling my nose. I had only visited a few times before but could never forget what it was like to be here. Like I could possess all the knowledge in the entire realm, and also like I would never know everything there was to know. It was oddly comforting.

The scholars who resided here were of all ages and types, but Shela was by far the youngest and most vibrant. While the Academy members chose to wear their habit of muted gray, Shela wore whatever bright colours she wanted and an Academy badge on a chain around her neck to signify that she worked there. When I had last visited four years ago, Shela was an unpracticed scholar, pestering the gray cloaks every day to hire her. She once stayed in the Academy for a week straight, refusing to leave until she had finished researching whatever it was she had come in there for. They were taken aback by her outgoing demeanor and peacock-like appearance and tried to point her in other directions. But finally at the beginning of last winter, her attention to detail and whip-smart memory could no longer be ignored and the Academy hired her as one of their own, tasked with helping the public with their research and pouring over her own centuries-old volumes in hopes of decoding old languages.

Since Shela's hire, younger fae were finding their way to the Academy gates, presenting obscure research they had done and attempting to secure their own spots. As I looked around the well-kept grounds, I was pleasantly surprised to find many fresh faces and youthful gray coats. It was good to see the Council of Scholars flowing with the new tide instead of trying to swim against it.

Spense was walking a step behind me. He was as calm and contented as he normally seemed, but there was something different about his energy. He was keeping his distance from me instead of confidently strutting at my side like he had been a prince his entire life. I couldn't help but convince myself that I had made him vastly uncomfortable. I glanced to my side quickly to see that he was still following me into the Academy building, and my stomach tightened when I met his eyes briefly.

I shoved last night to the farthest corner of my mind that I could. I had let my guard down, let myself feel something I had not for a very long time. And it was a huge mistake. I did not know what was to come of Spense in the near future; I had to keep my personal feelings out of it. I knew Spense was worthy of retribution, of finding his own place in Eira one day, maybe even in Nevelyn. And I would fight for him to get that chance. But only because it was the right thing to do, no reason other than that. Whatever his future may be here, it would not involve me.

When we reached the top of the stone steps and entered the Academy, I watched Spense's wondrous expression as he took it all in. It was awe-inspiring, I had to admit. Stone pillars held up walls decorated corner-to-corner with murals. The ceiling was impressively tall, made out of stained glass, and boasted a crystal chandelier bigger than any I had seen in the palace. The walls continued in two wings, which would wrap around and meet each other at the back of the building. Even from the foyer I could see the beginning of bookshelves down the wings.

The sun came down through the stained glass, creating beautiful rays of colour that bounced off of every surface. When it hit Spense I could see pink coming through his ivory skin, and his inky hair pulling a dark blue that reminded me of a raven wing.

"Stunning, right?" I asked, fixing my gaze on the mural in front of me. It depicted two Nordians on pegasi, meeting a drake in midair battle, a Dark fae on its back. I remembered viewing this last time I was here, thinking the Nordians brave to go to against the Dark. Now I found myself wondering where the honour was in a two-against-one fight.

"It's amazing," breathed Spense, even as his gaze hitched on the drake and its rider. "Where do we even start?"

I flagged down an elderly looking scholar, his gray robes matching his hair and lengthy beard. He smiled broadly when he realized who I was, bowing his head as he introduced himself as Ichabod.

"I was wondering if you could help me locate scholar Shela," I said kindly, matching his smile.

His face drooped in confusion. "Shela? I believe she is busy at the moment. I could certainly help you find what you are looking for, High Princess. Just say the word, I am at your disposal."

I recognized the disdain in his voice towards my friend. Clearly, he didn't think her an adequate representation of the Academy. But I kept my smile neutral and added a queenly tone.

"How kind of you, Ichabod. I have no doubt you would exceed my expectations. But Shela is a dear friend of mine, and has already begun researching what I am looking for today. I wouldn't want all her hard work to be in vain."

Ichabod dipped his head. "Of course, my lady. You will find Shela in the Room of Forgetting, located in the South Wing. Would you like me to take you there?"

"I know of the place. Thank you for your help," I said, gently touching Spense's arm in a silent request to follow me.

I could feel Ichabod's eyes on us as we set off down the halls. Soon we were lost in the quiet hustle of students and scholars alike, cramped over desks or carrying mountainous stacks of books. Many did not look up as we passed, and those who did seemed not to register who I was. I savoured the anonymity, not caring at all that these fae were too engrossed in what they were doing to bow their heads to me. For once I felt like I was one with my citizens. This was how they really lived when they believed no one was watching.

We passed countless more murals as we made our way down the South Wing. Sometimes one would morph into another without breaking off. They would continue through corners and sometimes up to the ceiling. So much of our history was depicted on these walls. So much life and death and everything in between. I wanted to stop and study them all.

Finally, we reached an iron door with the words THE ROOM OF FORGETTING hand-painted in fading black ink. All the doors into the rooms in the Academy were iron, fortified and infused with magic to be flame-retardant to protect the precious contents inside. The scholars had gone to the Southern Isles millennia ago to learn about fire magic and how to yield it in a proactive way. In fact, I believed they still traveled there every decade to update their learning.

I pushed open the heavy door and spotted Shela instantly, sitting at a table near the stained-glass window with mountains of books swallowing the surface. The light coming in the window made it look like her hair was aflame.

The Room of Forgetting was large enough but the rows upon rows of towering bookshelves made it feel quite tight, even with the ceiling being high enough to need a couple ladders to clean the chandelier. There were not as many scholars in here and a hushed peace hovered over the room. I could've used a quiet space like this to study when I was growing up.

Spense snorted under his breath.

"What's so funny?" I asked, shooting him a look.

He shrugged. "Just thinking of the irony of looking for memories in a room named after forgetting."

I didn't reply but allowed myself a small smile as we walked through the room.

Shela didn't look up as we approached. It was only when I dropped the small basket of blueberry scones right on the page she was reading that she jumped back and realized we were there. I had been happy to make a pitstop on the way here to get the breakfast treat for Shela. It had given me a chance to take in the City of Scholars during daytime. The little bakery I had gotten the scones from smelled so divine that I couldn't help getting a cranberry one for myself, which had been delicious.

"How long have you been standing there?" she asked, as though it was a common occurrence for her to have to get startled out of her work.

"Not long," I said, smiling as she wasted no time digging into the scones.

She dramatically threw her hand over her heart. "You went to Daggan's Bakery? Ah, just the best! You really know how to bribe a girl."

Spense chuckled as he reached for an ancient-looking book on the top of the pile nearest him. The cover was faded but the title was still visible in a language I didn't recognize.

Shela slapped his hand away. "No touching! This volume is older than the entire building you're standing in. It could crumple into dust without proper care." She gently stroked down the spine of the book as if in comfort.

Spense was not deterred. His brows were furrowed together as he said, "I know this language."

I sharply looked from him to Shela. "What language is that?" I asked.

"It's an ancient dialect from before Diana's conquer. It was widely used by the Unseelie Courts and died out after the uniting of the realm. It took me forever to learn it. Strange that you would know it; perhaps you were a scholar as well." Shela was pensive as she took Spense in. I tried to keep my heart from beating too fast. Shela was one of the smartest fae I knew. I wouldn't put it past her to be able to piece together Spense's true identity.

"Wait, wait, *Diana's* conquer?" Spense asked.

"Remember the story I told you about the Seelie queen's daughter who became the first Queen of the Lights? Her name was Diana." I said.

Spense blinked. "You never told me you were named after the first queen."

"She's obviously too humble, Spense, dear," said Shela. I started to object, to say that it just hadn't seemed relevant to the story, but Shela kept talking over me. "Can you read what the title says?" she asked, tilting the book towards Spense.

"*'The Magic of Memory'*?" Spense ventured, his brow still furrowed. A black curl dropped over his face as he bent over the book.

Shela's eyes widened slightly as she nodded. "Exactly."

I wanted to somehow intervene, to keep Shela from digging further. What could I say that wouldn't sound like I was deliberately changing the subject? Truthfully,

Spense's ability to read the Unseelie language was intriguing, and I did want to explore that. It was getting harder not to let Shela in on the whole story.

The sound of hushed voices and slight giggling broke our conversation. A few tables over from us, half-shrouded by a bookshelf, were a group of young female scholars in gray coats. They were taking turns looking at us and whispering to each other.

Shela rolled her eyes and said in a daringly loud voice, "I'd think that if *I* were a new hire wanting to prove my worth, I would spend less time loitering around *private* conversations and actually do something of use." Her words were pointed enough, and the group started to scatter.

"Damn gossips," Shela muttered. "You have no idea how much I regret appealing to the Council to hire young scholars."

I watched them leave, glancing over their shoulders at me to get one last glance at the High Princess. "This has to be handled with utmost discretion, Shel," I said, kicking myself for not being more discreet. I could have worn a hood, at least.

She nodded. "They may gossip among each other, but nothing said here will leave the Academy; that I can promise you."

"Do you have a meditation room? I want Spense to start there."

Spense's eyes flicked to me, but he said nothing.

Shela called to one of the young gray coats who had settled at a desk with two massive red volumes on it. "Raya! Come here."

The young female snapped her head up in surprise and joined us at Shela's desk. Her long blonde hair was enviably shiny and smooth, cascading loose around her shoulders like water down a stream. Raya bowed her head to me before addressing Shela.

"I take it you know who this is?" Shela asked.

Raya nodded, not meeting my eyes. No doubt she thought she was in trouble for eavesdropping before.

"Good, so you know how important it is for you to do exactly as I say. I need you to take this handsome male here to Quiet Room B and show him how to use the *gotu kola*. You will then leave him be and make sure he is not interrupted. Clear?"

Raya looked to Spense and back to Shela, a relieved smile forming on her face as she realized she was not about to lose her job. "Yes, that's not a problem."

Shela smiled too-sweetly. "It better not be."

I looked to Spense. "Trust yourself. Don't fight it." He nodded to me, looking a little confused but still holding that confident air around him. He followed Raya to the door. I felt an uncomfortable twinge in my gut when she looped her arm through his and laughed too-loudly at something he said. Pathetic.

"Do you enjoy hazing the new scholars?" I asked Shela once they were out of earshot.

She grinned. "So much." She put an elbow on the desk and rested her chin on her hand, sighing greatly. "Hate to see him go, but love to watch him leave."

I rolled my eyes as I settled down in a chair across from her.

"Speaking of nice touchies, where is my windswept

captain today?" Shela pushed a stack of books towards me.

I picked up the first one off the pile. *Healing Trauma Through Elemental Magic & Memory Training: The Extensive Guidebook.* "He's apparently too ill to help us read all day."

"You don't believe he's truly ill?"

I crinkled my nose. "I want to believe him because he's never lied to me before. I'd like to think he's above being petty. His favourite thing is making sure I'm "protected" so it just seems out of character for him to stay home, you know? Although I could smell the sickness seeping from his room."

Shela hummed as she flipped through pages of the book she was perusing. "Mm, matters of the heart can be so messy."

My eyes flicked up to her. The queenly thing to do would be to ignore the obvious bait. But I was already doing a terrible job so far of being Heir; what was one more deviance?

I sighed. "Fine, I'll bite."

Shela smiled innocently. "You mean to tell me you are wholly unaware of Aedan's feelings for you? It's glaringly obvious."

I blinked in surprise. "Aedan? We're *friends*; always have been. Yes, he may be a bit jealous of the time I've been spending with Spense. But that's just because we've always had the most time for each other until recently."

Shela looked at me like she didn't think I actually believed what I was saying. "*Or*, he's jealous because you're giving all your attention to this dark, mysterious, beautiful, built-like-a-mountain male. You will admit he's gorgeous, won't you? You're not in that much denial?"

"Well, yes, I mean — I suppose, if you like that kind of — "

"Diana, he's quite possibly the most handsome fae I have ever laid eyes on. Truly, how you got two amazingly gorgeous males to fight for your attention is inspiring."

I held up a hand. "Wait, now you're trying to tell me that Spense *also* has feelings for me? That's absolutely not true." Last night flashed in my mind, a reminder of how reserved Spense had been towards me since then.

Shela held up her hands. "Look, I don't know *what* it is, but there's a force between you two. It's like magnets. You obviously care deeply for each other, even if it's not inherently romantic." With that, she went back into her book, flipping pages faster than any normal fae would be able to read.

I stewed in this for a while, trying to come to terms with what Shela was saying. Before long, my head was spinning in confusion, and I could no longer concentrate on reading.

"Hey, would you be able to get me into the Secured section now?" I asked, keeping my voice low.

Shela slammed her book shut, a wicked grin on her face. "I thought you'd never ask."

*

Once Shela had slipped me past the incredibly old crone sitting at the desk that guarded the entrance to the Secured library, she left me alone and said she would be back in a few hours to get me back out. She had mentioned that being the Heir to the entire realm, I could likely just walk in without any resistance. But I didn't want to risk being denied, or worse, being asked what I needed from the shelves. Better to ask forgiveness than permission in this case.

I knew Spense would be preoccupied for a few hours at the very least. The *gotu kola* herb that the Academy provided for meditations was extremely potent. Rubbing it on one's temples could induce a coma-like brain state where it would be the easiest to meditate. I had experienced the effects of *gotu kola* twice before and both times was treated to a three-day hallucination. Normally the herb lasted a few hours, but I was one of those few who had an adverse reaction to it. Lucky me.

I felt a bit of shame for sending Spense away to meditate on his own. I hadn't even thought of how the *gotu kola* might affect him differently being Dark. I told myself that this was an important theory in regaining his memory and that he probably was grateful for the space away from me. I couldn't allow myself any distractions in my one chance in the Secured library, anyway.

The air in this room was thicker. The books felt like they had life to them, like old magic that had barely a wisp of light left. As I passed the numerous shelves, I noted horrendous titles like *Summoning Demons Through Portals* and *Tales of Urdan the Great: How A Group of*

Thieves Became the Mightiest Army in History. I hated to touch them, but I added them to my growing pile in case they held information I needed. I could see why they kept these volumes hidden away from the public.

Something I couldn't understand, though, was why they kept seemingly helpful and ordinary books here as well, like one book that held all of the Northern Peninsula's royal lineage and one that showed multiple uses for an herb called *gingko biloba*.

I felt vastly overwhelmed when I finally sat down at a desk with a dozen volumes of varying size and length. I settled in and lost myself in a sea of words and phrases in various languages and texts, most I didn't even understand. I was only skimming pages until I came across a passage from a book about realm-jumping.

While opening a portal, you must be cautious that you have enough power to draw from (see page 367 for power sources). Otherwise, you risk creating a rift. A portal is a perfectly safe, user-friendly piece of magic that will allow fae to cross through, entering the realm of their choice. Whereas a rift is a failed portal that is unstable with the risk of collapse. You will know it is a rift from its small size and ominous nature. Those who try to travel through a rift will not only have no control over the destination they travel to, but will also experience grave side effects such as dismemberment, brain alterations, total organ failure, or death. If you come across a rift, DO NOT try to travel through. As well, do not try to close it. Rifts will inevitably collapse on their own, and you do not want to be anywhere near the vicinity when they do. Now, let's talk about traveling through a portal while with child…

My heart thundered in my chest. This bit of information alone was worth the trip to the Academy. Spense's memory loss came from traveling through the rift. It was entirely possible, I reasoned, that he had not intended to come to this realm at all. I had to warn my mother to stop guarding the rift, to not allow anyone near it. I wondered if I could get an expedited messenger to the Western Shores before she left. Or I could just command the guards to step down as within my power as Heir. Either way —

Diana.

My breathing stopped. The voice from the rift in my dream.

At once, the table and library dissolved underneath me. I was standing in the forest again, looking into the rift.

Yes, Diana. You know now what must be done.

I forced air into my lungs.

Restore me. Heal me. Fix me.

I took a step back, and another, and another. But I wasn't moving. I had no option but to look into the outpouring of light from the rift while I was fixed in place. Waves of grey sludge reached towards me.

It is within your power. I will show you what you can really do. It is only a matter of time, now. Come to me.

Whatever had its hold on me let go, and I wrenched myself back into consciousness. My magic swirled around in confusion, raised to strike at the sign of my rising fear. Was the rift *watching* me? How horribly disturbing.

I had pushed the chair back from the table, far

183

enough that my back was pressing into a wall of books behind me. When I leaned forward, several large volumes crashed to the floor.

I heard voices from the front of the library and following footsteps.

Shit.

Hastily, I grabbed the book off the table and retreated farther into the Secured section. I wound further down the halls until I reached an alcove of shelves that looked like it hadn't seen a visitor in centuries.

I crouched down among the shelves to hopefully remain undetected. My eyes caught on the spines of the books at eye level. I tilted my head to the side as I read: *The Rule of Jweira.* I had never heard that name before my ritual and now had seen it twice. That couldn't be a coincidence. I stuffed the book under my arm as I heard footfalls getting louder towards me.

"Diana?" Shela's voice hissed. "Are you in here?"

I stood up. "Thank Gaia it's you."

Shela beckoned for me to follow her. "What are you doing in here, throwing a party? I heard the crash from down the hall."

My mind spun for something to say. Adrenaline was still coursing through my body. "Sorry, I tripped backwards and fell into the shelf."

Shela let out a soft chuckle. "I will be inspecting those books for damage and billing you for the repairs, you know."

I let out a sigh of relief that she believed me. "How did you stop the gray coats from coming in here?"

Shela just waved a hand at me. "Don't worry about it. You got lucky; I was coming to get you anyway. Spense is out of his meditation. I figured we could reconvene. I found some books that might be helpful on regaining his memory as well."

We wove through the books and Shela led me out the way we came after confirming the coast was clear.

"That's great," I said. "I just found out something that I need to pursue immediately; we'll need to head back to Nevelyn as soon as possible."

Shela gave me a serious nod. "I'll send the books I found with you, then." She gestured to the two books I was holding under my arms. "Is that all you need?"

I grimaced. "Shit, I left a pile—"

We ground to a halt as Spense rounded the corner, a giggling Raya on his arm. She wavered when she saw the seriousness in both mine and Shela's stature.

"We've got to go back to Nevelyn immediately," I said, meeting Spense's eyes as he pried himself from Raya's grasp. "Did you discover anything in your meditation?"

He did not look away from my face. "No."

A lie. I could almost taste it, the way the word floated sour in the air. The audacity to not even look away as he spewed the lie was enraging. I narrowed my eyes, wanting with so much conviction to expose it.

This isn't the time, a voice in my head said. *You'll have an entire day's ride to interrogate him.* That was good enough for me.

"Fine, let's go. We're going to grab Aedan on the way. I'll explain on the road."

Spense fell in with me as Shela led us through the halls back to the entrance, Raya's crestfallen face left in the dust.

At the foyer, I swept Shela into a hug. "Thank you so much for all your help, Shels. Seriously, I don't know what I'd do without you."

Shela smiled warmly at me. "Not be able to function, probably. Happy to help. But don't wait so long to visit next time, okay?"

"You're welcome to come to the palace anytime you like, you know. Might be easier for you to come to me considering all my new queenly duties," I teased.

"Don't let being Heir go to your head, darling," Shela purred. "We both know who gets more work done in a day."

I laughed. "Fair enough. Either way, I will not let it be so long until our next visit. I will have to return these books, anyway."

Shela waved us away. As we made our way off the grounds, we heard her call out, "Don't forget about my offer, Spense! You know where to find me!"

THIRTEEN
My Best to the Queen
SPENSE

Diana was silent as we walked at a rather uncomfortably fast pace back to the house. I was used to gentle quiet from her, but this was full of tension.

"Are you going to tell me why we're in such a rush to get back?" I was trying not to let my annoyance show. I wasn't done in the Academy, I wanted to stay longer, find more books in the Unseelie language.

"Are you going to tell me what you saw in your meditation?" she shot back, looking straight ahead.

I fell silent. Hadn't she realized that I hadn't wanted to tell her in front of others? Here I'd thought we were trying to be discreet.

A small part of me offered up the fact that I could have just said that to her and maybe deep down I really didn't want to share what I'd seen.

"We just need to get on the road. We'll talk then," was all she said, her voice terse.

I opened my mouth to defend myself but decided against it. For whatever reason, Diana was not in a space for that. I could practically see the emotion coming off her in waves. What was it? Anger, irritation, worry all came to mind. But none really fit. I could tell at least some of it was directed at me, especially after my foolish lapse of emotional control last night. Certainly, she'd kept her distance from me today because of it.

So I gave Diana the space she wanted as we set quite the pace through the City of Scholars' streets. They were manicured and well-kept, much like the grounds of the Academy. Hope flared in my chest that maybe we could return here one day. It lit and fluttered for a half second before it was stomped out by the reminder that I was still and would always be a prisoner.

We were almost back to the house, passing the street where we had stopped for scones, when an eerie hush came over the road. Diana halted in her steps, a phantom wind blowing her hair around her like a tunnel. The gentle spring sunshine disappeared, the street falling into inky blackness. It was way too dark outside for the middle of the day. My magic thrummed inside me, on high alert. There was something dark here, it was undeniable. Curling, methodically slow shadows appeared, encircling us.

Diana whipped around to face me. I expected her to be full of confusion, worry even, but she looked like a hardened warrior as she searched for the source of the shadows. Even through the darkness, her magic's light radiated off her, creating a terrifying and striking image. In this moment I feared her more than the shadows.

"Show yourself!" she yelled into the nothingness.

A chill went up my spine as a wickedly sinister voice chuckled darkly. It came from everywhere and nowhere and reverberated in my head painfully. I spun around in vain, looking for a source it could be coming from.

"You're a feisty one, Diana, princess of the North. If circumstances were different, I might admire that about you."

My legs almost gave out. This was the voice from my meditation, eerie and oozing with power.

"Who are you?" she called out.

The shadows swirled, taking shapes and dissipating as quickly as they formed. Finally, they settled into a vague, hovering silhouette of a large male. My heart leapt. He did not show his face, but instantly I knew it in my mind. He reached out a shadowed hand to caress Diana's cheek. She brought her fist up into it, causing the shadows to part around her hand and reform on the other side.

"I am exactly who you fear I am, child."

She hesitated, giving me a chance to take a step towards her and shout, "What do you want?"

The shadows surged to me, gleefully wrapping around my entire body. My own magic rose to meet it, delightfully even in match. I was sickened at the rightness I felt when it enveloped me. I pushed my own magic outwards in a shield, keeping the shadows at an arm's length.

"I want my realm back, of course. I am nearer than I have ever been to my return. I thought it polite to reacquaintance myself with the throne I will soon be seated on."

Diana's lips curled into a snarl. "You will never sit on this throne." Her voice was pure steel.

"My best to the queen." The shadows chuckled again, slowly fading outwards, dissipating as sunshine returned to the street. It was like it had never happened at all, save for the rotten feeling in the air.

Diana's warrior façade did not falter, but she was visibly shaking. I touched her forearm lightly, to which she jumped but did not pull away. She met my eyes, her breathing audible. Without another word, she grabbed my hand and took off at a run.

*

Diana did not slow down when we got back to the house or say anything other than telling Aedan we were leaving—now. The latter had jumped to his feet and joined us downstairs, although much slower than Diana was moving. To his credit, he did look like he was recovering from his mysterious illness, although he still looked quite pale, and there was a faint *sick* smell to him. I had only meant for him to be sick through the night, but there was a horrible part of me secretly enjoying the fact that he was still suffering for his hurtful words.

"What of the bags?" I asked when we arrived at the stables.

Diana wasted no time hopping aboard Finnvarra, tossing a handful of coin over her shoulder to the barn owner as she spun her around towards the gate to the stable grounds.

"I'll have them sent back to the palace. We don't need the extra weight."

I mounted Plum, gathering my reins, and turning her around in time to see Diana's chestnut hair flying away from us. Clearly, she wasn't waiting. I urged Plum forward, her hooves pounding down the dirt road as we raced after her. I didn't look back for Aedan, but I could hear his mare behind us. I wondered how he would fare on this hellish ride back. It was grueling and tiring to do the day-long trip at a comfortable pace; trying to run all the way there would be incredibly exhausting for all parties involved. Except maybe Finnvarra, I amended. That beast had more fire in her than the entire Southern region.

It wasn't until sunset that Diana slowed, allowing us all to catch our breath. The horses were lathered in sweat, as was I.

"We're about halfway," she said, her pace finally allowing for us to ride side-by-side. Aedan trailed a few feet behind, his pallor worse than when we'd left. His mare, Kali, was truly a saint as she kept balance for both of them.

"It will be well into the early morning hours when we arrive," she continued. "But it is pertinent that I speak with my mother as soon as possible." She might have aimed at an apologetic tone, but only queenly firmness came through.

I nodded. "Hey, that was... disturbing, back there. Are you alright?"

Diana looked to me, her mask slipping for the first time. "I, uh, I don't know." She fiddled with her horse's mane before continuing in a soft voice.

"I can't help but feel it's my fault."

"How could you even think that?" I asked, matching her quiet tone.

She shook her head, hair falling in her face. "Everything that's happened; the rift, you, the regions' unrest, the shadows, all of it started after my ceremony.

The ancestors, they told me—" she broke off, the words sitting unspoken on her lips.

I watched as she quietly collected her thoughts. It took long enough that I thought maybe she wouldn't share, but she finally said in a newly calm voice, "My ancestors told me that darkness is coming; and that I have to stop it." She waited for my reaction.

"That's quite a strong conviction to give to an unpracticed, young Heir."

She shook her head. "Don't you see? This is all because of me—whatever path I'm supposed to take, however that shapes me into the ruler I'm supposed to be—it's putting others in danger. And I can't do anything about it. I couldn't even banish those shadows! How many more will be hurt, or even killed, before I stop all this?"

The air loosed from Diana's lungs, a great relief to her as her shoulders sagged slightly.

"You're telling me you think all this—me crashing your ceremony, the rift, the shadows—it's all a test set out by your ancestors like some sort of game to get you ready to rule? That's insane, Diana."

She looked at me incredulously.

"You dare to say that my ancestors are insane? You don't know *anything* about our rituals."

I almost laughed, but at the sight of her face I held it in. "No, what I'm saying is you're too caught up in what happened in your ceremony. True, I don't know the intricate workings of your sacred practices. But I do know the fae here. I've lived among them for almost a month now and I can tell you that they are *good*. So why would your ancestors be any different? The fae I know would never jeopardize the safety or peace of its own just for you to prove yourself worthy."

Her gaze bore into mine as I continued. "Listen, maybe it's coincidence that you happened to come of age during the time of these changes, and maybe it's not. But I believe with my entire soul that you are not causing this. *You* are the only way this realm will triumph over the so-called darkness coming."

Diana held my gaze for a beat longer than necessary before blinking a few times and looking away. "I guess I was so freaked out I hadn't thought it fully through."

I nodded, fixating on a knot in Plum's mane.

"Thank you," Diana said.

"For what?" I shrugged, putting on a playful smile. "All I did was point out the obvious."

She rolled her eyes. "Can't give you any compliments, they'll go straight to your head. Besides, that's a lot of sass coming from someone who *supposedly* can't even do a simple meditation."

I sobered from that. "Hey, look, I didn't mean to lie, I—"

Diana cut me off. "It's fine, just tell me now and I won't hang you for treason against a princess." Her small smile was still there, reassuring, but I couldn't help wondering how frequently hangings happened in her peaceful region.

"The meditation—which, by the way, you didn't mention how useless I would feel during—was pretty hazy. I remember a very tall, dark, young male. He was trying to talk to me, but it sounded like he was speaking underwater. I could only make out a few words. From what I got; I think he was berating me for not working hard enough."

Diana took in my words, her eyes pensive. "Do you think it's a memory of a time in your life?"

I sucked on my teeth. "I don't think so, actually. It just didn't *feel* like a memory. It felt like I was being… visited. And—when we saw the shadow take form into that male, I instantly put the face from my meditation onto him. I know it sounds crazy, but I think it was the same fae."

"It doesn't sound crazy, Spense," Diana said seriously. "Because I think the shadows were from the King of the Dark Realm."

At her words, my mind instantly blacked. Suddenly, all I could see was the tall male's face, young and handsome, with dark, membranous wings protruding from his back. He had a twisted smile as he sat with a leg crossed over his knee on an ivory throne—made of bones, I realized as my gut wrenched. He wore black leathers similar to what I had arrived in and a long, impressive red cape.

"King Urdan," I gasped, the vision swirling away as fast as it had come. For a minute I thought I might pass out as I regained my vision and balance atop Plum.

"What?" Diana said, her brow furrowing. "That would make him over eight thousand years old."

We locked eyes. Her face shifted as she took in the urgency on my own features.

"It's Urdan. I *know* it is."

Slowly, she nodded. "I believe you."

Teasing, I asked, "Is eight thousand old for a fae?" I got a tight smile from her then. "About twenty times older than we normally live," she said. I was thankful for her smarts, for realizing I was actually asking about lifespans, and for not minding that I didn't know. Always so intuitive.

We were silent save for the horse's hoofbeats for a few moments.

"If the darkness is King Urdan, then he's closer to invading then we think. Being able to manipulate magic through realms? It's unheard of. I don't know how my ancestors think I can stop this." Diana stared into the forest; her eyes blank. I could practically see the wheel in her head spinning uncontrollably.

"Hey," I said, steering Plum closer so I could reach out and gently place a hand on her arm. I eyed Finnvarra's pinned ears apprehensively as I continued, "One day at a time. You have so many fae around you who will help you. I'll help you."

Diana looked at my hand on her arm, shockingly pale against her. She met my eyes, her hazel irises showing worry for the first time since I had met her. "I just don't know how to fight against someone who's been waiting eight millennia for his chance at revenge."

To that, I didn't have an answer. The shocking realization that the ancient Unseelie King came to me in a meditation and then again appeared to me as he declared his plans to take back the light realm hadn't even set in yet. All I knew, without question, was that there was indeed darkness coming, and Diana was the only way through it.

"That's enough rest," she said, spurring Finnvarra forward. "Let's go home."

We rode for the next few hours without speaking, pausing once to allow the horses to drink from the River Nord. As hoofbeats sounded in my head, all I could think of was King Urdan's wicked grin.

FOURTEEN
Queen Mask
DIANA

It was well into the early hours of the morning, but that didn't slow me down as I pounded on Queen Vera's chamber door. The guard standing outside was still trying to stop me, sputtering in vain as my fists drowned out the sound of his words.

It had occurred to me on my way here that she may not be back yet from her journey to the West. That had almost stopped me in my tracks, until I had seen the guard posted outside the entrance to her chambers.

The heavy door opened; my mother's face visibly annoyed as she stepped into the doorframe. She was still dressed in riding leathers, her hair intricately woven into a braid suitable for traveling. She must have just arrived home.

"Diana," she said, her voice concerned as she ushered me inside. "Whatever are you doing at this hour?"

"I've just arrived back from the City of Scholars —" I began.

"The City of Scholars?" My mother pressed a hand to her temple. "Is that why I have a rather passive-aggressive letter from Lord Daqin on my desk about proper social calls?" Whoops. Had forgotten all about that stuffy old lump. I made a mental note to send him an apology letter.

"Yes, just hold on. This is really important. Spense and I were ambushed by these shadows. It wasn't from this realm. I think it was King Urdan—"

"Diana." Vera sliced a hand through the air, her magic temporarily barring my voice from making sound. "Slow down, child. I just got back from discussing shadows in the Western Shores—which I assume you know about." She raised an eyebrow at me to which I averted my eyes. "My head is a cluttered mess, and yours doesn't seem to be much better. Why don't we pick this up tomorrow morning?"

"*No*," I urged. "The shadows were *here*. In this region. They spoke to me! King Urdan said he is coming for the throne, and that he's closer than he's ever been to invading the realm."

My mother was silent for a few beats. "I suspected this was the Dark fae's work when I was informed of the shadows. I saw them in the Western Shores; they're horrifyingly strong. It has no entity, nothing to banish away and yet remains like a poison on our lands. If they have come to the North, that is very grave indeed." She gave me a sideways look. "Whyever would you think King Urdan could still be alive? It is likely one of his offspring."

I blinked. "He practically told me. He said that he was *exactly who I feared he was*. And… I've heard that voice before, in a dream. All I could think of when the shadows were around me was the story of the Unseelie.

It's Urdan, I know it."

"That does not correlate—"

"It is King Urdan!"

"*Diana Lightbringer, you will stop this now.*" I flinched at her use of our family name.

"Why are you angry? I'm helping to solve this; we know who's behind the shadows now," I said.

"I am angry, Diana, because you put yourself at risk for a fruitless vacation to see your friend!" Vera's face had her queen mask on, her voice dripping in authority as she stared me down.

"That is not fair! Spense had a successful meditation in the Academy, he recalled a male figure in his life, telling him to work harder. I know this sounds crazy, but when we saw the shadow-figure he said he saw the same face on him. I think it's all connected, mother."

"How do you know Spense isn't behind all of this? The shadows only started appearing when he cut through the realm. I fear he is leading you astray on purpose, Diana."

I set my jaw. "Spense is not the Dark, evil, harbinger of doom you think him to be. He saved the life of one of our younglings if you don't remember." I was wavering dangerously close to a tone my mother would not tolerate.

"That may be, but I still believe it to be stupidly reckless. Why did you even feel it necessary to make the trip there when you could have used one of the meditation rooms at the palace?"

"I had some of my own research to do." I folded my arms over my chest.

"Such as?" my mother drawled.

"I was reading up on rifts. They're *failed portals.* Which means someone out there is trying really hard to make a real one. Rifts are extremely dangerous; it's only a matter of time before they collapse. You have to get the soldiers away from it — we won't get a warning. They're in grave danger."

Vera sighed once through her nose. "You think I didn't glean that information myself when the damn thing first opened?"

I blinked. "But — the soldiers — "

"Are serving their duty to this region. To Eira." Her tone made it clear I was not to push farther.

"You don't care about their lives?"

Oops. Pushed it anyway.

Magic flared around the queen, filling the room with the sweet tinge of lilac. "Of course I care, child. It is a horrible day anytime we lose one of our own. But tell me that your training didn't fail you. Guarding the rift is essential. These soldiers are not doing so unwillingly." Her stare bore into mine. I knew it would be fruitless to argue; these soldiers would lay down their life for the North flag.

"Will you at least order them to stand farther away from it?"

Vera waved a ringed hand. "I have already done so."

For the first time in my whole life, I didn't know if I believed her.

Quietly holding in my seething anger, I tried a different angle.

"Have you ever heard of *Jweira*?" Vera shook her head once. "That's the name of the emerald Queen Diana used to drive the Dark fae out of the realm. She told me herself when I was in the Sacred Pool," I said.

My mother was contemplative. "I didn't think it was still alive," she mused.

I threw my arms in the air. "But you knew it had an entity, its own magic? When will you stop hiding things from me!"

"You are treading on thin ice. You dare accuse me of hiding things from you? I am more than two hundred and twenty years old, Diana. I've forgotten more about this realm than you have learned in your decade of studies. I may not tell you things if I wish. That is my right. And it feels like a dagger in the heart to learn you don't think I have your best interests in mind. Don't you think if it was important, I would have told you? I didn't tell you about the emerald having an entity because I didn't think it important. Never in my wildest dreams did I imagine that I'd ever see it with my own eyes. By the time it made its way into your ceremonial hair, I knew you'd have felt its magic by then. Forgive me for saving my precious time from idle, needless chat!"

My mother was panting, her rant echoing in the air. I swallowed, the air feeling thick around my throat. I felt sick, outraged, hurt. I wanted to bite back but the energy to do so was fading away like ice in summer. It was worthless to try; my mother would get the last word. The more I alienated her from me, the less she would trust me with court information.

"I'm sorry, mother," I said, the words tasting like

bile on my tongue. "I'm only trying to help. I'm feeling overwhelmed with everything going on, with my ceremony at the head of it all."

Vera's face softened, nodding. "I feel that way as well. I will tell you this: I have the shadows under control. You need not worry yourself with them."

Anger swelled up in me again. Clearly the shadows were not under control. In fact, control was quickly slipping farther and farther from the palace's grasp.

"I want to help," I managed to say in an even tone.

"I appreciate it, Diana. But right now, your focus is on retaining memory from Spense. If it truly is the King of the Darks at our doorstep, then we will need to know absolutely everything we can about him."

I nodded, feeling more dissuaded from my mother than I ever had. It suddenly seemed unusual to me that she had only spent one day in the West and claimed to have a handle on all the shadow business.

"Where's Delios?" I asked, suddenly aware of the wolf's unusual absence.

"He's out. Try to get some rest, my dear," Vera said, guiding me towards the door. "I have scheduled a party for the day after next, an impromptu celebration of spring. I needed a way to get the court officials and their closest allies all in one place without raising suspicion. We will meet after the party to discuss these shadows in greater detail."

My head spun. She wasn't going to wait until Summer Solstice anymore to meet with the regions. This didn't bode well for Spense, especially if my mother didn't believe my warnings about King Urdan.

Without a word, I was shoved unceremoniously out the door, where the disgruntled guard gave me an annoyed look.

I set my shoulders in a manner befitting a princess, flipping my hair over my shoulder as I set off down the halls. There was more my mother wasn't telling me. She seemed glaringly unconcerned about the shadows, even though she spoke the right words to believe her seriousness about the matter. I reached deep into my magic, where I read others' energies and the emotions they were putting out. Vera seemed... locked up. Like she was stifling her energy to avoid being scrutinized.

I had made it to my rooms, but I didn't go inside. Instead, I spun on my heel and left the palace. I needed a walk.

FIFTEEN
Water's Edge
SPENSE

When we arrived back to the palace, the guards at the gate looking stressed and confused at our late hour, Diana instantly bounded up the steps and disappeared inside the iron doors. A guard helped Aedan off his horse, the latter waving his hand to decline being escorted inside. He hobbled away, assumedly to where he would crash and sleep for many hours before bouncing back to his usual arrogant self.

I took the horses back to the stables, which was thankfully empty. I couldn't fathom what atrocities the stable hands would say to me after my fight with their own.

I was feeling too restless to sleep, so I decided against going back to the palace and instead found myself on a path leading into the forest. My feet walked of their own accord as I pondered all that had happened today. It did not feel like mere hours had passed since I had walked the Academy halls. It felt like a lifetime ago.

Urdan's face was ever-present in my mind. Finally, something familiar to me. Something I recognized beyond waking up in this realm. It troubled me that this glimpse into my memory depicted the dark and evil that

I worried about. What was worse: I couldn't shake the feeling that I knew him on a deeper level than a regular citizen would know his king. He *knew* me. His magic was like mine.

It was almost dawn by the time I finally allowed myself to feel the wariness creeping into my bones. I didn't know how far I had gone into the forest or how to find my way out. Sleepily, I wandered until I found a semblance of a path. *It must lead to somewhere*. I changed my course, following the worn dirt. Slowly, the trees thinned. Day was breaking overhead, making the horizon clearer.

The path spit me out in a large clearing, flanking a mesmerizing pond in the middle. I walked down to the water, thinking I would have a drink before following the path out of the meadow. But as I neared the pond a haze came over me. The waves seemed to shimmer, even though the sun was not yet high enough to cause the effect. *It's magic*, I realized. I could feel the light magic, so akin to Diana's, pulsing out over the shore.

Come, it seemed to say. *Swim. Splash. Play.*

That didn't seem like such a bad idea. Ignoring the fact that it was mid-spring, and the sun hadn't even created its morning mist yet, I shrugged off my shirt and pants. Standing in my undershorts, I obeyed the pond's silent command. *Come. Swim. Learn.*

I was standing at the edge, about to dip my foot into the water, when a clear, shrill voice rang through the clearing, lifting me from my reverie. "*Stop!*"

My head snapped up. Diana was sprinting towards me, her eyes wild as her hair whipped behind her.

Beautiful. Powerful. Light, the pond said. I agreed.

"What are you doing?" she yelled, grabbing my shoulders, and ripping me away from the water's edge.

The pond was silent, the oozing magic subsiding from my consciousness.

"I—I just… the pond, it wanted me to swim," I said, breathless.

Diana took my arm and led me farther away; towards the path she came from. I was hyper-aware of the warmth of her fingers on my cool skin, as I was—

"Um, my clothes."

Diana seemed to just realize I was practically naked. A flush appeared on her neck, spreading up her cheeks. "Oh," was all she said as she held out a hand, my clothing flying across the clearing into her palm. She hastily stuffed them into my arms.

She didn't slow down as I attempted to pull my clothes back on whilst keeping up with her.

"You're lucky I found you. That's the Sacred Pool. Had you gone in, I fear you would not have been returned."

My stomach flipped once. "What's its deal?"

Diana, seeing that I was again fully dressed, slowed so I could walk beside her. "That is where we commune with our ancestors. I don't know how they'd react to a Dark paying them a visit."

I looked back, the pond now barely visible through the trees. I could still see the magic shimmering around it. It was almost funny to picture Diana, soaking wet in the pond, communing with her ancestors, swimming around in ghostly form.

"Probably best I don't go for a swim then," I said in a half-joking voice.

"Probably," Diana agreed with a wry smile. She seemed — easier. Back to how she used to act around me. Any lingering awkwardness or anger from the events in the City had dissipated.

I bumped her with my shoulder gently. Her magic misted around me at the touch, filling me with the smell of cedar. My own magic flitted to the surface, reaching out to softly intertwine with hers.

Diana inhaled audibly. She blinked a few times at the ground before meeting my eyes. *Beautiful, powerful, light.*

It almost hurt, to look at her purity, her goodness. She was light and kind and whole, everything I feared I was not. She looked at me with an openness in her face, one I knew meant something we were both afraid of. There was not an ounce of her that did not trust me. *Stupid,* I thought. *Stupid to trust what we don't know.* And, I realized, there was not any part of me that didn't trust her either.

When she looked away, I realized I had been staring a bit too long. Shaking my head gently, I cleared my throat.

"How did it go with your mother?"

Her magic sucked away instantly. Diana's face became hard, her features closing back up again.

"That bad, huh?"

She scoffed. "I am not agreeing with many of my mother's decisions as of late," she said, twisting her emerald ring around her finger.

"But you normally do?" I asked.

She paused. "I've never really been privy to her decisions before. I suppose I'm struggling with the fact that I'm finding out who my mother truly is."

I wanted to tell her that I understood but didn't know how to explain why I did.

"Did you get any sleep?" I asked.

"No," she said. "Did you?"

"Nope."

We both smiled softly, shaking our heads at the whirlwind that was the past few days. I walked with her in peaceful silence as the palace came into view ahead of us.

When we finally came into view of the rhododendron bushes lining the path through the palace gates, I saw two small figures standing at the gate point at us and then take off at a run, meeting us halfway.

Two small females, one was Diana's maidservant—Maisie. She had been a silent presence at every palace dinner, standing against the wall like she was glued there. The other I did not recognize, dressed in page's clothing, with the Northern wolf insignia on her chest.

"Diana!" Maisie gasped, panting slightly from her run. "The guards told me you were back. But when I couldn't find you in your rooms, I was worried you'd taken off on another journey again. Wouldn't put it past you to take off into the East without telling anyone."

Diana shook her head, allowing her breathless friend to keep step with her as we continued walking back to the palace. "Just needed a walk."

The other female piped up from behind us. "High

Princess, I have a message to deliver to you with utmost haste!"

Diana looked over her shoulder and beckoned the young page forward. "What is it?"

"Seamstress Beltain requests your immediate presence. She wished me to convey how urgent she believes the matter to be."

I could see Diana grapple to hold back a laugh. "Thank you, message received." The page scurried away.

Maisie rolled her eyes. "Gaia, you'd think that the palace was on fire with a message like that." Diana laughed gently with her. "But in all seriousness, I wouldn't wait too long to go. She's been in a frenzy about getting everyone fitted for the last-minute party."

I glanced at Diana. "Party?"

She sighed. "My mother's latest decision." She met my eyes, her face pinched in disregard.

Maisie clasped her hands together. "I, for one, am excited! A chance to see everyone and have a nice party to tide us over until Summer Solstice. It'll be fun."

Diana shook her head, her hair falling around her. I wondered how she'd wear her hair at this party, cascading down around her like she normally wore it, or up around her face in a more intricate fashion.

"I'd like to see if you dance the same in front of royalty as you do in bars," I teased.

She shot me a glare. "Too bad you won't be there to find out."

"Are citizens not invited?" I asked, surprised.

"Citizens may attend, but *you* may not. It's too risky

one of the court officials will sense your magic. They're not glamoured to forget you, remember?"

I nodded, taking notice of Maisie's pointed stare at her feet, tucking a piece of her honey-coloured curls behind her ear. *I wonder how many palace secrets she holds underneath all that hair,* I mused.

"Besides," Diana continued. "You don't want to go anyway. These parties are stuffy and boring and horribly long. Enjoy a night away from all the royalty." Maisie made a small noise of upset.

I agreed mildly, parting ways with the females as they went to find the bossy seamstress Beltain. I made my way back to my own room, glad to finally lay down and get some sleep.

As I drifted into unconsciousness, I thought about the exclusive party I was not invited to. I very much wanted to go, to see how Diana interacted with her peers, to be a part of royal festivities. And a part of me I wasn't sure if I liked wanted to see just how perceptive these high court officials were. I could be stealthy, avoid their scrutiny.

Yes, I think I would like to attend this party.

My magic tingled in agreement.

SIXTEEN
The First Diana
DIANA

After being poked, prodded, and squeezed into dresses of all types, I was finally released from the clutches of seamstress Beltain. She was a tall, skinny female, with hair so ebony black I couldn't see the individual strands. Her withered hands were not gentle as she expertly tucked fabric to create her masterpiece. Her voice was prim and slightly judgmental as she and Maisie discussed my gown for the party the day after tomorrow, which my mother had now dubbed Midspring Mania. I had zoned out completely, my thoughts on what decisions might be made now that the courts were all together again. Decisions on Spense.

Spense. Every time I thought I had a handle on who he was, my viewpoint was flipped completely on its axis. Usually, I had no trouble at all gaining insight on one's character—quite quickly, too. It was as natural to me as breathing. Spense felt like a blank canvas, his self-portrait full of lines and swirls that changed every time I looked. What was worse, he didn't know himself any better than I did.

Our encounter at the Sacred Pool confused me as well. I knew the Pool was its own sentient magic, fueled by the lives and deaths of my ancestors. Since I highly doubted they would have insight to share with Spense, the only thought that remained was that the Pool sensed a threat to Eira and wanted to eliminate it. Truly lucky timing that I stumbled upon him before he waded in.

A picture entered my mind unwittingly: Spense, standing at the edge of the Pool, his black hair curled around his temples as he breathed in the magic in the water. Stripped down to only his undershorts, his ebony tattoos a stark contrast on his pale skin. His body all hard lines and muscle. The pink scar that ran across his abdomen from his journey through the rift. How the V at his hips dipped—

Whoa. Enough of that.

I tried to will away the flush that had crept up my neck and face.

I had asked Maisie to not allow me any visitors until dinner, which was now only in a few hours anyway. I sat on the floor, leaned against my bed, with a cup of peppermint tea and the books I had borrowed from the Academy.

When I had first entered my room, there was a giant stack of books left on my bed, wrapped in brown paper and twine. A note on top read: *Saw these at your desk in the Secured section. Not very smart of you to leave your top-secret research lying around. If any of these books are harmed, we're in serious shit. These ones aren't even supposed to leave the Academy. You owe me! -S*

Shela had sent me all the books I'd been leafing through in the Secured section before my vision had caused me to send a bookshelf flying. The one about the portals, books about Dark history, and even the royal lineage I had grabbed for fun. I seriously owed Shela — big time.

I started into the pile, feeling overwhelmed. The urgency of the court officials' imminent arrival spurred me on as I flipped through the pages of the ancient tomes.

I read many Dark history books that were heavily biased on their evil nature. They mostly depicted how King Urdan came to power from an outside viewpoint. They named a few of his most trusted lords and captains, whom I did not recognize. Any books that were actually written by the Dark were likely extinct in this realm.

That felt like a waste of time as I eyed the sun's drooping descent. I stacked the books to one side, settling on the small novel I'd found after retreating farther into the Secured section: *The Rule of Jweira*. As soon as I touched it, thrumming energy filled my body, instantly recognizable as the energy from the morning of my ritual day. Remembering that the emerald was in my room, I retrieved it, keeping it safely inside its iron box, which I set beside me as I opened the book. My body became detached from my mind; I saw my hands move in front of me, but I was unaware of my telling them to do so.

The first page was a beautifully drawn portrait of a just as beautiful female who stared through the page ethereally. She was dark-skinned and bald, her sharp cheekbones and jawline boldly demanding attention.

The emerald started pulsing green light. Slowly, I picked it up, resting it in the palm of my hand as I peered into the effervescent body of the gem. Lowering my magic ever-so-slightly, I allowed *Jweira* to touch me with its own magic. Gasping as the ancient magic swirled in dancing waves around my consciousness, I was vaguely aware of my vision fading around me.

Fear burst through me; my magic pushed against *Jweira*, fighting to keep it at a distance.

Something old, older than I had ever known, awakened inside the emerald. It reached for me with outstretched magic, bearing itself wholly. There was darkness there, I could see plain as day. But the light was evenly matched, giving the picture of a perfectly balanced, perfectly harmonized magic. *What are you?* I contemplated, sending a tendril of my magic towards the pulsing gemstone.

Let me show you, it answered.

I didn't know why, but I felt a strong sense of ease as I gently lowered my barrier and allowed the emerald to slip in. It was warm as it tingled with my own magic, twirling and languid, never static. At first it felt different, foreign, but in almost no time at all *Jweira*'s magic was an extension of my own, perfectly symmetrical. I was delightfully shocked.

It has been so long. A releasing sigh. *It is nice to know you, Diana. You are much alike the first of your name.*

"You are *Jweira*?" I asked, staring unseeingly, feeling the gemstone in my hand radiate warm energy.

Indeed.

"Can I ask—you are an emerald, how do you... where does your magic—?"

The emerald laughed softly, the sound like the purr

of a mountain cat.

That is a long story, my child. Perhaps it is easier if I show you instead. Let me give you a memory that is over eight thousand years old.

"How?"

In lieu of answer, I felt *Jweira* push deeper into my consciousness, into the core of my magic. This part of me, this very essence and beating life force of every particle of magic in my being, resided here. It had never been seen by anyone. I should have felt the desire to protect it, put walls up around my most vulnerable and precious essence. Instead, I found myself perfectly at ease with the emerald making itself at home. It settled into my core, *Jweira's* voice a thrum in my head.

Relax, Diana.

Black came over me like a veil, shimmering down my body. When it finished, I was standing, the smell of lilacs wafting over me, a cold draft slipping around my shoulders.

I opened my eyes. I was standing in a large throne room, decorated lavishly with flowers and greenery. The stone walls were lined with wisteria, giving the room a feeling of being outside in nature.

Look.

Sturdy hands gripped around my mind, turning my head gently to the center of the room, where a female fae sat on the iron throne, her legs draped over the side lazily. She was naked, I realized suddenly. Her auburn hair cascaded down her back and front, long enough to reach her lap. A crown of emeralds sat upon her head, commanding power from the room. Her face was concealed by a white wolf mask, leaving only her eyes in view, which were strikingly blue.

At the back of the throne, slightly to her right, stood a youthful female who watched the one in the throne carefully. A shock went through me. It was Queen Diana. The female in the throne must be her mother, the Seelie Queen.

Before them stood *Jweira*, dressed in black armour, her stunning features prominently showing displeasure as she regarded the queen with fervor.

"Thank you for accepting my invitation to meet with me today, Princess Jweira," said the Seelie Queen, her voice dripping in sweetness.

Jweira eyed the guards in the corners of the room. "I didn't realize being subdued and dragged across the border to your enemy's palace against your will constituted as an invitation these days, *Your Highness.*"

The Seelie Queen laughed, twirling a piece of her long hair around a ringed finger. "You'll have to excuse the theatrics. I did not think you would come of your own accord."

"And now that I am here, what exactly do you want from me?" Jweira crossed her arms, her voice cold.

The Seelie Queen sat up, her hair falling around her like a mist. "Why, your help, of course."

She stood and paced across the room to where Jweira stood, cupping her chin with her jeweled hand. Jweira did not break eye contact.

"I have heard whispers of your great power, Jweira," The queen said, her voice soft like a lover. "You stand at your father's right hand, helping him to acquire whatever he so pleases. And nary a soul can even come close to defeating you in battle."

Jweira wrenched her head away from the queen's grasp. "Whatever he so pleases? I think the words you meant to say were '*taking back what was stolen from him*'."

The queen's reaction was masked, but her sneer showed itself in the flaring of magic around her.

"Regardless, I cannot ignore his behaviour any longer. It is making me look weak. Therefore, I offer you a deal: bring me King Urdan's head and I will allow you to rule the Unseelie Court unencumbered — so long as you keep to your lands."

Jweira glared at the Seelie Queen, her stature never failing. "And if I don't?"

"Then you, too, will become a casualty in my war on the Unseelie." The queen turned, her hair swishing as she stalked back to her throne and sat back down. Diana stood motionless in the same spot.

Jweira smiled savagely. "I will delight in meeting you on the battlefield, Lady." With that, she turned on her heel, her footsteps echoing as she paced to the throne room door. She reached out a hand to grasp the handle, but was stopped in her path as two guards stepped forward, blocking the exit.

The Seelie Queen's voice rang across the room. "Ah, but you see, declining my generous offer was not on the table today."

Jweira drew a sword from her hip, the metal singing as it came free from its sheath. The blade glinted menacingly as its wielder swung it in an arc around her head.

The Seelie Queen waved a hand, bored. "A swordfight? What are we, common soldiers? Show me your *power*, girl."

The queen snapped her fingers and the sword in Jweira's hand became hot. The metal turned red, heat coming off in waves. Jweira dropped the weapon in disgust.

"Don't make me ask again."

Without warning, a crack came from the stone wall, a massive chunk of it flying across the room, in direct path to where Jweira stood.

The Unseelie Princess lifted her hand, magic pulsing outwards, crumbling the stone around her like powder.

The Seelie Queen clasped her hands. "That's more like it." She sent piece after piece of the wall at her, and when that did not deter Jweira, she summoned flames from the hearth and began hurtling those across the room as well. Jweira handled it all with ease, dissipating the threats without sending any of her own back.

Finally, the queen was exasperated, annoyed her toy wasn't playing the way she wanted it to.

She beckoned to her daughter, who still stood quietly behind the throne. "Diana," she said. "Show our guest what you can do."

Diana did not say anything as she glided to the center of the ruined room, Jweira watching her every move. She got to her knees, placing her hands on the marble floor. Closing her eyes, she connected to her magic, sending it deep into the ground below. The room started to shake violently. Foliage crashed to the floor. The Seelie Queen lay draped on her throne, watching in glee as Jweira's face turned worrisome for the first time.

There was a bubble of magic around Diana and the queen, shielding them from the effects of the earthquake. Jweira had to work faster, her magic less calculated and more desperate as she fended off the entire room crumbling around her.

Diana then sat up; her face tilted at the sky. She opened her hands, sending magic out of her at an alarmingly fast rate. Thunder rolled overhead, angry gray clouds forming above the room, which was now missing most of its ceiling.

Rain came pouring down, soaking everything except those protected by magic bubbles. A crack of lightning forked down into the room, almost undetectably fast. Jweira was struck, screaming as her body was wracked with electricity.

The Seelie Queen laughed mirthlessly, waving her hand, ordering Diana's storm to finish the job.

Jweira's body rose into the air, suspended by her magic, which flared around her like a wraith. The lightning still coursed in her veins; her eyes wholly white as the colour of pure electricity. She screamed again, this time a warrior cry, blasting the lightning back out. The room was charcoaled. Diana's protection had been stripped away; her face blank as she reached deep within to pull out more magic. She seemed in a trance, her body moving robotically as she wielded magic that was dangerously close to being empty.

The Seelie Queen stood, her hands still on the arms of the throne, as she stared up at Jweira's power. "Magnificent," she breathed.

The rain continued to pour down, meeting Jweira's body heat and creating a mist around her.

Jweira lowered herself slowly to the ground, her eyes returning to their regular dark colour. "Let me leave this place," she said, her voice thundering with power.

The Seelie Queen put a finger to her lips. "It is clear you will not expel your power in killing me, which is truly a shame. It is unwise for me to continue trying to kill you by force, so you see, that leaves me only one choice."

She turned to her daughter, who sat on the broken marble, staring blankly as she awaited her orders. "Diana, my dearest, come forth." The girl shuffled forward, her drained energy clearly visible in her shaking legs and drooping eyes.

Jweira eyed the queen. "What have you done to her?"

The Seelie Queen stroked her daughter's hair gently. "I have made her into the perfect princess. She was just a little too perceptive, this one. Always demanding I explain my actions to her, as if I owed her any explanation behind my decisions. Obedience is necessary when one is gifted with immense power such as hers. If she is to be queen after me, she must be shaped in the proper way."

Jweira was disgusted. "You've made her into your mindless slave?"

"Mindless? Oh, no, she has a mind, of course. It's still in there somewhere, underneath her unyielding desire to serve me and only me."

"I will be glad to see a merciless, selfish, worthless

ruler like you dethroned. You do not deserve the crown that sits upon your brow." Jweira spat the words at the queen's feet. She sent a shiver of power her way, blasting the crown off the queen's head, which landed between them in a pile of broken emerald.

The Seelie Queen grew enraged. Red flame burst out of her, giving her the appearance of being on fire. She lifted her daughter into the air in front of them, Diana's still expression unchanging.

A knife appeared in Diana's hands. She looked down at it and slowly brought it up to her neck. Jweira's eyes grew wide as she ran towards her.

The Queen watched as she continued to pulse power. Diana lay the knife against her throat, pressing in gently. A line of bright red blood snaked down her neck into the bodice of her dress.

"No!" shouted Jweira. She pushed her hands out, sending an immense ray of white light into the room. The queen was blasted back, Diana dropping to the ground in an unconscious heap. The rain ceased immediately.

The Seelie Queen clambered to her feet, laughing maniacally. "You are unmatched in power, indeed. I will surely win my war when I add you to my collective." She strutted back to Jweira, who raised her hand warningly.

"Over my dead body."

"Now, now, that's no fun," The queen tsked. "I won't miss your attitude, that is for certain."

Jweira's magic flared around her protectively. It was wavering in some places, clearly exhausted. "You mean to take my power from me? Impossible."

The Seelie Queen nodded gravely. "Yes, a shame that one's power is not transferable. I will have to settle with the next best thing—keeping you along with it. Not my first choice, as I'm sure you can understand."

Jweira shook her head. "I will take my own life before I let you enslave me like your own blood."

"Speaking of my own blood, thank you for not letting my only daughter die. Not only would it have been a real inconvenience, but now your magic is drained like a riverbed in summer. Makes my job a lot easier." The Seelie Queen rubbed her hands together, magic flying off in sparks. She sent her hands out in front of her; a black orb appeared around Jweira. She struggled inside of it, pushing her limbs against it, but it stretched with her, almost skin-tight now.

"My father will kill you for this," spat Jweira, her magic pulsing inside the orb without affect.

"I do hope he pays a visit soon," cooed the Seelie Queen. "How ironic to kill him with his own daughter's power, whom he has come to avenge. What a story!"

Jweira seethed inside the bubble, staring down the queen with every inch of hate and spite in her body.

"Now, where to put you?" The queen's gaze landed on the pile of broken emerald at her feet, a shadow covering the wolf mask hauntingly.

"Ah," she said softly. The emerald pieces began to glow, melding together until they formed one giant gem. The queen raised one hand towards Jweira and pulled her closer, until the black orb disappeared inside the emerald, trapping Jweira inside. The queen studied the emerald, green glinting off the white of her mask.

The last thing I saw before the world melted around me was the Seelie Queen's head turning directly towards me and staring me down with her eyes of ice.

*

Gasping, sputtering, I tore around my room, looking for something to throw up in. I settled over a water basin, breathing heavily. The emerald was still in my hand. I could still feel its formidable power, even as its colour was fading. Finally the nausea subsided, and I could think clearly again.

The Seelie Queen. Diana. Jweira.

Plots. War. Lies.

I know that was a lot to process, Diana. I'm sorry that it had to be you. But I'm sure you have been told by now that you have a big prophecy to fulfil.

I held the emerald up to my face, as though I could look it in the eyes.

"You're lying. The Unseelie were the thieves, the rogues, the villains, not the other way around!" It couldn't be true. Everything I had been taught and preached my entire life, shattered like the broken emeralds in the memory. And yet, as I said the words, I found myself not truly believing them.

History is written by the winner of the war, Diana.

I got up from where I knelt at the basin, pacing around my room, thoughts spinning around my head uncomfortably fast. My skin felt itchy everywhere, like I was in a body not of my own.

You are chosen to bring back the balance between the Dark and Light, to undo what the Seelie Queen did eight thousand years ago. Finally, I could show myself to someone worthy.

"You mean to tell me that in eight thousand years of rulers, *none* were worthy? I am of their blood, am I not?" I asked, incredulous.

There is much you still do not know, Diana. I will help you when I can, but I am afraid this memory is really all I can offer you. I do not recall much after I was entrapped.

I threw my hands in the air. "That's just wonderful. Shatter my entire existence and leave me to pick up the pieces on my own! I am barely keeping my head above water, I don't understand what I am to do with this information, or how I am to bring about balance. I need help."

I don't have the answers you seek, but I can be your guide. I still remember my life at the Unseelie court. Keep me on your person wherever you go, use my knowledge. I will stay with you.

I focused on my breathing. Lies. My entire history was lies. The Seelie Queen had been perpetrating attacks on the Unseelie, who fought back. Jweira, the Unseelie princess, had been stolen to use against her father. Queen Diana, my namesake, had been nothing more than a thoughtless shell of a female.

I must have voiced my agreement, whether out loud or in my head, because Jweira said: *I have expended a great deal of energy today. I need to rest a few weeks before my power will be at full capacity again. I will sleep, so to speak, until the time comes that you need me. Even though I won't be able to talk with you, I will keep my consciousness entwined with yours.*

I felt Jweira fading. "Wait!" I called out. A slight pause in the magic. "You said earlier that I am alike to the Diana I am named after... but how can that be true, with what I just saw?" Hurt pooled in my stomach at the comparison.

Like I said, there is still much you do not know. The first of your name had her own battles to fight, but I think you will like her redemption story.

With that, I felt the emerald fade around me, the magic draining until just a spark was left, lingering in mine like its own piece of jewelry.

I sat with my thoughts for a while, soaking in the memory I had just witnessed. I could not help the feelings of betrayal that washed over me. Did my mother and family know of this? Were we all just complying sheep, happy to blindly believe what we were told? Everything I had ever been taught was now teetering on a ledge. If my realm's history, the steadfast story we all believed so fervently, was a lie, what else was?

A knock sounded at my door, causing me to jump a foot in the air. Casting a glance out my window, I could see the sun was almost set, sending rays of orange and red over the valley. I was expected for dinner very soon. Could I even attend in this state? I felt ill with this revelation.

I opened my mouth to tell Maisie I was unwell and would be skipping dinner, but before I could, she poked her head in the door. Her blonde curls bounced around as she grinned, telling me I had a surprise visitor. Hastily I grabbed all the books from the Academy and shoved them under my bed.

Without further warning, she swung the door open

wide, revealing my good friend Jamey from the Western Shores. She was dressed in usual Western attire, lightweight clothing for their heat and her hair tied back neatly in a braid. Her dirty-blonde hair was shining, healthy from all the sunshine in their region, despite her somber demure.

Shela's complete opposite, my friend was usually reserved and unexcitable, except in the rarest of occasions. Her calm and calculating nature was enviable to someone like me who aimed to be queenly in all endeavors. Maisie would not be able to tell that this quiet was different from her usual kind, but I could feel in the energy around her that she was troubled.

"Jamey, hi," I said, hugging her gently.

"I'll be back in a few minutes to collect you both for dinner," Maisie said as she left the room, closing the door softly behind her.

"I wasn't expecting you until tomorrow. Is everything alright—your region, how is it?"

Jamey shook her head, settling in the chair at my vanity, twisting it around to face me. I perched on the edge of my bed. Highly casual for two regional princesses, but we were old friends.

"The shadows have mercifully stopped since your mother's visit. I don't understand why, and my grandfather will not divulge that information to me. But the fae who were attacked in the village; they are still asleep. If you can call it that. We have called for healers from all realms to help. Nothing has worked thus far." Jamey studied the ring on her index finger, a family crest bearing the symbol of the West, the grizzly bear.

I leaned forward. "I'm so sorry to hear that. I'm

positive they'll find a way to restore them." As I said that, uncertainty settled in my stomach. Our healers had never seen a situation like this before. What if they couldn't be cured?

Jamey smiled weakly. I could see the past month had taken a toll on her. She was a long way from taking up her role in the region's court, but she felt a responsibility for her citizens, nonetheless.

"And how are you doing, Diana? I expected to find you a little more excited to be chosen as Heir, and yet you look as if you have seen a ghost."

I stifled an ironic laugh. "I have been going through my own troubles since ascending," I said, my eyes resting for a millisecond on Jweira's box on my bedside table. I had slipped the emerald into the bodice of my dress. I could feel it now against my ribs, beating softly alongside my heart, keeping perfect rhythm.

Jamey nodded. "I would imagine so. I heard of the Dark fae you have been fostering. I'm sure his slimy essence has taken a toll."

I sucked on my teeth. A simmering heat was rising in my belly. Spense was the farthest thing from slimy, and with new information come to light about his heritage, I wasn't sure the Dark were all that bad either.

"Well. Shall we go to dinner?" I asked, offering her my arm. I probably could have steered the conversation in countless over harmless directions, but I found myself without desire to continue speaking with my old friend. I had even less excitement about having dinner with the officials from the West. Friendly as they were, I was not in the mood for politics — or for seeing my mother.

As we left my room, Maisie opened the chamber

doors for us. We passed through the doorframe, and I breathed, "Tell Spense not to come to dinner tonight," in her direction. It was barely audible, but an ever-so-slight nod from my maidservant confirmed she had heard me.

And so I walked down the palace halls to the dining room, once as familiar to me as the back of my hand, feeling like a stranger in my own world.

SEVENTEEN
Vastly Uncomfortable in Her Personal Space
SPENSE

"I don't believe we have met."

Steady, blue eyes bored into mine, pinning me to the spot. I had been told an embassy from the West was staying at the palace for a few nights leading up to the party, and to keep away from them. And yet here I stood, unwittingly meeting the party in the halls as I looked for Diana.

They were all dressed similarly in lightweight clothing and sandy hair. About a dozen of them, assumedly on their way to the dining hall, had stared me down as I passed them. Too late, I realized that servants in the palace would probably have stood off to the side, waiting for them to pass before continuing on my way. Thankfully, it did not pique the interest of the group, who kept on their path.

All except one.

She was remarkably poised for her young age, reminding me of Diana. She seemed to hold herself in very high esteem as her gaze raked over me.

Unflinchingly, I let her look me over before bowing

my head slightly. "You have no interest in meeting a servant such as me, I am sure," I said, keeping my eyes down. Even as every instinct screamed at me to pull myself to my full height, to tower over her with my size and magic, to demand her respect. Such an ugly part of me. I pushed it farther down, tucking away any tendrils of magic that were peeking up to investigate.

The female scoffed. "If you truly are a servant, you are not a very good one."

Hot temper flared through me, disgusted take out.

"Apologies," I muttered as she gave me one last, inquisitive look and continued on her way.

Rotten, arrogant fools. Who gave them the right to believe themselves better than the workers in the palace who did more in a single day than the royals could even think of? The more time I spent in this court, the more it showed how truly special Diana was.

I hadn't seen her since she rescued me from my attempt at swimming in the Pool. That night, as I was getting dressed for dinner, Maisie had informed me to lay low for the time being. So I kept my head down, worked at the stables, and avoided as many fae as I could in the palace.

And yet now I itched to see her. If not to get some magic practice in, then to see what else she had learned about the shadows we had encountered. She had not sent for me or come for an afternoon ride, and I feared I wouldn't see her until after the party tomorrow evening.

So, ignoring the part of me that insisted it was a stupid idea, I made my way to her chambers, keeping to the side wings and servant passages that I had discovered during my nightly trips into Nevelyn.

The thought occurred to me that she could be keeping away from me because she did not wish to see me, which slowed my steps slightly. I shook my head once and regained my pace. Such childish, adolescent thoughts. I had not been so in my head since —

A memory almost broke through. I furrowed my brows, trying to will it back. But it was gone as quick as it came. Frustrating as it was, hope surged through me. My memories wanted to come back. They were trying.

I was nearing Diana's hallway when I bumped into Maisie, who looked at me with shock as she carried a giant bundle of sparkling fabric in her arms.

"Spense — what are you..." Maisie's eyes narrowed. "Oh, no, Diana has requested that she not be interrupted tonight. She's not even dining with her guests. I'm sorry, but you can't see her."

I put a hand over my heart, channeling Shela as I feigned hurt. "What makes you think I was going to see her? I was only taking a walk through the halls."

Maisie rolled her eyes. "I'll tell her you stopped by." She looked at me expectantly, waiting for me to turn away from the hallway I was pointed at.

I dipped my head, turning back the way I came and letting her follow me back down the halls. When she turned left, towards a servants' stairwell that led to the kitchens, an idea sparked. I made my way down to the kitchens as well, dodging the stares of more than a few cooks and servants. Securing a plate of food for the princess included using my best charm and a bit of over-emphasis on how overworked the poor princess was that she had to skip dinner. A burly female cook gave me an empathetic look before shoving a giant plate of meats and vegetables into my arms, telling me to come back should the princess still be hungry. I highly doubted that she even ate this much food in a whole week, but I agreed as I made my way back towards Diana's rooms.

I didn't know what made me so confident that she would be willing to see me after ordering Maisie to keep visitors away, but I didn't question it. Maybe that made me a fool.

I rested a hand on her chamber door, feeling her magic there, smelling her cedar scent. Another scent lingered lightly — the female who stopped me in the hallway before. She must be a friend of Diana's. While I definitely didn't want to risk another run in with the wretch, the light scent suggested she was long gone. Good enough for me.

I knocked twice, short and to the point. I heard her footsteps as she came to the door, blinking in surprise as she took me in. As usual, her hair was loose and falling around her shoulders, nearly long enough to reach her abdomen. She wore a casual tunic, her bare feet giving her no extra height as she craned her neck to look up at me.

"Hey," she said, smiling softly. Her demeanor was quiet, focused. From the stack of books on the floor behind her, she had clearly been busy at work, reading.

Her eyes landed on the plate of food. "Oh, is that for me? Thank you — I'm starving!" She grabbed the plate from me and started munching on some sliced vegetables. When we stood there silently for a moment, she held out the plate, offering me to share.

"Sorry, I shouldn't have interrupted you," I said, taking a step backwards. Suddenly I was hyper aware of my intrusion. This was a mistake. I shouldn't be here, inserting myself into her personal life.

Diana shook her head. "Not at all. I could use a break. And a fresh pair of eyes."

She opened her door wider, allowing me to step in and then closing it behind me again. Her antechamber was simple for the Heir to the realm. Beautifully carved furniture bedecked the floor, with hand-woven carpets under them, all pointed around a large fireplace. Her walls were mostly bare, save for one portrait of her as a youngling with her mother, smiling broadly. She led me through another set of doors, where her bed stood in the middle of the room. Windows taking up the entirety of one wall showed a magnificent view of Nevelyn, the city lights visible from here.

Diana sat down on her floor, clearly resuming the spot she was in before. She placed the plate of food next to her, in easy reach. I felt vastly uncomfortable in her personal space, like a fish trying to walk on land. So I mirrored her, taking up a spot on the plush carpet across from where she sat cross-legged.

Wordlessly, she handed me a book. She was clearly quite alright with me here, in her bedroom. I pushed away the array of thoughts that came with that fact as I perused the cover. *A Dark History.*

"You want me to read this?" I asked. *That was stupid. Why else would she hand you the book, moron?*

She shrugged. "I've already read it, but it would be

nice to see if I missed anything. You can just skim it."

I nodded, flipping open the front cover. Just as I was focusing on the words, Diana said, "I'm glad you're here. It's nice to have a partner in all of this." I knew she didn't just mean reading through this stack of books.

I met her eyes, matching her smile. Such a warm, pure smile. She held it for a beat before looking back to her own book. I watched her for as long as I dared, taking in the way she bit her bottom lip as she read, the way her brow furrowed just slightly. She was so endearing, even in such a mundane task.

Ignoring the warning that sounded in the back of my mind about where my thoughts were headed, I put my head down and read the first sentence of the book.

EIGHTEEN
Fire
DIANA

Spense was in my room.

I stared at the page of the book I had been trying to read for the past ten minutes, hyper-aware of the fact that I had invited a male — not to mention a Dark male — into my private chambers without even thinking about it. Rumors flew for less.

He'd only come to give me food, which was so kind of him. And I invited him in because... why? Because I wanted to explain to him why he had to lie low for a couple days? Because I had new information that might trigger a memory?

Because I wanted his company, I resigned to myself. Did he even want to be here? He looked uncomfortable, sitting on the floor, resting his chin in his hand as he stared through his dark curls at the book I had practically thrown at him.

I popped some grapes into my mouth from the plate he had brought me. Clearly Ada's handiwork. They crunched loudly.

"I did find some information about rifts while we were at the Academy," I said. Spense looked up, smiling that confident grin. "Do tell."

A thought crossed my mind that I was foolish to divulge this, that I was only telling him because I would say anything to break the tension.

No. This is pertinent to him. He is trustworthy.

"Rifts are failed portals. They're caused when the creator doesn't have enough magic to finish the project." I closed the book in my lap. I wasn't getting any progress reading it, anyway. I'd reread the page I was on twice now without retaining a single word.

Spense ran a hand through his hair. It seemed to go smoothly; I wondered if he could feel his horns even with the glamour. "What's the difference between the two?"

"Portals are a safe and effective way to travel through realms, whereas rifts are unstable and risky. You have no control of your destination, and you're likely to be gravely injured in the process. One of the side effects listed was brain damage—memory alteration. I'm positive you went through a rift."

Spense sighed shakily. "That sounds right. Unfortunately, that just asks more questions. Was I even trying to get to this realm? Was I the one who attempted the portal at all? I'd like to think my magic is strong enough to see it through its entire creation." The corner of his mouth turned up slightly.

"The dangerous part," I said, ignoring his bait. "Is that rifts are bound to collapse. It's not a matter of if, but when. And when they do, it's disastrous."

Spense uncrossed his legs, rising to his knees. "Aren't there soldiers guarding the rift right now? They need to be warned." He looked ready to march into the forest and retrieve them himself. My heart tightened to see the good in him.

I nodded. "My mother did not seem worried. It is more important to her that nothing gets through the rift. She knows our soldiers will eagerly lay their lives down." I sighed once. Everything was so complicated. Being a queen seemed like trying to hold a dozen plates at once, constantly rearranging, never truly resting. Waiting with bated breath for one to drop.

The Dark fae nodded gravely. He sat back on his ankles, his eyes deep in thought. "I wonder if we could repair it—turn it fully into a portal."

"The book said it was impossible," I said, shaking my head. "And, if we did somehow manage to open it, what would we do? Parade you around the realms until someone recognizes you?"

Spense didn't laugh. "I don't know, I just feel like my memories are tied to the rift. My brain was altered because of it. If we fix the rift, wouldn't that fix me too?"

The room exhaled with that breath of shared insecurity.

"You're not broken, Spense," I said softly.

"Aren't I?" We stared at each other for a few seconds. "What happens if I never find out who I am? I'll be broken forever."

Sadness flooded my chest. "Even if you never find out about your life before coming here, that doesn't stop you from figuring out who you were—who you *are*. That will get clearer every day; you just have to keep being true to your inner self. And who you are isn't broken. Do you think anyone truly knows who they are, through and through? I certainly don't. It's the path we walk in life, always evolving. In the end, maybe we aren't meant to fully know."

Spense smiled softly, his gentle gray eyes the colour of rainclouds. "Your kind words never cease to amaze me. I thank Gaia every day that it was you who was sent to help me. If it had been anyone else, I might not even be here anymore." The words settled between us, making my heart clench. I opened my mouth to say something, anything. I wanted to tell him that I was grateful for him, too. For changing my perspective. For making me better. But I hesitated too long.

"I'll always be Dark, Diana. That can never be changed. Even if by some miracle I can live out my life here, in Eira, I'll be living in secret. I'll never be able to show these." He gestured to his head, his magic swirling as he removed the glamour on his horns. It had been so long since I'd seen them, I'd almost forgotten what they looked like. Seeing them now, the dark, gently curved horns peeking from his mess of curls, he looked... complete. Like he had been missing an integral piece of him before. Something that was unplaceable.

I swallowed. "I'm going to tell you something. But you have to promise not to utter a single word of it to another soul."

Spense's face was wary as he nodded, his brows knitting together.

His face was mostly unreadable as I recounted my conversation with Jweira, and the memory she had shown me. What I was prophesized to do. Why I had been holed up in my room for two days trying to piece together the puzzle.

Letting him stew in it, I gently said, "Being Dark doesn't correlate with being evil. I knew that after our first day together. I have been exposed to so many lies and deceptions in the last few weeks that I have no idea what's even true anymore. I've been trying to make sense of what's up and what's down but I'm so confused. It's given me a better understanding of what you must be feeling. But I know for sure things are changing. Who knows what the future holds?"

After a moment, Spense cleared his throat. "Thank you. You have no idea how much I needed that. And I promise — I won't repeat any of this."

I smiled at him. I had no idea how much I'd needed to share that, either. Having another know this heavy truth felt like a knot coming loose in the pit of anxiety that was my stomach. Even if he couldn't help me with the storm that was undoubtedly coming my way, I relished in his solidarity. Someone else knew. I wasn't alone.

He picked up a thin, hand-bound book from the mess of tomes between us. Clearly ready to ease away from the heavy conversation, he read out: "*A Comprehensive Lineage of the Northern Peninsula Royals.*" A wry smile crept onto the corner of his mouth. "Are you in this?"

I tried to snatch the book away, but he was faster. He opened it up to the last page, where I would be the newest entry.

He grinned wickedly. "*Diana Lightbringer, born to Vera Lightbringer and Jago Harwell. Seventy-eighth generation. Named for our first Queen Diana, the Conqueror of the Darks. Born close to the Spring Equinox in the year 8200. Light brown hair, hazel eyes*—the title was no joke, this is comprehensive as hell."

I stuck out my tongue. "Tell me the picture is half-decent, at least."

Spense studied the portrait. "Hmm, the likeness is there, but you look a lot older in real life," he teased.

"It's all the wrinkles I'm getting from dealing with you."

"Don't forget the gray hairs."

I laughed, savoring the way it made my chest feel lighter. I reached my arm across to him. "Can I see?"

Instead of placing the book in my outstretched hand, he unfolded his legs and got up, settling himself beside me in one smooth movement. Our shoulders brushing, he held the book so we could both see.

I laughed as I took in the portrait. "I remember sitting for that painting. I was probably fifteen." I flipped the page, my stomach clanging once as I met eyes with my mother, her youthful, take-no-shit face a hard reminder of everything I had been dealing with lately. I flipped again, taking in the familiar faces of my great-aunt, Lily, and my grandmother, Maeve.

We looked through the females of my history, the queens who had sat on the throne long before I existed. Most I recognized from my schooling; some were unfamiliar. All held that steadfast look in their eyes, daring me to challenge them.

Spense asked, "You got this at the Academy? Don't you have books like this here, in your own library?"

I nodded. "We have mountains of lineage papers and books—too much to read in one lifetime. But recording all of the queens in one volume is not something I've ever seen. I mostly grabbed it for fun."

Spense continued to leaf through the pages. My brow furrowed as I thought about how odd it was for this book was hidden away in the Secured section in the Academy. And as nimble, pale fingers turned another page, I realized why.

Iave.

I slammed my hand down over his, stopping him from turning the page. He looked sideways at me, confusion in his face.

There she was. The first face I saw during my time in the Sacred Pool. I was not mistaken. Her molasses-dark skin and curly black hair. Her strong, stunningly beautiful face. The only difference was that instead of eyes that were pure light, hers were dark brown.

"I have never seen Iave in *any* official record in my whole life. Who made this book?" I breathed.

Spense turned the book over a couple times, looking for an author or footnote. "It doesn't say. Looks homemade."

Suddenly aware I was still gripping Spense's hand, I let it slide away, off the page. My hand felt cold in the absence of his heat.

I read the stats it included about Iave.

Iave Lightbringer. Born to Opal Lightbringer and Terrence Severin in midwinter, 1208. Died 1236, unmated and unmarried, after ruling for eight years. Survived by her daughter Kvista Lightbringer, born 1228 out of wedlock.

Father unknown. Unseelie sympathizer.

I slumped against my bed. Questions on top of questions on top of more questions piled in my head. Every time I turned around, there was something blowing up a part of my life I thought I knew.

Unseelie sympathizer. That was likely the reason she had been excluded from my teachings in the palace.

Spense searched my face, his eyes concerned. "Are you alright?"

Sighing, I nodded slowly. "Just more changes to the world I thought I knew."

After a minute of silence, Spense asked hesitantly, "This says she was unmated. What does that mean?"

Mentally, I searched through all of our lessons in the forest, all of the history and workings of the realm that I had taught to Spense. Had I really not mentioned the existence of soulmates?

"I'm sure you understand the concept of marriage," I started, to which he nodded. "Being mated to someone is more than that, more than a negotiation or strategy. It's finding your soulmate, the fae who matches you evenly, perfectly. It's not something you can choose or predict. When it happens, you know you've found the one your soul belongs with. The bond between a mated pair is unbreakable. It's beautiful." I thought wistfully of the father I would never know, my mother's true match; gone before she could enjoy life with him.

Spense's voice was low. "Have you... found your mate?"

I laughed shakily. "Gaia, no. You'd know if I had. When a mating takes hold, usually after an act of true love, each partner is marked with matching tattoos on their left arms."

Instinctually, I looked to Spense's arms, remembering his tattoos. For a heartbeat I felt something squirmy in my gut as I wondered if he had a mate. Did things work the same way in the Dark realm? In my heart of hearts, I thought it must be the same. Weren't we the same species after all, banished to separate realms?

Something like relief washed over me when I noted that he only had tattoos covering his right arm. His left remained bare; his pale skin almost luminous in the moonlight washing through my window.

Spense smirked, catching my gaze. "Looks like I'm a free agent."

I rolled my eyes. "I'll send a warning out to the town."

"In all seriousness," he said, his voice contemplative. "I would think a bond like that would be able to survive a memory-altering trip through a rift. If it's as unbreakable as you say."

Gaia, I hoped so. The undeniable strength and tenacity of the mating bond was one of the only truths I still held on to. If that, too, was a lie, it could be the brick that sent my wall crumbling.

I gave him a half shrug. "It's definitely not something that's ever been tested before. What if you do have a soulmate desperately awaiting your return in your realm?" I meant to put an easy humour in my voice; I kicked myself internally when it came out sounding more like despair.

Spense ran a hand through his hair, touching his horns absent-mindedly. He hadn't placed the glamour back over them yet. A small touch of pride surfaced in my belly at the show of his comfort around me. "I think I know myself well enough by now to say with full authority that if I had someone that special, that I couldn't live without, then I wouldn't have left them in another realm."

Softly I said, "You could have been sent through against your will."

Spense studied my face then. "Why are you so determined to make me believe I have a soulmate waiting for me?"

Because it would be easier. Because then I would be able to have you here, in my room, without wondering what your horns feel like, or how much of your shoulder is touching mine. Because I'm scared of what I think is happening.

"I would just hate to be the one waiting, only for my love to return with another."

He wet his lips, holding my eyes. "You've experienced it before." It wasn't a question, but an acknowledgement.

I looked away, shame prickling in me. He had seen that right away. Was I truly still so weak about what had happened six years ago? I would be a horrible queen if I couldn't hide my emotions.

Spense touched my arm comfortingly. "You don't have to tell me."

I wanted to. I had been living in this hurt for a long time, letting it consume me as I pretended to ignore it. In my short time knowing Spense, nothing felt too secret to share with him. Hell, tonight alone I had told him more than anyone in Eira knew. I wanted this feeling in my chest to lighten, to leave forever. It didn't have to own me anymore.

I swallowed.

"When I was sixteen, I was sent to Mt Nord to live there for the entire summer, so I could learn to fight in their traditional ways. Customary royal training. It was the first time I experienced real freedom, unaccompanied by palace officials. The Nordians — they're so rough and wild. The females were way too intimidating for me to grow close to, and the males were no better. The flirting was out of control. But they all respected me enough to leave me alone — that or they were scared of the crown's retaliation if they touched me. My combat instructor was more outgoing than the others. Maverick. He was so full of confidence, of swagger. Only eighteen but he acted like he ran the place. He was the only one brave enough to pursue something with me. I was untried. I loved the attention. I fell so hard in love with him, and he told me he loved me too. We spent the summer doing everything together. When we weren't training, we were sneaking off somewhere. He showed me the most beautiful spots in Mt Nord, mountains and sunrises and places where the sky touches the river, all while telling me I was the best view. I thought he would be my forever. I was actually offended every morning that I woke up and the mating tattoo wasn't there." I huffed a laugh.

"By the end of the summer, I was a formidable fighter. I could hold my own in the sparring ring and was a *very* adept pegasi flyer." I smiled at the memory of being in the clouds, sailing on phantom winds, and moving faster than I ever thought possible. "But I had to return to the palace; I had five more years of training to complete. I wrote to my mother a few times, asking to stay, saying I hadn't learned enough yet. I don't know whether she saw through me or just didn't care, but she didn't entertain it for a second. I'm grateful for that now.

"Maverick said we would make it work, that he would come down to visit me and when I was done my training he could serve in the Queen's Army. It seemed so ideal at the time. I wrote him a few times when I was home, but I never heard anything back. Finally, after a few months, he sent me a three-sentenced letter saying that he was sorry, he had found his soulmate and whatever we had was over. I was sad, of course, and angry that it wasn't me. But I understood. I respected the sacred bond of mates.

"When an emissary came down with the rest of my trunks, I sent Maisie to receive them with an ulterior motive in mind—that she would find out who Maverick's mate was. I was genuinely curious, having met most of the females while in Mt Nord. When I saw her that night, she cried while telling me that the emissary had no idea what she was talking about. That Maverick had no mate. And he had already moved onto his next mark." I looked down at my hands, twirling my emerald ring.

"I felt so stupid. I gave my entire heart to the first male who gave me attention, so freely. Looking back now I see that I ignored some pretty obvious red flags.

But I was young. I was angry at him, but I took it out on my family, for not preparing me enough for real life. I stopped trying in my lessons, stopped riding, stopped spending time with my friends. I was consumed by the betrayal. It wasn't until my mother shipped me off to the Gaian Abbey that I was able to heal. I've never been with a male since then. Mostly I've just been too busy, but if I'm truly being honest with myself I think I'm scared to get my heart broken again."

Silence hung in the air, almost deafening in my ears. There was so much buzzing tension around us, I could have probably created a lightning strike with it.

I could feel Spense's eyes on me, waiting for me to look at him. Finally, he placed a hand on my cheek and gently turned my face to his. The calluses on his palms grazed my skin, but I was glad for it.

His face was so soft, so yielding as I drank him in. Just as I had hoped, I felt the weight of that story, of the hurt I had held onto for so long, float away like butterflies in the wind. Something reignited in my chest at the lightness.

I'd never heard Spense's voice so gravelly, so tender, as he spoke next.

"You deserve so much more than that pig. You're strong, you're wise, you're merciful. Not to mention beautiful. I can't imagine how horrible someone would have to be to take advantage of your warm heart."

His voice lowered to a soft whisper. "I'm sorry this happened to you. I wish I could take it away."

His hand was still on my face, which was now dangerously close to his. My heart was beating wildly in my chest. My mind was spinning, dizzy with the relief of the confession. Dizzy with what was in the air between us.

I felt his magic touch mine, soft and gentle, asking permission. My magic accepted greedily, feeling his warm, dark purple essence matching my snowy white; it misted lavender around us. It felt so right, so incredibly natural. So much so that I didn't hesitate when I closed the gap between us, pressing my lips to his.

At first, I worried that I had misread everything. Spense was frozen in surprise.

Then fire erupted.

His lips moved over mine, drinking me in, slow and methodical and targeted. My heart was beating without control or rhythm. I swore I could hear his, echoing frantically against his chest. It was an understanding, a joining of magic and feeling that had been waiting so long for this moment. Spense was soft and strong and completely open to me, his heart unguarded.

Had kissing always been so earth-shattering? I had been out of the game for a while but couldn't recall ever feeling something so right that it sang in my very bones. I wanted to feel this way forever.

I placed my hand on his hip, comfortably within reach of my arm. Realizing too late how intimate that was, I made to move it up, resting it on his chest.

But the damage was done. Spense's kiss became urgent, his feverish lips matching my own. His tongue swept in, tasting me. I did not feel scared, or worried, or even remember why I had been hurting in the first place.

All I knew was here and now, and that Spense's hand was tangled up in my hair, and that I wasn't very far from gathering the courage to put my hand in his mess of curls, to wrap my fingers around the horns that stood there.

I was vaguely aware of how loud our breaths were getting. I didn't care. I slid my hand up his chest to the nape of his neck, where I twined some silky black hair around my fingers.

I could feel his hand trail down my back, leaving tingles in its wake.

Any reasonable thought had left my mind, tossed to the side at the first feel of his lips. I just wanted to soak him in, to sit here on the floor all night with him wrapped up in me.

Clearly, that was too much to ask.

A bang sounded at the door, accompanied by a small gasp.

I sprang away from Spense, shock racking through my body. I knew who I would find at my door. Her honey-dipped magic was flared in surprise. Maisie, hurriedly picking up the box she'd dropped: the culprit of the loud bang. She moved back and forth over the threshold, clearly vastly uncomfortable and unable to decide what to do.

"Sorry, sorry, sorry," she was muttering. I opened my mouth to request she wait in the drawing room for a minute, but before I could, Spense was standing, making his way to the door. The absence of his magic from mine felt wrong and cold.

"It's fine, Maisie. I should really get going." The

confident grin he usually wore was gone, replaced by a shaken ghost of a smile. He sidestepped Maisie through the door, pausing behind her to meet my eyes once more. I offered him a sheepish smile, to which he gave me his wicked grin and left, sending a thrill up my spine.

I looked at Maisie through squinted eyes. I would be hearing about this for a while.

"I... should have known," she said, light dawning in her eyes. "No visitors allowed, and then I see him on his way here. Of course, you've been so different lately."

I still felt dazed. "What? No, he came to bring me some food. It... just kind of happened. I don't even know what it means." I rubbed my eyes, realization setting in. What we had just done was all sorts of stupid.

That didn't stop it from feeling so right.

"Please, Maisie, you can't breathe a word of this to anyone," I pleaded, thinking of the unending shit I would be in if my mother caught wind of this. She wouldn't understand. She couldn't even comprehend the idea that Spense wasn't some evil, plotting Dark. She would absolutely combust before accepting that he was the only fae in my life right now who I trusted completely.

"Of course, Di, you know I would never." Maisie's face was solemn. She set down the box she'd come in with on my vanity. "I'm sorry to have interrupted at all. I forgot to bring you the jewelry for Midspring Mania. I was going to leave it in the drawing room, but I thought you would still be awake, that you might want your tea topped up—"

I waved her off. "It's probably a good thing you

interrupted. I don't know what might have ended up happening."

Maisie wiggled her eyebrows. "Well it looked like it was headed *somewhere*. You and Spense, huh?"

I wacked her arm playfully. "There is no 'me and Spense'. We just got caught up in the moment. This could never work between us. This would never be allowed."

My friend shrugged, bending down to clean up the pile of books discarded all over my floor. I helped her, making two neat piles that we placed on my desk.

"Last time I checked," she said finally. "You were the damn High Princess."

I blinked. Maisie never swore, even a milder word.

"I know I wasn't sure about Spense in the beginning. I'm still not. But I'm sure about you; one hundred percent. If this is something important to you, that makes you happy in this crazy whirlwind that has become your life, then I think you need to honour that."

My body betrayed me by nodding, even as my brain offered up a million reasons why I should definitely stay away from whatever this was.

It was an ember, sparked and ready to catch flame. I worried what would happen when the fire started.

NINETEEN
Playing Queen
DIANA

When Maisie first showed me the dress Beltain had created for me yesterday, I worried about being able to pull it off. Made of shimmering fabric that reflected every light, it hugged my form all the way to my knees before flaring out in a beautiful train. It was strapless and backless, the neckline swooping in a V down to my ribs, much lower than I'd ever been comfortable with before. It was a Queen's dress.

Now, swishing the fabric in between my fingers, I was excited to wear it. I was the damn High Princess, and I would make sure everyone knew.

If normal dining traditions were to be upheld, then I would be placed at my mother's side, with Embris beside me. The eldest of the region leaders would be across from me on my mother's other side: Kashdan. The aging Prince of the West was a good male, albeit prone to overindulging at parties. I was confident I would be able to loosen his lips about the shadows once the night kicked off.

Plotting how I would gain the most information from the other regions as possible was the only thing keeping my mind off Spense. I was still a hundred different types of confused about that. Us.

If my mother wasn't going to involve me in the court politics, I would involve myself.

It was something that might prove difficult by the end of the night, considering the lack of sleep I had gotten. My mind whirled a hundred miles a minute and the rate that it switched back and forth from Spense and the deceit unfolding in front of me was giving me whiplash. Honestly, it was a miracle I got any sleep at all.

Maisie helped me into the skin-tight gown, gasping in delight as she adjusted the train around my slippered feet. She led me over to the mirror, which she tilted so I could see my whole body.

Shock murmured through me. She had lined my eyes with black kohl and applied blush over my cheekbones. She'd painted my lips a bold red and swept my hair over one shoulder, pinning it in place to the side as the rest cascaded in waves down my back. My chest and curves were on full display, moving the fabric so it looked like it was a river, constantly in motion. Jweira was on a delicate white-gold chain around my neck, the emerald pulsing warmly over my collarbone.

I had never looked so regal, so beautiful before.

I had never looked like a Queen until now.

*

I entered the formal ball room to the exact reaction I had been hoping for. With Maisie slightly behind me, she dropped the gown's train around my feet just as the guard at the door announced my arrival. To complete the effect, I unspooled a piece of my magic to flare around me just slightly. It would be felt, rather than seen.

There was a whoosh as air left the room. Stares from every pair of eyes in the room warmed me as I made my way across the floor, joining my mother at the dais in the back of the room, where two ivory thrones sat. The thrill could be felt down to my bones.

Some, mostly court officials, remembered themselves and snapped their gaze away, bowing their heads slightly as I passed. Others remained how they were, slack jaws and wide eyes. I was no longer the young princess they had known for two decades, the one who raced through Nevelyn on horseback, leaving her cares in the wind. I was the Heir. Their future queen.

As I climbed the dais, I locked eyes with my mother. She was beaming, her pride clear, consuming her whole face. "You are mesmerizing, darling," she murmured to me. I almost felt guilt in that moment, for how I planned to scheme around her back tonight. Her harsh words slammed into me as I took my place at the throne beside her. *I may not tell you things if I wish. That is my right.*

What about my right, to know about the kingdom I would someday lead?

Vera stood, her ivory white gown flaring around her. She held her arms out, to silence the crowd, but they were already hushed from my entrance. I barely hid my smirk.

"Good evening, friends. Thank you all for being a part of our newest tradition, a feast to celebrate

Midspring! I trust you will find everything you are looking for tonight, whether it be food, drink, or dance. And let us not forget the grace of our Mother Gaia for leading us successfully through Spring. Enjoy!" With the end of her speech, the light orbs on the wall changed from their bright white hue to a muted green, creating an intimate ambiance.

Conversation sprang immediately between the guests. Music started from the band in the corner of the room, an upbeat, folky tune. Servants rushed in, offering bubbly alcohol from chutes and appetizers on skewers. These would continue for a few hours before dinner was served—a chance for casual visiting. Dinner was the time that alliances were renewed, and politics were discussed. Because after dinner, the dancing would begin, and would not stop until dawn had broken over the horizon.

A group of three Northern court officials nearby were joined by Lord Nimshar, his Eastern finery on full display tonight. I had already thought of how I would appeal to each region leader, what words to say to slip into easy trust with me. Nimshar was a prickly male, prone to arrogance and pride, but he was also cunning. The elusiveness of the Eastern Plateau notwithstanding, he would be the tightest lipped of all my marks tonight.

A small touch at my elbow had me turning to see Aedan, dressed in a crisp navy suit, smiling genially at me.

"You look beautiful, as always, Diana," he said softly, pressing a kiss to my cheek.

"Thank you, Aedan."

"I wondered if we could have a private moment? I want to apologize for what happened at the City of Scholars. I cannot begin to tell you the embarrassment I feel—"

I cut him off, resting a hand on his arm. "No apology needed. It was out of your control. I'm just glad you're fully recovered." I hardly remembered him being in the city at all. So much had happened since then. Was it truly only a few days ago that we were there?

Aedan's smile was so genuine, so pure. For the tiniest heartbeat, I saw it. What Shela had theorized about his feelings for me. I always saw familial love in Aedan's eyes, and maybe it was because I was aware of it now, but for a moment his eyes betrayed longing, a different kind of love that had been festering for years.

I dropped my hand from his arm. Waves of uncertainty washed over me, while my mind spun. Should I be treating him differently? Was I unconsciously doing something to lead him on?

Clearly, my face had slipped from its regal composure I had practiced in the mirror for so long this morning. Aedan had been talking this whole time, something about smelling cherries while he had been sick, but he trailed off. His brow furrowed, and he took a step closer to me. "Are you alright?"

Mercifully, we were joined in that moment by Jamey, who seemed to float in her gown of deep purple. She held a flute of clear fizzing drink daintily as her keen eyes surveyed the room.

"Evening, Princess, Deputy Captain," she said, her voice elegant.

Aedan, ever the picture of politeness, took her hand and gently pressed a kiss over it. Jamey watched with half-lidded eyes.

"No need for titles between friends, J," I said, bumping her with my elbow.

Jamey studied me for a beat. "There are a lot of important fae here tonight. You never know whom you may need to win over with dazzling social etiquette."

The words had a slight sting to them. This was on par with how our conversations had been going as of late. The night I dined with my family and the Western officials; it was to great surprise that I found myself irritated beyond belief at my longtime friend. She spoke like a stranger, with an air of self-righteousness that rubbed me the wrong way. *Jamey's changed*, I thought to myself.

Or maybe I have.

I spotted Lord Daqin, the representative for the City of Scholars, munching on a plate of candied pecans across the dance floor. And he was alone. Perfect.

"Well, do let me know if you find a fae here tonight more important than I, *Lady Pinois*," I said, my tone clipped. Gathering my train, I inclined my head in a slightly mocking way, leaving them as I slipped through the throng of bodies crowding the room.

I didn't turn around, even as I felt my friends' stares at my back.

A wizened, quirky male, Lord Daqin was a true embodiment of the city he maintained. His tweed suit was much too large for him, causing him to appear smaller than he already was, and his glasses gave him a glossy, fish-eyed look.

As I approached, he hastily disposed of his plate on a passing servant's tray and wiped his fingers on his trousers.

"Lord Daqin," I said. I had to press my lips together to keep from laughing as he bowed, the tilt of his head revealing he was wearing a wig over a bald spot.

"High Princess Diana, how pleasant to see you," he squeaked.

"Likewise. I wanted to express my deepest apologies for my abrupt departure in the City of Scholars. I had been planning a social call with you when we were summoned back to Nevelyn with an emergency." I gave him my best queenly smile, allowing a bit of soothing magic to wrap around us.

Daqin's face was reprimanding at first. "Yes, well, that was quite the embarrassment for me indeed, as I'm sure you understand." But his face softened, smiling back at me. "All is forgiven, my princess. Sometimes these things cannot be helped."

I took his hands gently, the old male blushing slightly. "You are too kind, Lord."

He waved me off, his flushed face beaming.

"I trust you know of the reason we had to leave so quickly," I said, keeping my voice low as I leaned closer to him. He looked around before leaning in as well, his face full of worry.

"Queen Vera did fill me in, of course. What a terror!"

I nodded gravely, fueling his exuberance. "Indeed," I opened my mouth to continue but his wheezy voice filled the pause.

"And that poor girl — oh, Gaia protect her."

I snapped to attention. I hadn't heard of this, though I wasn't surprised at this point.

Playing it cool, I asked, "How is she doing?"

"She's been sent to the Western Shores, to be kept with the other shadow victims. I've been told the healers are thoroughly stumped on how to save them." Daqin's voice turned raspy. "An attack in my own city — and a new recruit from the Academy to boot. Raya's poor parents have been inconsolable."

Blood thundered in my head. I had seen Raya, spoken to her, the day the shadows trapped Spense and I. She had been attacked. This was my fault — I should have done something, warned somebody.

Lord Rentin, the representative for Nevelyn, waved to Daqin from a few feet away and came to greet him. I politely dipped my head and left, leaving them to catch up.

The shadows had attacked after leaving us. Why only one fae, when there were entire villages in the West being sacked? Doing my best to keep my queenly repose, I scanned the room for a conversation to join. If I stood still too long, I would surely be swept into something I did not want to be a part of. This I knew from years of experience. I spotted Prince Leo speaking with Jamey, but to my great grievance Sir Hestor was with them, who would no doubt be keen to speak with me now that a healthy amount of years had passed since our last encounter.

Prince Kashdan's booming laugh echoed through the ballroom.

I snatched two flutes of bubbly from a passing server and followed the laughter to my next mark.

*

I spent the remainder of the welcome hours filling Kashdan's drinks and charming him with anecdotes and stories from the palace. By the time dinner was called, his cheeks were blushed and rosy, his smile unwavering, and I was exhausted.

"Let me escort you to the table, my dear," he said, offering me his arm.

After settling at the royal table that had been assembled on the dais, Vera stood and made a toast to the entire room. She invited High Mother Cretis to lead us in giving thanks for the food, and then conversation erupted over the sounds of cutlery scraping plates.

"My dearest Vera," boomed Kashdan. "Why haven't we seen more of your fine prodigy at the regional meetings? She is quite an impressive young princess, you know. Lots to say about her kingdom!"

My eyes flicked to my mother, who graciously accepted Kashdan's praise. "You are so kind, my old friend. Diana will join us in due time. Her full-time priority right now is working with our... *newest guest.*" Her tone dropped an octave on the last words.

Kashdan drained his wine goblet, gesturing at a servant for more.

"Ah yes, and how is that going? I'm sure we'll be getting an official update later, of course, but if you had a bone to throw my way... ?"

"It's going quite well, Prince," I said, keeping my voice steady as Vera's gaze bored holes in the side of my head. It must have killed her that I had spoken before she could formulate the perfect non-answer.

"Well, you say? Meaning you have gotten the information we seek?"

The hush that went through the officials at the head table was impossible to miss. I kept my voice low as I continued, though I knew it would make no difference with these gossips.

"Meaning that while, yes, we have uncovered some important clues, it is more important to learn that he is no threat to us."

Kashdan set his goblet on the table rather forcefully. "No threat to us?" he repeated, his voice incredulous. "He is spawn of an evil, vile, malevolent race. Having him here, in Eira, is hugely unnerving, especially with his skills and motive unknown. Vera, how could you let this happen? She has been ensnared in his mind games!"

My mother put a calming hand out, but it had no effect as I slammed my own flute on the table. The delicate glass cracked, spidering up from the spine to rim. Bubbly started to drip all over my hand, the table.

"Is it so hard to believe that he is redeemable? I'm sure you have all done horrible things in your long lives that you have sought and received forgiveness for," I said, addressing the officials that were all staring at me now. Thankfully, the rest of the party was as loud and unaware as could be.

Bubbly was reaching across the table, spilling over the side. I sent a net of magic out to catch the alcohol before it landed in my lap. Letting this be the distraction that kept me from erupting, I soothed the liquid back into the flute, which sealed itself neatly at my magic's urging.

When I looked up again, my mother's face was furious. The officials were either looking down at their plates or staring at me in disgust. Amatha, the lovely, quiet wife of Kashdan's, was watching me in disbelief.

"How can you use our water magic so far away from the West?" she breathed. "And so *well*?"

I looked at the flute. Shock rippled through me. I had never been able to wield water this well, even while I was in the West.

Vera changed the course of conversation towards Kashdan's son's upcoming nuptials, and the table fell into an easy, albeit quiet, lull of talking.

The rest of dinner passed without further drama, leaving me to sit in my own fury while pushing food around my plate. When I was queen, no one would dare challenge me at my own damn table, in the palace my ancestors had lived in for eight millennia. When I was queen, there would be no room in my court for old-fashioned bigots.

It was a relief to stand and breathe air into my lungs again when dinner ended. The band struck up a fast-paced tune, and soon everyone was flocking to the heart of the ballroom to dance. As officials left the table, none even glanced my way, save for Prince Leo, who gave me an evaluating look as he descended the dais. I held his gaze the whole time. I may have made a spectacular show of embarrassing myself, but I was still the High

Princess.

The damn High Princess.

*

"Dance with me," Aedan's breath tickled my ear as he appeared beside me.

"You must have the stamina of our war horses if you have not tired yet," I teased. The deputy captain had not even been able to leave the throng of dancers without being approached by another female requesting a dance.

Aedan chuckled. "With any luck, this will be my last of the evening." As I saw the yearning faces of beautiful fae watching Aedan intently, I knew that would not be true.

I took his arm and allowed him to spin me into the heart of the dancing. We danced to an old fiddle-heavy jive, one with words that came from an unused language. Our bodies found the rhythm with ease, a reminder of the years of lessons we endured together growing up.

"Kind of feels like old times, right?"

Old times? Nothing in my life felt like "old times". Everything was upside down and inside out. Everything I thought I knew had been shattered before my eyes. I had seen things that I never thought possible. How could he think that a stupid party could make everything right again? He only said that as a way to gain sentiment towards a time where Spense had not yet entered our lives.

"The old times are so far behind us I don't think I

could recognize them anymore, Aedan." I said.

His brow furrowed but he said nothing as we continued our duet.

At the end of the dance, Aedan led me to the outskirts of the floor. "Diana, I know things have been really stressful for you right now. I want you to know I'm still here, you can lean on me to bear some of it for you. You don't have to shoulder it alone."

My heart ached. I couldn't think of words in the moment to express how much I loved him, my old friend, my partner in crime. He had always protected me, never let me hide in another's shadow. And now I knew that he had pushed his personal feelings for me to the side for our friendship.

What would he think if he knew what I had done with Spense?

Aedan pulled me into a hug, his arms a comforting weight around me. Once I thought it would not be so hard to love him, to spend my life with him. But as I breathed in his familiar pine scent, my head resting in the crook of his shoulder, I knew I didn't want comfort and familiarity. I wanted fire and passion and adventure. I wanted to shatter old ways of thinking and abolish the outdated thoughts on Darks. I wanted Spense at my side.

He pulled away, his blue eyes searching my face. I gave him a small smile. Aedan opened his mouth, but paused as his gaze settled on something behind me.

"May I cut in, my princess?"

I turned to see Prince Leo smiling like the snake he wore over his breast pocket, his tanned skin contrasting beautifully to the deep black suit he donned. His scent washed over me, the smell of the ocean and tropical fruits that didn't grow in the North.

"Of course," I said, taking his hand. As he escorted me into the frenzy, I turned to give Aedan a reassuring smile, which he did not return, his brow furrowed.

Leo and I began a series of turns and spins, his skill obvious as he followed the music. "You made quite the impressive show at dinner," he drawled, his voice smooth as glass.

"My passion gets the best of me sometimes," I said as he spun me away from him and then pulled me back.

"I find it endearing. I would imagine your ideas are not alike to what your court has to say." Meaning my mother.

I settled my gaze on him, thoughts whirling about where this was headed. "And your ideas, Prince Leo? Where do you find them aligned to?"

The Prince of the Southern Isles laughed darkly. "You are just as quick as I'd hoped."

Without warning, he halted our dance, leading me across the ballroom, out the glass double doors to the stretching balcony. The cool night air was a pleasant shock to my hardly covered body. I hadn't realized how warm I had gotten. The stars winked in the black sky, the full moon's glow flooding us with light.

There were over a dozen fae on the balcony, some out for a breath of fresh air, leaning on the railing, watching the River Nord snake down the mountain. Others were tangled up in dark alcoves, bodies writhing in the cover of night.

Leo led us to a stretch of railing that was mostly private. "You are a rare treat in these boring courts, beautiful Diana," he said, his eyes on the view below us. "It is not often indeed that I find someone as likeminded as me."

I watched him through narrowed eyes. I didn't know much of Leo, as he had only taken over his father's throne two years ago. And what I did know him to be was shady and conniving. Disgust roared through me at the thought of us being alike.

"I have plans for my region that will shake this realm to its core. After eight thousand years without change it is time a new leader stepped up. Have you noticed how the land seems to grow less and less vibrant, the animals harder to sense? Perhaps not, as you are still so young. In my years, I have seen the withering of this realm. There was a time, long ago, when we lived in balance with our Dark counterparts. I believe this is key to keeping the land alive. The Folk have gone, without any attempts to invite them back. How will this land be in another thousand years, without the nymphs to invoke the magic, without the elves to tend to the wild?" Leo turned to me, his amber eyes ablaze with passion. "This land is dying, Diana, and I think you know it, too."

What I did know was that the energy around us had shifted, and I didn't like it. Leo was becoming unhinged, his words breathless.

"What do you suppose I can even do about it?" I ventured.

"To start, the rift that is currently sucking the life out

of your forest needs to be repaired, created into a true portal." He waved off the look of shock on my face. "Yes, yes, I know about portals. You are the most skilled in magic I have ever seen, and the other officials know it too. They fear you. I believe you can repair the portal with your own power alone, not even considering the depth of magical reserve in that emerald you wear."

Instinctively, my hand flew to Jweira. "How —"

"Once the portal is open, we can begin to bring balance back, starting with the Folk that have been absent so long. I can help you create a new kingdom."

"My mother will never agree to this," I said, my voice stony.

"She will hardly be able to stop you."

I imagined my world, my beautiful city, filled with nymphs and sprites and pixies. Elves and goblins and all the rest I had only read about. The Dark lived among us, blending easily into us, no borders, just one united race. I wanted that, yearned for it.

Leo used my silence as fuel. "Let us make an alliance, you and me. A marriage between the North and South will be unstoppable. It will be easy —"

My magic sliced through the air in a clean line of shock. "Marriage? You can't be serious."

"Not to fret, my dear Diana, it would only be for show." His lips curved upwards, an adder on the hunt. "Unless, of course, you found yourself wanting more."

I stepped backward, on reflex an arm of magic reached out on a phantom wind to slap Leo across the face.

I expected him to fly into a rage, but he chuckled to

himself, a hand stroking his red cheek. "Feisty, feisty." I didn't like the confidence in his stance, the propriety in his eyes as he looked at me. Cold crept up my bare spine, and I was suddenly aware of how much of me was on display.

I was not a queen, not yet. My confidence was shattering around me like the flute I had broken earlier. *Stupid, stupid, reckless.*

A warm hand was suddenly on my back, the smell of dark chocolate wrapping around me. I knew that touch — that magic.

"Princess Diana, your presence is required inside," Spense said, his voice dripping cool disdain at the Prince who sneered at him.

It was everything I could do to keep my hands from shaking as I followed Spense off the balcony, into the palace. As I looked over my shoulder, Prince Leo watched me with his snake expression. "Think about it," was all he said as I disappeared inside.

I leaned into Spense's touch as he guided me away — not back through the doors to the ballroom but through a smaller door I knew would lead us into a corridor that ran beside it.

Once the door whispered shut, I wanted to sag to the floor in relief. But instead I punched Spense in the arm.

"Hey!"

"What do you think you're doing here? You'll be recognized!" I grabbed the arm I had just punched and led him further down the hall, pushing him into an alcove that wouldn't be visible from the hallway. Even without guards in this hall, I knew Delios was around here somewhere. He hated crowds, so he would stay out of the ballroom, but he never wandered too far. There was something about how the wolf watched me that made me think he could whisper secrets to my mother.

Spense's head smacked against a painting of a wolf drinking from the River Nord. How appropriate.

"For someone who just saved you from what I assume was an unwanted proposal, you certainly don't care about covering me in bruises," he said, rubbing the back of his head as he smirked at me.

Gaia save me from that smirk.

I shook my head. "You'll get much worse injuries than bruises if you're caught. The officials are far from ready to jump on the forgiveness wagon."

Spense shrugged, a hand lazily going to my hip and tugging me closer. "I've already proven to you that I can handle myself in a fight." When I didn't smile, he contested. "I'll leave. I was bored in my room and thought I'd sneak a peek of what a stuffy royal party looks like. I think you undersold how much fun the dancing is." He grinned at me. "I saw you go out to the balcony, and suddenly, I could feel your magic wrapping around me. It was distressed, so I followed you out there. Who is that pompous male, anyway?"

I reached up to brush a stray curl that had fallen into his face. He shuddered slightly at my touch.

"Prince Leo, from the South. He's outrageously full of himself, but he made some interesting statements. I'll fill you in later. Thank you for saving me."

Spense smiled at me. "It might have been a bit selfish on my part. Now I get you all to myself."

A breath caught in my throat. "I have to admit, even though it's stupid, I'm glad you're here. I wasn't sure after what happened last night, maybe I overstepped —"

He cut me off with a kiss, gentle and soft.

My mind melted; any rational thought stripped away. I rose onto my tiptoes, wrapping my arms around his neck. One of his hands settled on my back, warm on my bare skin. The other cupped my face gently, holding me to him. I was on my tiptoes, and even then Spense had to crane his neck to cross the distance between our heights. Magic seeped from my pores, desperate for its own touch. White met indigo, a beautiful harmonic aura around us.

I was vaguely aware of Jweira pulsing lightly at my neck.

Spense nipped at my lower lip, sending a shiver down my spine that blocked out every other sensation.

This is not wise, a small voice piped up in my head. *Keep your focus.*

The fact that we were only a few feet away from every fae in this realm that wanted Spense's head on a spike was the only thing that drew me back from him. I lost myself in those gray eyes, the low lighting making them look smoky.

"Don't say it," he whispered, his nose still touching mine.

"Say what?"

"That this is a bad idea. That we're endangering each other. That your mother won't like it. Because I really don't care."

I was a fool. I was a foolish, silly girl, infatuated and

270

reeling and lost. I was in no state to be making such life-altering decisions. And if I was smart, if I was truly ready to play the part of High Princess, I would stop this before it started. But in that moment, I really didn't care, either. In spite of myself, a small laugh escaped me. "No one can know," I breathed.

He nodded, over and over.

"I have something for you." Spense pulled away, reaching a hand inside his tunic's breast pocket. He handed me a small piece of wrapping, which he had clearly done himself, judging by the rips and overall wrinkled appearance.

Gently, I peeled the wrapping away. A pair of small ruby earrings sat in my palm, set in a muted silver. A memory washed over me, one of Spense and I standing in the jeweler's section of the Marketplace, where he had seen me looking at these earrings.

"You — you remembered," I said, closing my hand softly around them.

Spense's answering smile was a touch sheepish — something he didn't wear often. "They're not the ones you originally liked. I did go back intending to buy them, but a stable hand's salary doesn't pay all that much. I actually made these from the ruby you let me keep from one of our lessons." I remembered that ruby — I'd assumed he'd sell it.

"Wait, you made these with your own earth magic?" He nodded. "I know I'm a great teacher, but last I checked you weren't even close to bending metals to your will." I studied the silver casing around the rubies. It was good quality, not the best I'd seen, but passible certainly in the jeweler's section.

He shrugged, the motion making him appear smaller. "I don't know how I did it, honestly. I kind of… let go of any thoughts and just allowed the magic to flow through me."

I slipped the earrings into my ears, replacing the plain emerald dewdrops that had been dangling there previously. I stored them in the frame of the wolf painting behind us.

"That's meditation, you know," I said, shaking my head slightly to test the dangle of the rubies.

Spense looked at me with such an open expression, so much trust in those eyes of steel.

I continued, "I wonder if you worked with metal in your life before. I could probably get you an apprenticeship with a jeweler —"

I was cut off when Spense ran a hand through my wavy hair, smoothing it out over my shoulder. "I'm not so sure I even want to remember my life anymore," he breathed, the admission a soft whisper in the air.

Instinctually, the part of me that was the High Princess found that to be a red flag. *Why not? Has he already learned something damning about himself? Does he think he'll be killed after his memories return?*

But the part of me that was here, the traitorous, hopeless romantic young girl that looked into his intent gaze brushed all those thoughts aside.

I must have been wearing the internal grapple on my face, for Spense took my hands and led me into the hall. "Let's dance," he announced, making a beeline for the pair of doors into the ballroom.

I tugged back on his arm. "That is a *horrible* idea."

He feigned looking hurt. "You don't want to dance with me?"

"It does make me nervous that you probably don't remember how to dance, and I may end up with bruised feet," I teased. "But you will most definitely be recognized and very likely attacked if you show your face in there."

Spense grinned wickedly, clearly hoping I'd say that. He let go of my hand, waving his arms around him in a dramatic affair. It did have flair, I admitted to myself as dark purple magic swirled around him. My nose was filled with the smell of summertime fruits and chocolate.

When the magic settled, I was no longer looking at Spense's familiar face. In his place was a plain fae with no outstanding features. Dusty brown hair and unremarkable brown eyes. My own magic moved in me, unsettled by the fact there was a glamour close to it.

If I strained myself, really focused, I could see the glimmer around him that was proof of the deception. A simple glance his way would not provoke any second thoughts. It was an impeccable glamour.

"How did you do that?" I breathed; my brows knitted together.

He shrugged again, the face he was wearing delightfully proud of himself. "There's more to my magic then we both realized. I'm certainly having fun testing it out."

Spense reached out his hand to me again, the tanned skin so different from his usual pale pallor. I bit my bottom lip. Even with his impressive disguise, there was still a lot of risk to him parading around the dance floor with the High Princess.

He wiggled his eyebrows, a motion so confident and cocky and unfitting of the face he wore that I almost laughed. Surely one dance would be fine.

"One song, then you go back to your room and *stay there*."

Spense only grinned.

Gaia help me.

I took his hand.

TWENTY
The Daedal
DIANA

Even in my iridescent statement of a gown, the throng of
bodies and the music beat growing rhythmically were
enough to keep me mostly unnoticed as Spense guided
me to the center of the room. I expected the free alcohol
had played a part in that as well, I noted as I took in the
easy sway of the dancers, their sweat-glistened faces,
relaxed eyes.

I had been unable to stop myself from glancing at
my mother in case she reacted. Vera had been in the
same spot all night—at the head of the long dining table
with Princes and officials on either side of her, speaking
in low tones. She did not give me a second glance as I
paraded under her nose with her greatest enemy.

Either Spense's glamour was that good, or I was
severely low on the queen's perimeter tonight.

A jivey song was vibrating across the room, the band
musicians putting more effort into their movements and
strums than I thought possible after so many hours of
playing. Spense swept me into his arms, and with an
ease I hadn't felt all night, I begun to dance with him.
Keeping one eye on the officials and one eye on the not-
Spense face in front of me, I was able to enjoy myself.

It was a slight tug at my heart when the dance ended. I made to pull him off the floor but was tugged back when the next song started. I knew it instantly: The Royal Daedal. Aptly named for its complex and sophisticated routine, this was not a dance for the untrained beginner. As a youngling I had spent hours practicing this with Aedan, tripping over each other and getting so dizzy we couldn't see straight. It took us years to master the steps.

Many of the dancers were leaving the fray, using this unattainable routine as a break for refreshments. It was getting too light on the dance floor, too easy to wonder who the High Princess was with.

"Spense," I hissed. "Let's go."

The sharp first dance note of the Royal Daedal rang through the air. The song launched forward, giving no time to ease into the complicated steps.

And we were dancing it, foot for foot.

Spense demonstrated perfect form as he spun me around, one arm at my waist and the other holding my right-hand outwards. I followed his lead as we maneuvered around the other couples, twisting and dipping with every demand.

He knew the Daedal. How did he know the Daedal?

I looked at him in sheer surprise, to which he only raised his eyebrows slightly as if to say, "Don't ask me."

This was clearly muscle memory, Spense's body moving fluidly with sheer confidence. The only dancers brave enough to join were officials or part of the court families. They had learned the Daedal as part of their training.

A sparkling truth sat in my mind: Spense was high-born.

Millions of questions webbed from that realization. Most overlapped with the same ones from the first day he arrived here, bloody and barely alive. Something new stood out, clicking into place. If Spense was a part of the Dark courts, then his absence was surely missed. Wouldn't someone be looking for him?

I got my answer in the memory of a shadowed form, speaking to us in riddles in the City of Scholars.

King Urdan.

The shadows had only started when Spense had arrived, that was no coincidence. With the rift currently bridging our two realms, it was plausible that the shadows could slip through. If they were only looking for Spense, then the attacks in the Western Shores didn't make sense.

Frustration settled in me. New information was supposed to help put the pieces together, not create a bigger puzzle.

I looked at Spense as we danced, at the utter easiness with which he spun me around. He was still so much of a mystery, the complicated earth magic, the expert glamour, the Daedal.

All trains of thought were effectively derailed as we entered the last half of the routine. This was where the true skill lay, and proof of stamina. I didn't expect Spense to misstep or trip and was proved right as we twirled and twirled. Despite the steep difference in height, our bodies fit together everywhere we touched. We were like magnets, I thought, remembering how

Maisie had described us. Where I went, he went too. Where he led, I followed.

Around and around we went, the train of my dress catching every light as I spun. Spense's expert hands guided me through the steps, one hand warm on my waist, the other gripping mine with intensity.

I could see Spense's gray eyes through the glamour, the steely colour looked strange on this foreign face. His gaze did not waver from mine as we followed the Daedal, dancing and twirling and spinning.

The final crescendo rose, demanding the dancers to quicken their pace, hasten their steps. On and on and on we twirled, never missing a beat. I was beginning to sweat, but I barely acknowledged it.

Spense's magic was seeping out of him, creating a dark haze around us. Mine rose to meet it eagerly. Any rational thought had been silenced in the first half of the Daedal.

We danced and danced, colours blurring together around us as we spun too fast to make out the world beyond the two of us. Those gray eyes became softer, his face more recognizable. His floppy black hair was sticking to his forehead, damp with sweat.

The song hit its last note. Our bodies collided together as we came to an abrupt halt with the music. The silence rang in my ears deafeningly. My low panting was loud in my mind as I realized Spense's glamour was gone, melted away like ice in summer.

Why was it so quiet? Where were the cheers that always followed the Daedal?

Suddenly aware of myself, I let go of Spense's hand

and backed up a few steps. I broke our gaze to find every other pair of eyes in the room on us. I looked back to Spense, who was running a hand through his hair. It snagged halfway — on his horns, which were very much visible. Being the same colour as his hair did not camouflage them in any way. There could have been a sign above him that gained less attention.

Oh, shit.

The magic around us was still swirling, the mix of dark and light happily overlapping. I hastily pulled mine back inwards as I smoothed my dress, trying to find something to do that would keep my hands busy. Instantly, like a seal breaking, whispers broke out through the room, words flying at breakneck speed towards intent listeners.

I didn't want to look at the dais, where I knew my mother's furious face would be. I really, really didn't want to, but my traitorous body did it anyway. I saw Aedan first, his face a mixture of shock and hurt. Embris was beet red, his face twisted in rage. The officials' expressions portrayed confusion or disdain as I followed the table to its head.

I thought fury awaited me in Vera. Instead, I found something much worse: disgust. The sight of it burned shame through my whole body. I wanted to run, to hide in my room away from all these eyes that I had proved my incapability to be queen to.

Nimshar's voice rang through the ballroom, loud and clear: "Does anyone care to enlighten me on what that *Dark* is doing with our High Princess?"

The fae gathered around us whispered intently,

never taking an eye off Spense. Their tones became more hurried, fearful, as they slowly backed away from us. Wide eyes stared at me from every angle.

I took Spense's wrist and dragged him off the dance floor, hoping to use the crowd as a shield long enough to hide him somewhere.

"Seize the Dark!" It was Kashdan's turn to chime in.

Guards who had been stationed at each door started towards us. We were definitely not getting out without a fight, and even then, the chances were slim. This had to be done civilly. If it looked like he was trying to escape, it would only further their ideal that Spense was not to be trusted.

I changed our course and walked straight for my mother. This met some resistance from Spense as he realized where we were headed, but with a few darts of magic into his arm he subsided.

Vera clapped her hands, using magic to send the sound across the room, effectively cutting off every conversation. Her smile was queenly—and utterly fake. "Please excuse this interruption, there is nothing to fear here. A simple misunderstanding. Let us carry on with the celebration." Magic was dripping from her voice, flooding into the words, calming those who heard them. With a small flourish from her hand, the band started up playing again. Slowly, shaking their heads slightly, the guests began to return to their dancing and socializing.

I had never seen my mother do a glamour before. I hadn't even known she had the power to command a room this size. A bitter edge crept into my thoughts. I'd always thought taking away someone's free will was a violation against nature.

Satisfied we would have less of an audience, Vera descended the dais, her smile sliding off her face. Fury replaced it. The officials gathered around intently, sneering down at Spense. I caught Prince Leo's eye, who surveyed us with an interested look, one eyebrow raised.

My mother grabbed me, her nails digging into the soft underside of my upper arm painfully. *"What have you done,"* she hissed, her voice only audible to me. I chanced making eye contact, which was a mistake. I shrunk away from her gaze, her blue eyes pure ice.

"What is the meaning of this, Vera?" Prince Kashdan had stepped forward, his eyes wary as he looked at Spense. "Why do you parade this Dark around like royalty? I was under the assumption he would be under lock and key for the safety of our citizens."

The others murmured in agreement.

"He would never harm anyone," I said, my voice steely. "Spense saved the life of a youngling drowning in the River Nord. He's not who you think he is."

Vera motioned at the guards to grab Spense. "We will discuss the matter in my council room. Officials only," she added, her gaze stern as she looked upon Aedan and Jamey. "For now, the Dark will be sent to the holding cells under the palace." Hands wrapped around Spense, pulling him out of the room.

He watched me as he went with them, quiet and strong. *Don't struggle,* I tried to convey to him. *I'll make sure nothing happens to you.*

The princes and officials filed out into the hall, following a Northern councilor who lead them. I started after them, ignoring the stares of my friends. My mother stepped into my path. "Where do you think you're going?"

I sidestepped her, picking up my pace. "The council room."

"Was I not clear? Officials only." A wave of her magic wrapped around me, filling my nose with the scent of lilacs. I slashed through it angrily.

"How dare you try to glamour me! I have every right to be in that room, I am the High Princess of Eira!" I had to be there. No one else would stand up for Spense.

Vera stared me down, unrelenting. "You lost the right to be in that room when you made a fool of our entire region tonight. I will have enough of a mess to clean up without you in there making it bigger. Go to your room and stay there until I retrieve you."

She flicked her hand, and a guard appeared at my side, placing a hand on my shoulder. I wrenched away, glaring. Vera gave me one last look, shaking her head once, and turned away. She walked down the halls, her heels clicking.

"No, mother, please! I'll take the punishment for tonight; it was my fault! Don't punish him. Mother!" Words spilled out of me as she walked away, a guard's strong arm the only thing keeping me from chasing down the hall.

"Let's go, my Lady." I let him steer me away, in the direction of my chambers. I looked over my shoulder as we walked and didn't turn around until my mother's shape disappeared around the corner.

Once we were nearing my room, the corridors became empty and quiet.

"Sorry to do this," I whispered.

"Did you say something, miss?" The guard slowed,

and that was all I needed. I sent out my magic to wrap around him, enclosing his own, blue-tinged essence. He blinked in surprise. I tightened my fist, my magic following suit around him. His face became blissful as the endorphins rushed to his head.

Sleep.

With a final twist of my hand, he slumped to the ground, snoring.

I swallowed hard, bile rising in my throat. There was no going back from this now. I had enforced my will over his.

I only did it because I had to.

Spense needs me.

I won't ever do it again.

Taking a steadying breath, I sent magic around the guard to sit him up against the wall near my door. His head rolled to one shoulder, his mouth gaping open. It would have to do.

I took off at a run to the council room.

TWENTY-ONE
Scars & Shadows
SPENSE

I had messed up, big time.

How could I have been so blindingly stupid?

Next time think with your head, idiot. Leave the other body parts out of it. I paced the small confines of the cell I had been locked in. After winding down a hundred steps and into a dimly lit hallway, I was unceremoniously deposited into a cement room with bars along the sides, the guard telling me that this entire floor was warded against magic, and not to try anything stupid.

It was too late for that, I thought grimly.

My feelings for Diana were a messy jumble of desire and respect. Kissing her felt like a piece of myself had returned. When I was with her, I didn't even care about my former life, about who I was. She believed I was good, and that was enough.

When I had seen her with that slimy male from the South, I'd known from the tension and his roaming eyes what he wanted from her. It had filled me with a disgusting sludgy emotion I realized was jealousy. I had only come to peek in through the doors. I hadn't wanted to enter into the den of wolves, but I couldn't resist when

I thought of her choosing me over him. Then dancing with her, the desire, the feel of her magic with mine...

It had all gotten away from me; the glamour, my magic, all of it. I had done the equivalent of stripping down naked in front of the entire party.

I was as good as dead.

Even Diana could not save me from this.

I continued to pace, my foot sliding slightly through every turn in what was likely a layer of algae from the dampness down here. My options were both slim and neither were to my liking: wait for a sentence or try to escape.

"Would you stop with all the pacing? You're making me dizzy." A voice sounded from my side. I whirled around, peering through the bars of my cell. There, in the next dank room, was a huddled figure almost hidden against the dark wall.

"I thought I was alone down here," I said.

"Well, sorry to burst your bubble, but the world doesn't revolve around you, boy." The voice was rough, but undeniably female.

I tried to see through the darkness to make out the figure's face. "The irony of that is hilarious." My hand went to my head, where my horns were still on full display. I hadn't had a chance to replace the glamour, and wouldn't be able to now that I was in this magic-stifling cell. I could already feel the discomfort around my limbs like a dull ache — suffocating my magic.

My neighbour lifted her head slightly, her hood falling back a touch to reveal a mess of blonde hair tucked into her cloak. "Don't tell me you're one of those useless Princes from the visiting regions," she said drily.

"Those pricks are the reason I'm down here."

The female stood, coming to stand by our shared bars. She let her hood fall back from her face, revealing chocolate eyes and a large scar that ran from her temple to her cheek. She was familiar, I realized. I had seen her at the Leaf and Stone on a couple occasions, keeping her head down, never staying long.

"How'd you get those?" she asked, staring at my horns.

"How'd you get *that*?" I countered, my gaze resting on her scar.

She huffed once as we stared, her lips curving slightly.

"Malia," she said by way of introduction.

"I've seen you before—at the pubs by the Marketplace."

Malia eyed me warily. "That's unlikely. I'm akin to a shadow when I go there. Who did you say you were?"

"I didn't. But you're a pickpocket, aren't you?" Her silence was answer enough for me. "Is that why you're down here now? Were you trying to steal from the party-goers?"

Malia's eyes narrowed. "I was nicking stuff from the royals — small busts and some jewelry. Figured they'd be too busy getting drunk and bragging about themselves to notice. One of them even left a pair of emerald earrings in a picture frame! Damn rich bastards. I got caught grabbing those." She shrugged. "They're usually pretty easy on thieves—I'll spend a few days scrubbing the latrines and be on my way. It's why I stopped running opium, penalty on that is a few years in a prison similar to this."

If only I could ask: *what's the penalty on a realm-jumping mortal enemy of the queen who just showed himself to her entire court?*

"Why steal at all? Why not make a living legally?" I asked, realizing afterwards how that could have come off as intrusive, since she was having no qualms with sharing.

Malia met my eyes. "You must not be from around here, huh?" When I didn't answer, she continued. "Fae who are born with little to no magic don't have much choice when it comes to employment. Physical labour is pretty much it. I was born with shit-all, so unless I wanted to spend my life breaking my back while those who are stuffed to the brim by pure luck peered down their noses at me, criminal was the way to go."

I furrowed my brow. "I didn't know fae could be born without magic."

She scoffed. "Oh, the magic-havers will all tell you that it's there, deep down, and we just don't know how to reach it. Believe me, I've tried everything. It's an empty well."

A flicker of empathy pooled in my stomach. I remembered all too clearly what it was like to reach for my magic only to come up empty. I had felt powerless.

"I'm sorry," I murmured.

Malia sneered. "I don't need your pity, boy. I'm doing just fine without the burden of having a second entity inside me."

"Yes, I can see that," I said, pointedly looking at our

surroundings. "Although I suppose my having magic got me into this mess."

Her eyes flicked back up to my horns. I almost shrank back into the shadows of my cell. I had grown used to hiding them from everyone.

"Is there a way out of here?" I asked. I could see questions pooling about who I was, why she'd shared so much, and I hadn't.

Malia blinked. "Your magic is useless down here, but that doesn't mean one couldn't find a way-out using brains and slick fingers." One side of her mouth lifted into a sly smile.

I felt a matching grin rising. "Do you think if I got a guard to come into my cell, you could nab his keys?"

Malia's smile widened, showing rows of pearly whites. "You're in luck," she said, her voice wicked. "Pickpocketing just happens to be my specialty."

*

"HELP! I need help!"

The guard standing at the entrance into the hallway of cells turned around, his face suspicious as he neared me.

I had used one of Malia's stashed knives — where she hid it while they searched her, she did not share — and ran it along my lower arm. It was shallow but the skin was tight there, meaning it would bleed substantially. Already, the smell of blood was standing out against the stale stench of rot down here. Blood dripped down and pooled in my hand, where I held it against my side.

The guard could obviously smell the blood and see it in my hand, but didn't know where it was coming from. He let himself into my cell, eyeing me as he did so, and stuck his keys into a giant loop on the side of his trousers. "Try anything, and I have permission to make you regret it," he said gruffly.

Like he could take me in a fight.

I had positioned myself in the back corner, where the guard would have to stand next to the bars to look at me. I kept feigning pain as he stood exactly where I'd planned, holding my arm tight to my body. The guard grabbed my arm and wrenched it away from me. I gritted my teeth — that actually had hurt. I fought my first instinct to land my other arm into his gut.

"How'd you do this?" He surveyed the bloody mess, looking for the source of the bleeding. Quickly, I glanced once at Malia, who was quiet and nimble as her hand darted through the bars.

I groaned loudly into the guard's ear to mask the sound of keys. He stood up, annoyed, and tore a strip from the bottom of my own tunic to wrap around my arm.

"Wuss," he grumbled as he made to leave.

Malia was at her own cell door, using the keys she'd nabbed to unlock it. The guard froze as he saw her, his hand going to his empty belt loop. I used the opportunity to punch him in the gut. He doubled over, grunting, and I sent another fist into his jaw, right in the spot where I knew he would instantly go down.

And he did.

I stepped over his body, joining Malia outside the

cell. She then locked the guard in and tossed the keys down the hall.

Grinning, my heart pumping, I said, "Let's get out of here."

Malia grinned back. "Hope you saved a few of those punches for the way out."

I broke into a run, and she kept time with me. "You're in luck. Punching is my specialty," I said over my shoulder.

"I never knew someone with magic could be so fun," she said. "In another world, I think we could be friends."

I smiled in spite of myself, in spite of the situation I was in and all the hopelessness that was my future. "I'm Spense," I said. "Pleasure prison-breaking with you."

Malia took the lead, swerving down hallways that she clearly had memorized. "Likewise, Spense," she said, flashing another grin. "Likewise."

TWENTY-TWO
Reunion
DIANA

The queen's council room had been warded for centuries against eavesdropping. I knew right away that when I pressed my ear even to the thinnest wall—the northeast one, which was by some luck unguarded—I would hear only silence. It really was a helpful and smart addition to the palace unless you were an eavesdropper.

Thankfully, I had a way around that.

I was directly related to the castor of the ward, whose blood had been used to fortify the strength of the magic. All I needed was a few drops of my own blood and a little bit of coaxing to hear as though I was standing in the room as well.

I was not in the habit of carrying weapons on me, so I had to make do with a corner of a picture frame in the hallway. Red trickled down the soft skin of my forearm, the cut prickling uncomfortably.

Reaching out with my magic, I felt the shimmery ward melt into my touch, submitting to the pressure I force-fed it. It was sloppy, shaky work, not even close to the standard I held myself to when it came to my own magic. But it would have to suffice, for I could not get my damned heart to stop its wild racing.

My mother's voice floated through the wall. "Diana is young. I'll admit I thought she was ready to handle this on her own. It's clear I should have been supervising. She lost sight of the original goal, and I will take the blame for that."

Nimshar's sneer was almost audible. "I trust there will be an adequate punishment assigned."

A thud as a hand slammed on a table—likely Embris.

"The embarrassment of this public failure is punishment enough, Nimshar," my mother ground out, her tone vicious. "And I will have her present when we send the Dark back through the rift."

No. No, no, no. He wouldn't survive.

Another voice joined—Prince Leo. "I see you have decided again without consulting us what to do with the Dark. Are you so worried of his corrupting your daughter that you wish to abandon the sole reason we have kept him alive?" There was a slight pause. I could practically see the adder-like smile as he continued. "Unless you have already procured the memories you seek."

I expected a reprimanding correction from Kashdan about speaking with one's queen, but it never came. The officials were all silent.

Vera's tone was icy. "I am going to ignore that blatant insult. It is clear the Dark has methods beyond magic to infiltrate us, and the risks outweigh the potential information we might get from him—should his memories ever return."

"So why not just kill him? If the roles were reversed,

the Darks would not have even hesitated to neutralize the threat," Kashdan asked.

"I would not see Eira sink to the level of the Darks. Besides, it is highly unlikely he will even survive a second trip through the rift." My blood was beginning to boil, my heart rate slowing from its hectic pace to a steady, determined beat that thudded in my ears.

"And if he does? The Dark Legion will know of all our secrets — he has, in fact, been staying in *your* palace."

"His memories of the North and everything else he experienced here will be taken before we send him through. Do you think me an imbecile?" Vera snapped. There was a hasty reply of muttered apologies. The tension in the room was nearly leaking out the wall.

Leo dared to speak. "If the boy somehow survives the trip through, wouldn't that prove it is safe to travel through? The Dark Legion will march on us. The only reason they have not yet is because they do not know if the rift is safe. I vote we keep the boy here, imprisoned, until we know what we're up against."

"I vote we send our own army after the boy to teach the Darks a lesson about invading us!" Nimshar jeered. There were a few loud agreements.

Another voice chimed in, "Just kill him and be done with it!"

Hands slammed down on the table. "That is enough!" Vera said, her voice dripping in authority. I recognized it now as magic wrapping around her words. It made me wonder how many times she had used it to win arguments before. "I am your ancestral-chosen Queen; therefore, *I* have made the decision. I will not hear any more treachery come out of your mouths. The Dark's mind will be wiped, he will be sent through the rift, and we will close it behind him. With our combined power I expect we will be able to get it done."

A voice, probably Nimshar, started to argue again, but I could no longer hear anything beyond the blood pumping in my head. Anything the officials came up with now would be in vain. My mother had invoked her decision, and Gaia forbid she go back on her word. Her stubbornness would win out, even if it killed her.

That left me only one choice. I had to close the rift before Spense could be sent back through. It would have to be now, while they were still holed up arguing.

Hastily drawing my magic away from the wall, I took off running down the halls, ignoring the shouts of guards. With each one I passed, I sent a puff of magic after me, which they breathed in and instantly forgot they had seen me.

It's only to save Spense.

It's only to save Spense.

I tore through the halls, only pausing once to remove the slippery shoes I wore and tossing them over my shoulder before I continued.

My mind was a spinning wheel as I ran. What would happen once I closed the rift — if I *could* close it? I thought of what my mother would do. She had already suffered enough embarrassment, and there was no chance in hell I could convince her to let me keep trying to retrieve Spense's memories. Vera would want to wash her hands of this before her officials questioned her judgment further.

That meant closing the rift was a death sentence for Spense. But sending him through could be worse. What awaited him in the Dark realm if he even arrived there? He had already lost his memories, what if he became paralyzed, or sustained injuries that couldn't be healed?

I halted my trajectory so fast that my hair flipped around and whapped me in the face. I had to hide Spense first. Then, while the officials looked for him, I could focus my energy on closing the rift.

Spinning on my heel, I tore off in the direction of the holding cells deep underneath the palace. I gripped Jweira in my hand, feeling the warm steady pulse in my palm.

I hope you've rested up, Jweira. I'm going to need to your help.

*

After skirting guards and — with guilt washing over me — Maisie, I fled the palace and reached the stairs that twirled in a seemingly endless spiral underground. It looked like a cold cellar to anyone who didn't know what really lay beyond the wooden door. My bare feet made no noise as I took my first step down the concrete stairs.

Two strong hands grabbed me from behind, clamping over my mouth as they dragged me backwards, into the corridor. I was gathering a great deal of magic to blast at my attacker when they released me, spinning my shoulder so I could see my assailant.

Blue eyes bore into mine. "Aedan!" I hissed. *He had*

almost gotten the wrong end of some nasty air magic. "What are you doing here?"

"Me! What are *you* doing, you're supposed to be in your room!" Aedan had changed from his party clothes into black training gear, a blade strapped across his chest. "You're letting him out, aren't you? Gaia help me, Diana." He rubbed his temples, an exasperated sigh escaping him.

"They're going to kill him, Aedan. In cold blood. I can't let it happen."

I made to step around him, but he blocked me. "Diana."

"Please, Aedan. Pretend you never saw me." I didn't want to use magic on my friend. *Please don't make me.*

"I trust your mother, the officials. They say he's a threat. How can I ignore that?" His eyebrows had lowered, his face showing the pain he felt from being on my opposing side.

"Don't you trust *me*? Spense is innocent. He hasn't done *anything* wrong. I just want to keep him safe until my mother calms down. Until they can all think rationally again. Please, Aedan." Magic danced inside me, wanting to coat my words, but I pushed it back.

Aedan stared at me for a few beats before taking a long breath through his nose. "I didn't see you," he said, turning around and walking back down towards the palace.

"Thank you," I whispered. He turned once and gave me a look I knew all too well from all our adventures. One that said *be careful.* I nodded once at him and waited until he had disappeared into the palace before starting down the steps.

I heard frantic boot-steps making their way up the stairs, so I ran back up and plastered myself against the wooden door. A tall mass came leaping from the stairwell, followed by a small, lithe one.

"Spense?" I gaped. He whirled around, his eyes ablaze. They softened when they saw me. The second figure took off into the forest, not pausing to look back. "Who—what—"

Yelling voices floated up the stairs. Spense grabbed my arm and took off sprinting into the woods. "Later!" he called back at me.

We ran like hell into the forest I knew better than the back of my hand. I steered us away from the Pond, from the Abbey, deeper and deeper. It would be harder to scent us with the ancient trees leading up Mt Nord. These pine and evergreen giants had their own kind of earthly magic. It would protect us.

I only stopped when we reached the wide mouth of River Nord. Panting, I scooped some water from the river and hastily drank. Spense did the same.

"This river leads straight up Mt Nord. It's a day's hike up the mountain, and then you'll reach Spike's Passage. From there—"

"Whoa, whoa, slow down. What are you talking about, Diana?" Spense took one of my hands in his own, warm and firm.

"You have to hide," I urged. "They're going to send you back through the rift." Spense's hand became slack as his face drained of colour.

"How did you get out?" I asked, the fact that he had

just escaped the palace underground prison suddenly rising to the forefront of my mind.

"I had help," he said, smiling. "We got keys off a guard and ran like hell."

There was more to that story, I knew. There were a dozen guards stationed between the cells and the top of the stairwell. Just running could not have gotten him out. But there was no time to waste. I pushed his chest, trying to guide him in the direction of the mountain.

"I'm going to close the rift. But you're not safe here. The Nordians will take you in; they don't have to abide by my mother's command." I took off the emerald family ring I wore on my middle finger. "Show them this, and tell them I sent you. They'll take you in." I repeated.

Spense's hand curled around the ring I pushed into his palm. "What about you?" he rasped. "You shouldn't be risking yourself for me."

I shook my head gently. "Don't worry about me. I'll come get you when the time is right. Go, okay? Please."

He was right, of course. I shouldn't be risking myself for him. I was Eira's next ruler, and I had been raised my whole life to hate Spense's kind. But I had also been raised to trust in myself, my intuition, my sense of what is right. This wasn't about him anymore. What my mother was doing—it wasn't what she had taken great care to teach me that a queen did for her kingdom. It was a reaction of fear, of judgment, of the need to prove herself to the other regions. I would close the rift, and when she cooled off, I would explain it to her. That I was doing what I believed to be *right*. To be worthy of the title of Queen of the Lights.

Mercy over justice.

Spense closed the space between us, leaning down to rest his forehead against mine. I could smell his sweet scent wrapping around me. He nodded gently.

I stepped back before I could convince myself not to go through with it all. "It'll be okay, I promise."

He smiled grimly. "You're amazing, you know."

"I know."

He gave me a real smile this time, and I continued my instructions of how to get to the base camp of the Nordians. After repeating it back to me, I was satisfied he could make the journey there, and I sent him away. He jogged with his back to me, following the river. I only let myself watch him for a few moments before turning to my own path.

The nearer I got to the rift, the more I could feel the slimy magic in the air. It closed around me like a noose around my neck, thick and choking. The guards that had been stationed to stand at alert were nowhere to be seen, likely called back to the palace when Spense was realized to be missing.

When I came into full view of the small tear into the realm, Jweira became hot at my neck, almost unbearably. There was stirring in the emerald, and I hoped that her consciousness, or essence, or whatever she was, awoke to help me.

I stared into the rift. It looked back at me, pulling at my magic greedily.

Come, repair me, it crooned. *Let me take you to where you need to be.*

Closing my eyes, I spooled magic around me, sending it around the rift, leaving no gap or hole as it completed a circle. I wanted to rear back at the feel of the darkness ebbing from it. Vaguely, I wondered if its failure to become a portal was to blame for the icky nature, or if it was a reflection of the castor.

Yes, Diana Lightbringer. Yes, you have the power inside you.

"No," I said aloud. "I won't let you exist here any longer. I'm closing you for good."

"You mustn't, my dear child. The rift must be repaired."

My eyes snapped open at the sound of a real, female voice. One I recognized so clearly. She was standing there, her gray hair in its usual bun, her body transparent as it hovered before the rift. She looked at me with those kind eyes, her crows-feet wrinkling as she smiled. My heartbeat was in my throat.

It was my grandmother, Maeve.

TWENTY-THREE
Constant Motion
SPENSE

Follow the river, climb the mountain, Spike's passage, walk the cliff, under the clouds... follow the river, climb the mountain, Spike's passage, walk the cliff, under the clouds... I repeated Diana's instructions to me over and over as I jogged alongside River Nord. The water rushed in the opposite direction as me, clear and strong. I repressed a shudder at the memory of being in its waves.

What would I find in Mt Nord? The warriors there were tough, but I wouldn't struggle with that. I did wonder if I would be able to hold myself back from ripping Maverick's head clean off his shoulders if I encountered him. My anger had become a bit of a problem lately.

I spun Diana's emerald ring around my pinky finger. It was the only finger that it could slip all the way onto, and I didn't risk carrying it for fear of dropping it somewhere along the two-day trek. She was so good, so brave. Guilt pooled in my stomach thinking of her facing her unyielding mother, of how she might be punished for helping me. Already she had been forced to give up so much just to keep working with me. And why? Because I had kissed her?

No, I realized. She would have done this for anyone she deemed worth saving.

I stopped in my tracks. I couldn't run away to Mt Nord and hide like would be expected from a Dark on the run. Diana thought I was worth saving, but she was worth saving, too. Much more than my own life. She was important to Eira's future. She was the queen they needed. What would her punishment be for defying all the region leaders? Could she be prevented from becoming queen—did they have that kind of power? I should be there, to take the blame, to save her future.

I couldn't let her close that damned rift on her own. I had been through the blasted thing; it was extremely dangerous. She needed help.

Decisive, I spun on my heel and changed my trajectory. I didn't know my way around this forest—and had been steered wrong before—so I reached down into my magic and tried to quiet my mind, the way I had been taught to meditate. I could feel a faint thrumming in the back of my head, familiar enough that I trusted my gut to follow it.

It led me through the forest, my pace quickening as the thrumming got stronger. Twice I was spooked by deer running away from me, scared by my own loud sprint.

I could see a light in the distance, glowing so bright that it almost hurt to look at from this far away. Diana's magic was palpable now, her cedar smell strong even through the pine trees. The magic of the rift was mixed in there as well, mingling insidiously. It was dark, I realized, and it felt so familiar.

Pushing myself to run faster, I could see her figure, silhouetted by the light emanating from the rift. I was almost close enough to touch her now, to reach out my magic to help—

An arrow whizzed through the trees and landed in my calf, sending me hurtling to the ground. Pain flooded my vision. *Breathe, Spense. Breathe and think.*

It was all I could do to lift my head from my sprawled position on the forest floor. My vision was blurred around the edges, but I made out a dozen armor-clad males surrounding the rift. This was all hauntingly familiar. Embris was among them, his expression full of fear as he looked into the rift.

Following his gaze, I understood why.

A bubble of light had encased Diana and the rift, thoroughly trapping her inside. Magic flowed out of her like a waterfall, beautifully white and pure. She was glowing. She was talking in there, tone raised in emphasis, but her voice was garbled by the effect of the bubble. Was she talking to herself? Someone on the other side of the rift? My heart clenched at the thought that she could be calling for help.

"Get her out of there!" Queen Vera had entered the scene, her eyes wild as she took in her daughter and the bubble of magic.

Soldiers attacked the bubble at once, trying to pierce it with their swords and daggers, to no avail. It held strong, like hard rock. Vera let out an exasperated yell and shot a fiery zap of her magic outwards. It hit the bubble and instantly shot off it, effectively hitting a nearby soldier and blasting him ten yards back.

Embris' gaze had followed the soldier and now landed on me, laying in the grass and holding the skin below my knee tightly, trying to stop blood from entering the arrow wound site. "You!" he bellowed, pointing a finger at me.

Immediately, hands from behind me hauled me to my knees. I bit my tongue so hard to keep from crying out that blood erupted in my mouth. I spat. A cuff was placed on my wrist, filling me with dread. I instantly felt its effect—my magic faded around me like a mist. This was worse, so much worse than the arrow. I breathed in heaving gulps of air as the innermost part of me became inaccessible.

Vera stepped in front of me, her sneer vicious as her ice blue eyes stared me down. "You have been nothing but a thorn in my side. Whatever you have done to corrupt my daughter stops now." Her eyes flicked to the magic-binding band on my wrist, and then back to Diana, who remained in the bubble of light.

"I haven't done anything to her," I ground out, trying not to grimace from the pain in my leg. They had me bound and magic-tied, with blood pouring from my calf, but I would show no further weakness than that.

Vera snarled. "It seems your Dark magic is more potent than I thought. It clearly holds on her even while you are indisposed. She walked a circle around me, a wolf stalking her prey. Embris had come to stand at her side, motioning his childish son Aedan to join them. The young male's pale blond hair was disheveled, his fighting leathers hastily donned overtop a crisp navy suit. It was impossible not to see the similarities between father and son as they looked at me, but they differed in the expressions they wore. Embris was pure disgust and bloodthirst, while Aedan was reserved, confused.

"My queen, I think it is time we considered our last option," Embris said as his eyes left me to take in Diana's bubble. His eyes softened as he took in her form, her hands out in front of her, the warbled sound of her voice. *He cares immensely for her,* I thought. As did seemingly everyone in this forsaken land. They all doted on Diana, treated her as a special and bright young female. But when she voiced her opinion, they didn't listen. They wanted to protect her, obviously. And they would say it was out of love that they pushed her insights aside, forced her to their will. But was that truly love?

Vera nodded, never taking her eyes off me. She opened her mouth, likely to give the order of my execution, but was distracted by the light behind her growing blindingly brighter.

I tried to look around Vera, to see what was happening. The light was growing bigger and bigger, until I could only dare to look through squinted eyes. Diana was no longer visible. Fear bit at me, coursing through my veins.

The bubble exploded suddenly, the magic fracturing like ice as it traveled outwards. Embris grabbed Vera roughly, meaning to shield her from the blast, but she was able to deflect the shattering bubble away from them, inadvertently shielding me and the soldier that held me as well. The other soldiers that had fanned out around the bubble were now slumped on the ground, their moving chests the only indication they were still alive.

The light had settled slightly, no longer too bright to look upon, and now condensed into one place — Diana. She stood in front of us like Gaia herself, her arms outstretched, magic pouring out of her in a steady stream. The power emanating from her was palpable, sending shivers down my spine. Her eyes were not the hazel that I could spend an eternity looking into, but all white, they too pouring magic from them. She was beautiful and ethereal and unstoppable.

Something had gone quite awry in her attempt to close the rift.

Behind her, the rift had grown. It was big enough that someone as tall as I could walk through it without ducking, and wide enough for two to walk side by side. It was shimmering with magic, the waves in constant motion. It was no longer a rift, I realized.

It was a portal.

TWENTY-FOUR
Life Changes
DIANA

"Maeve?"

"How I've missed you, my dear child. I'm so proud of who you have grown to be." Maeve's eyes twinkled as she looked at me with love. Vaguely, I could feel my circle of magic tighten around the rift, closing in on it.

"Wh — how are you here?" I asked incredulously. "You didn't come to the Sacred Pool during my ritual." It was not the most important thing to note right now, but in this state, thoughts became words without any control.

"I wish I had the time to explain everything to you, Diana. I'm afraid you might not like what I have to say. This rift, you intend to close it. That cannot happen. Finally, the realms have been reunited again, finally balance is beginning to be restored."

I shook my head, causing my vision to blur around the edges. "You're not making any sense. I don't understand."

Maeve reached out a hand in comfort, resting it on the space above my shoulder. I placed my hand atop hers, hoping to feel her warmth, her familiar touch. But it fell through her transparent mist, landing on my shoulder alone. "I know, dear one. It will all make sense one day. For now: heed my words. Repair the rift into the portal it was meant to be."

I looked at the rift, its menacing ooze grinning back at me. My stomach lurched. "What will happen once I do?"

Maeve smiled, the lines on her face wrinkling. "Your destiny will begin."

I wanted to roll my eyes at the dramatics. "Seriously, what is it with you spirits? I can never get a full answer out of you. Why can't you just tell me what I have to do?"

"Our purpose is to guide, not to dictate. We can nudge you in the right direction, but you alone must decide how to march down your destined path."

"Yet here you are, telling me I have no choice but to repair this rift," I countered.

"You always have a choice, Diana," Maeve said gently. When I did not appear convinced, she continued. "Look around you, at your surroundings, at the energy at work. Can you feel it? The pulsing?"

Pulsing was all around me, thrumming through my body. I'd been certain it was Jweira, but now, reaching into my magic, I wasn't so sure. Jweira was hot and loud at my neck, whereas the pulsing was faint, coming from something else. I slowed my breathing, concentrating on its source. A gold line of magic was coming from the rift, wrapping around my hands gently. The pulsing was coming from there.

"That is the life force of this rift, given by its maker." Maeve watched me intently.

The life force was strong and powerful, but it didn't have any of the disgusting ooze, the dark, foreboding essence that I had been able to sense here and in my dreams.

"Where's the darkness coming from, then?" I asked. Now it was obvious to me that the two essences were separate, both glomming on to the rift for dear life, intertwined, but not the *same.*

"That is the other half of the fae. There is too much light here, but you have never known anything else, so you shy away from the darkness. But without dark there is no light. There is no balance in this realm, no countering force where nature can thrive. The light cannot live without the dark, and vice versa. Do you understand why you must open this portal?"

Slowly, I nodded. "The Darks must come back to Eira."

Maeve smiled. "You are destined to unite the fae once more, Diana. We will all be watching with pride as you do."

"Once more? The Seelie and Unseelie were never united."

"Surely by now you've realized that the history you were given is not what it seems."

I blinked. My whole existence, the North, Eira, being 'light'; it was all wrong. And the acceptance of that filled me with peace, not dread, not panic. I was destined to restore the balance. I would find out who changed the history books, and why. And I would not let it happen again. If I never learned the truth of my ancestral past, so be it. All that mattered now was the future, and making sure it was fair and just and inclusive.

"How do I repair it?"

*

I stood, arms flung out, as magic radiated out of me. The lifeforce of the rift had melded with the magic I had fed it, growing and growing until it was whole and beautiful and pure. The golden thread was now woven into its shimmery surface, twisting with a new white piece of magic, my own that I had given freely.

The calm and soothing feeling washing over me from the immense magic was unlike anything I'd ever felt before. Perfectly balanced between light and dark, no room for judgment, for unkindness. I just was.

I felt strong.

I felt powerful.

I felt *right*.

Slowly, the landscape before me came into focus, my vision returning. The edges still blurred, the haze of the magic around me like a fog.

Happiness swirling, I smiled as I saw my mother, and Embris, and Aedan, all gathered in front of me. But as I took in what they stood in front of, I faltered. Spense was on his knees, his magic cut off, and seemingly injured, from the reek of blood in the air. A soldier held his arms back with one hand, a sword glinting in the other.

"What have you done!" shrieked Vera. Their faces were all open in shock. I let go of the portal's magic as I came fully back to myself.

"I am restoring the balance of nature," I said, my voice coming out eerily calm. I looked into my mother's contorted face, her confusion and rage building up, and was not scared like I used to be.

"You have made a grave mistake, child, one you will *regret*," Vera said venomously. "He holds some sort of power over you, forcing you to free him, to open this portal and divulge secrets on our courts." She pointed a menacing finger at Spense. Spittle was flying as she spat words out.

"You're wrong," I said. "I want to explain, but you need to calm down." I was beginning to have an inkling of worry as I saw Vera's control slipping. Her queenly mask was terribly askew, her emotions pouring out of her in a tidal wave. Even Embris seemed to lean away. The air around her became lethal when her face turned to deathly calm, a vacant smile appearing.

She turned to the soldier holding Spense. "Kill him." It was Anten, I recognized with a shock.

He looked to me in hesitation, his blade unmoving. Vera shrieked in rage, blasting magic his way. He stiffened, his face glazing over, and lifted the sword high above his head. He was bringing it down on Spense's neck when the world stilled.

"NO!"

Magic blasted out of me more forcefully than I had ever known. White, snowy magic that sent Anten flying into the air, slamming into a large pine tree with a sickening crunch. Vera, Embris, and Aedan were forced backwards, my magic not sparing them as it took on its own volition.

The band around Spense's arm snapped off, disintegrating before it could touch the ground. The magic expelling from me wrapped around him, flowing down into his leg, stemming the flow of blood. The glamour around him disappeared like a mist in the sun, his black horns on full display.

I could barely get a breath in as I let go of the emotion that had elicited such a reaction from me. My arm was burning, but I didn't pay it much attention. Vera was staring at me in utter disbelief, her anger likely to return soon. "You've killed him," she whispered, turning to look at Anten's body, bent at an unnatural angle at the base of the tree. He lay unmoving, a line of blood trickling down his forehead.

No, not Anten, no. No, no, no. He was my loyal friend, my longest protector.

There was nothing inside me except shock. Empty, hollow, disbelief.

Embris and Aedan shared that look on their faces, but they weren't staring at me, or at Anten, or even at Spense's healed leg.

They were staring at my arm.

My left arm was now stinging painfully, like burning fire in my veins. I grasped at it in vain as I watched it change. My skin was swirling, the pale hue flashing through every colour all the way from shoulder to wrist. I was having an adverse reaction to the magic I had just expelled. I was combusting, being punished for killing an innocent. It was only fair.

But as the skin on my arm settled, inky black lines started to appear. They wove down my entire arm, creating patterns and lines and swirls, leaving a prickling trail in its wake.

No one spoke as the tattoo finally stopped moving and settled into my skin. This — this looked like a mating tattoo. But —

Spense had stood up, catching my eye. His face mirrored my own look of disbelief. For down his left arm, a matching tattoo swirled from shoulder to wrist. It was alike in every way, a perfect pair.

My soulmate.

Spense was my soulmate.

My arm still tingled; I wanted to scratch it, to relieve some of the burn. I wanted to stare at my arm, at those patterns, until I had memorized every single line. But I couldn't look away from those gray eyes that bored into mine.

For once, my mother had nothing to say. Her jaw gaped; her gaze fixed on my arm. I looked to Embris, who was deathly pale, and to Aedan, whose crestfallen face sent sadness straight to my heart.

Spense started towards me, taking my hand gently in his as we let the shock wash over us. I should say something, I should break this terribly awkward silence.

But I didn't get the chance before movement in the portal took my attention. The magic shimmered, pulsing with power as a shape began to take form in front of it. Someone was using the portal.

He appeared smiling devilishly, wearing a long red cape and clothing as black as night. Accompanying him were two membranous, leathery wings that protruded from his back, reaching far above his head in height. He leaked power as his handsome smirk sent shivers down my spine. Was this Death?

"It feels good to be back," he said, breathing in a deep smell of the forest. His voice was eerily familiar.

No, he wasn't Death.

He was the ruthless Unseelie leader, the one controlling the shadows, the one I'd encountered in the City of Scholars.

King Urdan.

TWENTY-FIVE
A Warm Embrace
DIANA

My heart slammed in my chest painfully fast. Jweira was pulsing hot at my neck, her essence flaring into mine at the arrival of the newcomer.

Not just any newcomer.

King Urdan grinned lazily as he returned my mother's stare. For once, she looked at a loss of what to do. Her soldiers lay unconscious around the portal, at least one of them assuredly dead, her only weapon being magic and whatever Embris, and Aedan were carrying. *Oh, Gaia, how many of these soldiers are dead? How many lost their lives because of me?*

Yet Vera still stared him down with ferocity and raised her chin in disdain. Delios had emerged from the trees and had his lip curled, growls radiating louder and louder from his large body.

"Leave, Urdan, before you lose your chance to do so." Vera's voice was still and icy. I wasn't sure I could keep mine from shaking if I were in her shoes.

Urdan chuckled drily, sending a vibration through the ground that I could feel in my legs. The magic that seeped from him was ancient and powerful, when it touched me I felt as if I were suffocating. I cast a small, invisible line of magic in between Urdan and I, drawing Spense closer.

Guilt wrenched in my belly. This was my doing. Maeve — she'd said this was my path. How could this be? It felt all wrong. Had this all been a ruse?

"You believe yourself powerful enough to force me back to that wretched realm?" Urdan shook his head, that infuriating smile never leaving his face. "No. I have spent millennia working to get back here, and now that I am, I will not leave this land. It was mine once, so shall it be again."

"You are but one. And gravely outnumbered," Vera said. Embris was at her side instantly, a sword drawn. Aedan hesitated before joining his father at the queen's other side, his eyes regarding me warily.

Urdan glanced around pointedly at the fallen soldiers. My heart clenched when my gaze passed Anten's lifeless body, tears stinging at my eyes. "Is that so?" With a palm outstretched towards the portal, he sent a jagged shard of magic into it. The portal stretched oddly, the wavy lines turning opaque and cloudy, until we could see through it. On the other side, heavy sun causing their weapons to gleam, shrouded in a forest much like the one we were standing in, was an army. Armed to the teeth and wearing the same black leathers as Urdan, in formation and awaiting their signal. There had to be thousands, if not more.

Vera paled, her bravado slipping. Urdan grinned once more, his lips sliding over sharp canines, making him look feral.

"Do you find no peace in your own realm? Why

must you take from us?"

Urdan snarled. "*Peace?* The land we were so unceremoniously dumped into eight thousand years ago is no friend of the fae. We are hunted and killed by an intelligent and ruthless species sent from the depths of hell. My court has faced terrible famine and droughts in the only place we are safe from those monsters. And do you know why?" His voice turned feline; his teeth bared. Our silence fueled him to continue.

"Because our magic is a poison on those lands. The only place where we are not being killed, we are the ones killing. Ironic. Without the Seelie to counter us, we are a drain on the land. And sensing from the imbalance in this realm, you are dying without us."

"You lie!" Vera shrieked. "You only lie, and you only take! Eira flourishes without your taint of darkness!"

"Eira will die in the very near future without us."

"Restore the balance of nature," I whispered under my breath.

Urdan's head snapped in my direction, his gaze raking over me. "Indeed child. I am almost impressed, but I know it was not your own smarts that led you to that conclusion." His eyes flicked to Jweira. "You *dare* wear that, parading it around like some sort of prize? I should kill you where you stand!" His face flashed in anger, making my heart thrash wildly in my chest like a caged animal. If everything I had been shown was true, he had every right to be angry; Jweira had been his daughter.

Spense stepped in front of me, his magic flickering

dangerously around him. Urdan began laughing maniacally, not deterred even as he easily deflected the white-hot strikes of magic Vera sent his way.

"What a grave disappointment, indeed," he said, his laughter fading to a sneer. "I had such high hopes."

"What are you talking about?" Spense demanded. His magic was becoming erratic — I could tell by the way his scent filled the area.

Urdan rolled his eyes. "You, of course. Did all functioning reason leave your brain along with your memories?"

I looked between the two of them. Spense was angry in his confusion, which only gave more power to Urdan. I placed a hand on Spense's arm, along the newly inked flesh. He shrugged away, pushing me farther behind him as he stared down the Unseelie King.

"How do you know about my memories?"

"Because I was the one who took them from you." He said it with such flippancy, such ease. "I couldn't risk our secrets being exposed. I had thought your fundamentals would remain with you, but clearly I was wrong," Urdan curled his lip as he looked at me, at our matching arms.

Spense shoved a large, violet blast of magic towards him, which I expected to be easily waved aside like my mother's failed attempts. To my surprise, its aim was true, hitting Urdan in the chest with more force than I had anticipated. The Unseelie King bared his teeth in anger.

"Watch yourself, *boy*," he cautioned, his tone deathly calm.

Vera spoke again. "I knew the boy couldn't be trusted. You admit to sending him here as a spy, an infiltrator?"

Urdan finally tore his gaze away from us to look back at the queen. "It was Spense's idea; he begged me for years to let him do this for the Unseelie, for *me*. I finally agreed."

"You're wrong!" Spense shouted.

"Oh, please. Enough with the theatrics, my son. It's getting quite trivial. By all means, have your memories back then."

His—

"Your *son*?" echoed Vera, her voice incredulous.

Urdan smiled darkly as he lifted a hand lazily towards Spense. A viscous, cloudy substance seeped from him into the latter's body, causing him to go rigidly still. I shook his arm, trying to get him to come back to himself. It seemed like hours as his eyes clouded over, and he began to tremble. He collapsed onto his knees, unseeing.

When Spense finally looked at me, his eyes were blank. He was lost inside his own mind.

I stood frozen. I wanted to do something, anything, but what could I do?

"Ironic, isn't it, *Vera*, that my son would find a mate in your daughter. The odds seem incredibly low, don't they?" Although Urdan's voice was as smooth as honey, his words were barbed, poisonous as a snake.

"If you had anything to do with this, so help me Gaia—"

Urdan put his hands up in mock sincerity. "Even I cannot influence the ancient magic of soulmates, Queen.

If you weren't so blind maybe you could see it as an omen. The inevitability of the joining of our two fae once more."

"That will *never* happen." Vera steeled herself, and without warning, sent an uncontrollably massive stream of magic at the portal. She screamed in effort as she sent more and more, grabbing Embris' hand and funneling his magic as well. The portal began to shake, the shimmering dimming substantially. Vera was closing it.

Ancient voices began screaming in my head.

No!

The agony; do not close us once more!

Mercy! Have mercy!

Stop!

Urdan's smile slipped as he realized he would be alone in Eira, his army unreachable. "*Bitch!*" he roared to Vera, whose satisfactory smile spread wider on her face. Urdan's expression became hard as he looked to Spense, and made his decision.

I knew it would happen before it did. I shoved Spense back, out of reach of the wild King. He growled, wrapping magic around his son's torso, and pulling him through the air. With Spense at his side, he leaped towards the portal.

Blindly, I jumped through the air, grabbing Spense's arm and pulling with all my might. I could hear voices behind me, my mother's and Embris' and Aedan's, probably telling me to let go, to get back. They didn't register. All I could focus on was keeping Spense from the grips of Urdan.

When the King felt my resistance, he snarled,

blasting magic as black as obsidian my way. I didn't have to make a conscious effort for my own magic to send it rippling over me like a harmless gust of wind. I flared my own magic out, hoping to hone in on his hand and cause enough pain for him to let go of Spense's vacant body.

Let go! I screamed in my head, magic coating my words.

A wall slammed down in my head, so jarring I was instantly stricken with a migraine, my body pounding everywhere in pain.

You think you can compel me, child? Me? You are unworthy of my son. The voice came barreling into my mind, unbidden, and rang through me so uncomfortably I could feel my vision fading as my body threatened to black out.

It was that moment of pause that Urdan used to squeeze through the portal, which was becoming smaller and smaller. The voices screamed in my head, along with voices I could hear outside my body.

Spense disappeared through the portal next, his arm tugging me along.

Pain was still blooming in my head, so crippling that I couldn't think, couldn't tell my legs to move.

My head was going to explode.

"Diana!"

"Let go!"

"Come back to us, Diana!"

I was unable to heed those words as I drifted into oblivion, my body finally giving into the pain wracking through me.

I'm sorry, I thought, willing the words to be aloud, so that my family might hear it.

Magic wrapped around me, a warm embrace, as I hurtled through the portal.

I'm sorry.

EPILOGUE

Hands were on me, everywhere. I couldn't see, but that didn't make a difference. Probably half a dozen soldiers were holding me back, easily recognizable by their rough grips and the smell of battle armour stinging my nose.

I was eerily calm as I fell to my knees, not feeling the ground when I hit it, not caring to distinguish the dozens of voices cutting through the air. It was all a background buzz. The only thing I could really hear was my own breathing, ragged and deep.

There was nothing. I was nothing. And, for some reason, I knew that I deserved this.

Slowly, excruciatingly slowly, memories of what had just happened began to resurface. And as they did, my heart shattered into a thousand pieces. Sharp and painful.

I was a killer. I had failed. My soulmate was lost.

It didn't even matter that the blindfold digging into my skull prevented me from seeing the weapons all around me, or that I was likely to die without warning in the next few minutes. The air felt thick and warm, the Dark magic strong, wrapped around the atmosphere like vines growing on a building. It was fitting that I die at the hands of those I failed. Maybe my ancestors would forgive me.

"*Diana!*"

The low voice stirred something inside me. Among the broken pieces of me, there was something there that was still alive. Beating.

My magic lifted its defeated head in curiosity. *We know him*, it seemed to say. Weakly, slowly, it reached out, daring to touch the magics in the room.

Instantly I found his. I clung to his purple magic like a life force, holding all the humanity I had left.

"Spense," I breathed. He was back, returned from wherever his father had sent him, deep within his own mind. He was here, with me.

Scents and feelings came sharper into focus. He wasn't quite back, I realized. Only half-conscious, his magic flaring wildly. My heartbeat quickened.

The hands on my body felt hot. Their magic was strong, stagnant. Too much. I was suddenly itching to get them off me, to get the blindfold gone, too.

But my body wouldn't fight, wouldn't even struggle. There were other forces at play. Spense's wild thrashing and calling my name went silent. "Take him to the infirmary," I heard him say. Him — the Unseelie King. The reason I was here, the reason Spense was lost.

I would make him pay.

Dark chuckling sounded in my ear, warm breath tickling my neck. I recoiled in disgust. "You sure are a fiery one, Princess." His voice turned steely low. "But know this: you will not best me in my own court. The only reason you are alive is out of courtesy to my son and respect for the ancient magic of soulmates. If you make a move against me, I will not hesitate to take you out, mated or not." I tried not to swallow, not to give him the satisfaction of seeing his words successful in scaring me, but my traitorous body did it anyway.

With a growl, he lifted my blindfold. My vision was heavily blurred, but I could make out dark marble floors, large windows letting in so much light that I had to squint. Urdan's face was right in mine, his breath stale and hot.

He reached for Jweira, which I hadn't realized was beginning to burn. The second his skin touched the emerald, his hand snapped back. He grunted in pain, lips curling into a sneer.

"Whatever you've done to her to make her fight against me, it will be undone," he threatened through clenched teeth. He snapped his fingers at the soldiers who were responsible for the hands all over me, and they dragged me to my feet.

"Take her to my son's room and wait for further instructions."

Without hesitation, we set off at a pace that had me tripping over my feet. If I hadn't been held up, I would have had to be dragged.

As Urdan left my line of sight, I heard him say in an eerie voice:

"Welcome to the heart of the Unseelie."

CPSIA information can be obtained
at www.ICGtesting.com
Printed in the USA
LVHW030757130423
744165LV00001B/1